MANIMAL

A.C. HESSENAUER

ISBN 979-8-218-76169-1

CONTENTS

1

THE SETTING. THE CHARACTERS.

Atlanta, 1935

It was a hot, humid day in Atlanta. The air hung thick and heavy with moisture, despite the rain that had fallen in sheets all morning. The street outside was barely visible through the grimy windowpanes streaked with condensation.

Jack Quinn sat with his feet on his desk; one foot propped on the other. An unlit cigarette dangled from his lips. He wore his fedora pulled low, his face hidden, as he read through the sparse sheets that lay in an open folder splayed across his lap.

His partner watched him, his disapproval loud, despite the silence that permeated the room. He sat erect at his desk, directly across from Jack, both feet planted firmly on the floor. The pen in his hand long forgotten, his stormy blue eyes fixed on what he could see of Jack's chin– on that cigarette that hung from his lips. He stared blatantly, but Jack didn't look up.

August Sullivan ran a hand through his long, dark hair. He cleared his throat. Jack turned a page with an air of lazy languidness. The veins that branched out like spiderwebs beneath the nearly translucent skin that framed August's eyes seemed to pulse as he watched his partner with mild contempt.

August cleared his throat once more before finally deigning to speak. "Go ahead; read it again. Read it as many times as you like. It isn't going to change anything."

Still, Jack did not look up. The cigarette clinging to his lip drooped a bit lower. August stared at it. It was barely holding on. The paper was stuck to his lip, and a part of it would rip off when he finally removed it, leaving a bit of itself behind.

"It's been a week, Jack." When that statement elicited no response, August's hand spasmed in a brief motion, as though he were about to slam his palm down on the desk. He blinked at the pen in his hand before setting it gently beside his notebook. The crisp white pages mocked him in their blankness. August sighed. "A week," he repeated, "and we're no closer than we were the moment we found the body."

His voice fell flat, somehow, in the protracted silence and stillness of the office. The rest of the station was out, presumably doing their jobs, unlike the two of them. As though sitting here, reading over that bloody case file was going to get them anywhere. He didn't understand it. It wasn't like Jack. It wasn't like him at all.

"We're partners; we already spend every waking minute together. I don't see how finding a body would bring us any closer, and I'm not sure I would want to be closer," Jack said in a bored sort of voice.

"You're insufferable, you know that?" August said evenly. "I was talking about the case."

Jack snorted. A short huff of air left his nostrils. His lips stretched slightly as though he were smiling at some private joke that only he was in on.

"Oh, for fuck's sake, Jack." August stood, pushing his chair back and planting both palms on the desk in one smooth motion. He swallowed, staring at Jack through narrowed eyes that had suddenly grown darker, those veins of his bulging slightly. "Just what the fuck are you playing at? Huh? We should be out there." He pointed at the grimy window. "Not stuck in here, sitting on our assess, waiting for an answer to fall out of the sky into our goddamn laps. We should go back to the cathouse; question everyone again."

"Jesus Christ, Sully." Jack raised his chin, revealing his face for the first time in what had felt like several hours to August. "That's a lot of cursing, coming from a preacher."

"I'm *not*–" August began, but he cut himself off, lowering his voice, forcing his shoulders down from his ears. "I'm not a preacher," he said quietly. "I'm serious, Jack. Someone out there must know something. Someone must have seen *something*."

Jack sighed deeply and shuffled through the folder. He held up a photograph and studied it for several seconds. "Dixie LaRue..." he said quietly, as though to himself. "What was your real name, darling?" He set the photo down and looked up at August. "And you think that if we show up there again, they'll talk to us this time? No one at the cathouse is going to want to spend time with a couple of dicks, Sully. Not for free at least."

August just shook his head. "You're hilarious, Jack." He frowned over at him. "What is it you're not telling me?"

"What makes you think I know something you don't?" Jack asked, his tone casual, like they were discussing the weather.

"Gee, I don't know, maybe it's because you've been sitting here all day, insisting we don't need to be *doing* anything?" August swept his arm out to the side, pausing for dramatic effect. But Jack remained unimpressed. "Meanwhile, there's a deranged killer loose on the streets..."

"Well, why didn't you say so? He's out on the streets? Right now? Then let's go get him."

August ran a hand over his face. "Christ..."

Jack tilted his head to the side, eyeing his partner with an expression of faint disapproval. "I never said we don't need to be doing anything. What I said was, there's no *point* in doing anything right now. There's a difference."

"Is there?" August folded his arms over his chest. He had removed his suit jacket and loosened his tie once he realized they were settling in for the long haul. It gave him a somewhat disheveled look that was particularly at odds with his typical dapper appearance.

He moved suddenly, pacing up and down the aisle between the rows of desks. "I've had it with sitting here. I've had it with this case." He faced the grimy window, staring through the streaked glass. "I've had it with this weather. And this whole garbage heap of a city." He turned to face Jack, loosening his tie further, in a rough motion, as though it was strangling him. "I need to..." he trailed off, unable to complete his sentence, his chest heaving slightly.

"Careful now, we can't afford to have you going feral. Only one of us can have an anger problem. You can't play good cop, bad cop with two bad cops, after all." Jack studied him for a moment before pulling a lighter from his pocket.

"Don't," August said, his eyes narrowing. "You know I hate it."

Jack raised an eyebrow at him, pausing, the lighter hovering below the end of his cigarette. "There are worse vices," he said quietly. August's eyes narrowed to slits, his veins pulsing, purple, morphing to black. Jack flicked his thumb down, igniting a tiny flame that flickered back and forth as he stared up at August, his brown eyes wide in mock innocence. Neither of them moved.

The bell clattered shrilly in the heavy silence of the office, and both men turned towards the door as it was flung wide.

A leggy brunette strode into the room. She had way too many legs—like eight of them. She wore a neat, trim, black dress, her narrow waist cinched with a belt. Her dark hair was pinned back behind her ears. Her hat sat at a jaunty angle, sporting a short black veil, pulled over her face, in stark contrast with her pale skin. Her green eyes were lined with dark kohl; her lips painted a shade of firehouse red that was *almost* indecent. She clutched a small handbag in one hand as she glided forward, her legs—rather, her tentacles, moving in concert with an odd sort of disconcerting elegance.

August stood there, mouth gaping open slightly. She moved past him with the barest of sideways glances, taking in his veins and all, as though he bored her already.

Jack rose to his feet, setting the folder on his desk, snapping his lighter shut, and tucking it back in his pocket. He removed the unlit cigarette from his lips. She placed a gloved hand in his, and rather than shaking it, August watched as Jack bent forward, until his lips just barely brushed over the black silk. She smiled down at Jack in a smug sort of way, reminding August of a cat.

"You made it," Jack said with a crooked grin.

"Made it?" She frowned down at the glove. "Heavens no, much easier to buy these days. But never mind that, I'm only fashionably late, aren't I?"

Jack returned her smile. "Naturally," he said magnanimously. "How could you be anything else?" He turned to August, with what could only be described as a shit-eating grin. "Sully, this is Miss Vivienne Gray."

August took several seconds to break out of his stasis. He shot Jack a dark look, uncrossing his arms and striding forward. He stopped short of Miss Gray, watching as Jack released her hand. August eyed it warily for a moment, then bent forward at the waist, his hair falling over his eyes, as he bowed deeply.

"August Sullivan, Miss Gray. It's a pleasure," he said, his tone somewhat clipped. He caught a faint floral scent that he couldn't quite pinpoint. It reminded him of something sweet, but with a dark undercurrent. Like the scent in the air just before it rained, mixed with magnolias, perhaps. And peaches. His heart rate quickened as Miss Gray seemed to study him for rather longer than was polite.

"Yes, well," Miss Gray said, giving him a small, tight smile. "Let's get going, shall we? I don't suppose either of you are in the business of wasting time?"

With that, she turned and left the office just as abruptly as she had entered, the bell clanging in her wake.

Jack plucked his trench coat off the rack by the far wall and moved towards the door after her. August stopped him, halting his progress with his hand held out. Jack walked into it, forcing August to put some force behind his outstretched palm, pressing it against his partner's chest.

"Where are we going, exactly, Jack? And what's with the dame?" His voice came out as a growl.

"Just cool it, will you?" Jack said. "We're finally going somewhere, okay?"

August tilted his head to the side, fixing Jack with a look. But Jack ignored him, pushing past his partner and out the door.

August waited only seconds before shrugging his jacket on, and following him, tightening his tie as he went.

2

THE CHURCH. THE PLOT.

August stepped out onto the pavement, and the humidity rose to greet him. He pushed it back down with both hands, and took a deep, steadying breath. His pulse was still racing. The disruption had been enough to distract him, pull him back slightly from the edge. But he hovered there, his nerves stretched taut, still on the brink. Jack was right. They couldn't afford to have him going off half-cocked. He was supposed to be the calm one. The reliable one. He needed to get his emotions back under control. Maintain his composure.

It was the case. It had set him off-kilter. Managed to crawl under his skin, invading his thoughts, waking, and sleeping, in a way their previous cases hadn't. He was unsettled by it. Practically unnerved, if he were being honest. And it was for that reason, more than anything else that Jack had said or done, that he was on the verge of snapping. Of losing control.

August knew what would happen next.

And so did Jack. Yet, he continued, with his little digs. His snide comments. Calling him a preacher. Almost as though he was egging him on. Like he wanted him to snap.

August felt his fists clenching at his sides, his grip tightening on the brim of his hat, which he held in his right hand, as he eyed the black Cadillac that sat idling at the curb across the street. He practically did a double-take as he realized with a jolt that Miss Gray herself sat behind the wheel.

Jack had claimed the passenger seat beside her, leaving August with the back seat as his only option. He combed his hair back off his forehead and slid his hat on his head. He could already feel the sweat beading on his brow, and he wiped it surreptitiously with the back of his hand, as he jogged across the street to join them.

Neither of them spoke as he climbed in. Miss Gray waited only a moment before pressing the gas pedal down with one curled tentacle. The car lurched forward, pulling away from the curb.

She wasn't a bad driver; just a woman, and she drove fast. Way too fast for comfort. Or decency. August found himself clinging to anything he could grab hold of. He cleared his throat as Jack and Miss Gray chatted in the front. About tea, of all things.

"Might we, um, slow down, just a bit?" he called out over the din of the engine. Miss Gray laughed in response, as though he'd said something witty.

"Don't mind Sully," Jack said, twisting to glance at August over his shoulder. "He's downright morbid at his worst, and maudlin at his best."

"Gee, thanks, Jack," August said, clapping him on the back. "A ringing endorsement."

Jack laughed, glancing back at Miss Gray. "That's just my bitterness talking; he keeps me on a short leash."

Miss Gray smiled in a knowing way, her eyes flicking up at August in the rearview mirror. "No easy task, I imagine."

August smiled back, somewhat grimly. "Someone has to do it."

Jack fished two cigarettes out and handed one to Miss Gray. She took it, placing it between her lips, leaning over as he lit it for her. August watched them, his eyes lingering on Miss Gray's lips, red as sin. His gaze drifted to the curve of her neck, before he tore it away, focusing on the view out the window instead.

They had left the streets of downtown Atlanta, heading towards the Eastside. Smoke curled through the open window and was quickly pulled away, as Jack turned and exhaled carefully. August kept his lips pressed tight. He was tempted to ask where they were going, but knew better than to think he'd get a straight answer from Jack. He was still making up his mind about Miss Gray.

The Cadillac continued its mad dash through the Eastside, then through open fields of farmland, the pavement beneath them transitioning to dirt.

The horizon lay in the distance, never drawing nearer, just out of reach past an endless flat expanse. As August stared at the desolate landscape, he felt a wave of melancholy sweep over him. There was something about the open fields outside the city that filled him with a sense of existential dread. When a church rose out of the field in the distance, off to their right, that feeling only grew stronger. A knot of anguish formed deep in August's bowels as he stared at the pale, white structure, cutting a swath through the backdrop of dark woods that lay beyond.

They slowed, and Miss Gray guided the Cadillac in a right turn. They shook and bounced down the bumpy road. Two ruts worn into the earth that could only lead to one place.

August drew in a long, deep breath as the car ground to a halt. Miss Gray turned and eyed him surreptitiously; her gaze swept him up and down. "Are you going to be alright, Mr. Sullivan?" she asked, looking him directly in the eye. He only stared back at her.

"He'll be fine." Jack grinned and winked at August over his shoulder, before pushing his door open. "He's a masochist, after all."

August was shooting daggers at the back of Jack's skull as he climbed out of the Cadillac. Thankfully, they all missed, lodging themselves into the headrest. He waited until Miss Gray exited as well. Breathing deeply, taking slow deep breaths in and out, he willed himself towards calm. He pictured his veins shrinking, retracting. He gave himself to the count of ten, then he pushed the door open and stepped out of the car.

While Miss Gray busied herself in the trunk at the rear, August steeled himself, eying the steps that led to the double doors of the church. Plain, but oddly ominous; black handles against faded wood grain. His eyes strayed to the roof. The peak. The plain white cross that perched there, like a cold proclamation of judgement, reaching into the heavens. He was barely breathing. He could feel his control, already stretched thin, ready to snap.

But to his relief, Miss Gray led them to the side of the church, rather than up the stairs, and then around the back. They walked past headstones. Some leaned, tilting, close to surrendering themselves to the soil, along with their namesakes. The headstones closest to the church were the oldest, if August had to guess. The stones became more upright, and less weather worn, as they continued their trek. The graveyard extended nearly to the treeline, the hum of cicadas growing steadily louder as they approached the edge of the woods.

Miss Gray walked with a long umbrella, using the pointed end as one would a cane, or a walking stick. She did not lean her weight on it, but she punctured the earth as she moved forward, with a brisk tap of the point into the soil, her many legs sliding and slithering over the damp grass.

She came to a stop beside a headstone, as unassuming as any other small stone in the graveyard. She glanced up at the sky. Locating the dim sun, shielded behind a veil of clouds, she lifted the umbrella and opened it, holding it between herself and the faint rays of daylight. August glanced back and forth between her and the invisible sun overhead. That explained her complexion.

"Here," Miss Gray said simply, nodding to herself, her green eyes swiveling to find Jack.

Jack pursed his lips. He fanned his trench coat out behind him dramatically, and placed both hands on his hips. He turned, surveying the ground beneath their feet, the surrounding headstones. He spun in a slow circle, studying the church, before he returned to the headstone Miss Gray had planted herself beside. "Here?" he asked, pointing at the ground at their feet.

"Yes," Miss Gray said.

"You're sure?"

"Yes. I'm quite sure."

Jack pursed his lips once more, expression thoughtful. He cocked his head to the side and then nodded briskly, seeming to have accepted her confidence.

"What's here?" August asked, frowning down at the grass beneath their feet, then at the gravestone. The engraved text was faint, but he thought he could just make out a name and a year: '*LANGSTON - 1892*'.

"This is where it will be," Miss Gray said, turning her cool green eyes on August. Once again, he found himself mildly unsettled by the directness of her eye contact, as though she was seeing more than just his features when she looked at him.

He looked away, studying the ground once more, as she observed him. "Where *what* will be?"

Jack turned, hands still on his hips. "Yes, well, I suppose it's just a matter of staking it out then, isn't it?" He studied the back of the church once more. "I don't fancy waiting inside, and not just because we'll risk you bursting into flames." He grinned over at August as he said that last bit.

"Very funny." August glared back, suppressing a shudder. "Waiting? Waiting for what? Just what are we talking about exactly?"

Jack turned to the treeline, studying the edge of the dark forest. "Yes, I like our odds in the woods much better." He turned to Miss Gray, one eyebrow raised. "Tonight?"

Miss Gray nodded, her expression impassive. "I believe so."

"What's tonight?" August frowned, looking back and forth between them.

"Right then. I suppose we'll have to make the most of it. It's our best chance," Jack said. He looked over at August. "We should've had something to eat before we left, you know; we could be in for a long night."

"Oh, don't worry. I packed plenty of provisions," Miss Gray said cheerfully.

"You're not staying?" Jack asked with a frown.

"I am," Miss Gray stated plainly but firmly.

"But that's out of the question," Jack said, as though he were faintly amused.

"I assure you, it isn't a question at all." Miss Gray met Jack's incredulity with her characteristically steady gaze.

"My dear Miss Gray." Jack fell into a relaxed stance, an easy smile coming to his lips. "I really must insist. Your assistance thus far has been invaluable. But to put it mildly, our foe is clearly formidable."

"I'm aware, Jack," Miss Gray replied, her tone conveying nothing but boredom.

"I'm not sure that you are..." Jack trailed off, shaking his head. "The scene we came upon was..." he trailed off yet again, with a shrug. "The details are not suitable for polite company, I'm afraid."

"I have never claimed to be such." Miss Gray's eyes seemed to crinkle slightly in amusement, the ghost of a smile on her lips. August swallowed thickly.

Jack was not to be deterred. "Miss Gray, I shall put it to you as plainly as possible. I cannot possibly allow you to stay. To do so would be to put you in danger. The scene of this particular crime is burned into my brain. Into my retinas. I have seen many, many unfortunate sights during my tumultuous, albeit somewhat brief, existence, but the sight of that woman, splayed–"

"Jack," August warned, taking a step towards them.

"Her heart was removed from her chest. Carved out. Whether with claws, or teeth, or a tool of some crude design, we cannot yet say. The skin of her abdomen was stretched, affixed on either side with–"

"Jack, that's enough."

Jack waved a hand dismissively in his direction. August watched Miss Gray. She did not appear to be the slightest bit perturbed.

"Her entrails–"

"That's quite enough, Jack," August barked, an edge to his voice now.

"Hush, Mr. Sullivan." Miss Gray turned her cool expression on him. "He need not stop on my behalf."

"...were removed from the cavity," Jack continued as though neither of them had spoken, Miss Gray stared into August's eyes. "There was the scent of... sulfur in the air. And on her skin, burnt... branded, as though with an unnatural flame, markings, containing text from the–"

"Oh for the love of God, shut your damnable mouth, Jack," August growled, his exasperation finally leaking through, his chest rising and falling rapidly.

Jack paused, turning to him as though he'd forgotten he was there. His mouth twisted in a wicked sort of grin, and he raised a finger, rested it on his lips, and cocked his head at the church. "Careful now, old boy."

August's glare could have cut ice. But as it was mid-June, and they were in Georgia, there was none in sight.

"As I said, you don't need to stop on my behalf. Nor do you need to continue. I've already seen it for myself." Both men turned to stare at Miss Gray. "It's going to happen again. Here. Tonight," Miss Gray continued, unfazed by the surprise written on their features. She stood there, under her black umbrella, her green eyes calculating behind her veil, her voice dropping to nearly a whisper. "The next murder."

3

THE CRIME SCENE. TEA.

"You cannot be earnest, Miss Gray." August shook his head; the tiny teacup he held in the saucer before him rattled slightly. He felt ridiculous.

"I've told you, her name is Vivienne, not Earnest," Jack said with mild disdain.

They sat on the blanket Miss Gray had insisted on laying out on the grass for them, enjoying a picnic beside the gravestones.

Miss Gray pursed her lips at Jack as she rolled her eyes at him. He picked them up and rolled them back.

She turned to August. "I assure you that I am, Mr. Sullivan," Miss Gray replied. Her tone held a hint of long-suffering patience. "I am intimately familiar with the crime scene from the first murder. And the second," she added, almost as an afterthought.

"That's not possible," August said, shaking his head. The teacup rattled again. He gripped the delicate handle tighter.

"But it is, old boy," Jack said, his tone sounding much more chipper than August felt it was decent to, given their current situation. "Miss Gray is renowned for her abilities."

"Prescience, being only one of them," Miss Gray said, inclining her head in Jack's direction.

"Prescience..." August began, trailing off, setting his teacup and saucer down on the blanket before him. "Really, Miss Gray–"

"Is it so hard for you to believe, Mr. Sullivan?" She tilted her head to the side, studying him once more. "I must admit, I find that not only intriguing, but somewhat ironic, coming from you."

August's features shifted, the veins beneath his eyes darkened, almost imperceptibly. "You say you're intimately familiar with the crime scene," he said, "perhaps you'd be so kind as to describe the victim's features."

"Please excuse him, he's not accustomed to..." Jack's voice trailed off uncertainly, as though he wasn't quite sure how to describe Miss Gray.

"With pleasure," Miss Gray said. "The victim was a young black woman."

"That was in the papers," August said, unimpressed.

Miss Gray continued. "If I had to guess, I would say mid-20s. Curly black hair, worn loose. Her eyes were brown, open, her pupils dilated. She was found naked," Miss Gray paused, then continued. "Jack has already described most of her... injuries, but I'll add that the markings were found primarily on her hands and forearms. Her veins were visible on her chest, above the... open cavity, as well as on her face." Miss Gray maintained eye contact with August as she spoke. "The veins beneath her eyes, in particular, were very prominent, as though she had expired while in a state of... arousal."

The silence that fell was thick. Heavy. August found himself momentarily at a loss for words. Jack sipped his tea idly while August recovered his composure.

"None of those... details were leaked to the press. The public. How–"

"I told you," Miss Gray said, "I saw her for myself."

"Yes, you said that," August conceded, "but I don't understand how."

"Miss Gray can see things, Sully," Jack said. "Sometimes, things in the present, or the past. And sometimes, the future."

"How is that possible?" August asked incredulously, his voice rising.

"Magic," Jack said simply.

August snorted, shaking his head, as he shifted uneasily on the blanket, tipping his teacup. Jack reached out, faster than humanly possible, and caught it before a drop had spilled. Miss Gray's eyes widened slightly as she watched him.

"It's true, Sully," Jack said, setting the teacup back on its saucer. "Miss Gray and I go way back." He smiled over at her. "She's helped me solve more than one case in the past. Before your time."

"I'm not offended, Jack," Miss Gray said softly, her gaze on August. "As I said, I am only intrigued. And amused."

"Oh, I amuse you, do I?" August asked.

Miss Gray appeared unbothered by the edge to his voice. "Your skepticism amuses me, yes." She smiled at him, her expression sympathetic, almost sad.

"Just because I–I am what I am," August said, his cheeks flushing, "doesn't mean I'm any more inclined to believe in magic, or whatever it is that you claim gives you this... prescience."

"August-" Jack began, but Miss Gray held a hand up, palm out, in his direction, her expression unflappable.

"I find that most intriguing, Mr. Sullivan," Miss Gray said. "I must apologize in advance for my brashness, but I have a feeling you'll forgive me." She smiled sweetly at him. "You are a vampire, Mr. Sullivan, are you not? An *upir*, in common slang. And your partner is... well..." she laughed. "Jack Quinn." She glanced over at Jack, and he bowed slightly.

"The one and only," he said with a self-satisfied grin. August shook his head, sighing.

"Add to that," Miss Gray continued, "and please, do correct me if I am wrong, that you've spent the past several months ridding the city of some of its most prominent... *undesirables*. I must confess, I find your skepticism not only amusing, but quite difficult for me to believe in myself."

August remained silent for several seconds after she finished speaking. He stared down at the blanket. His cheeks flushed hot, purple veins pulsing beneath his eyes. Jack studied his neck, or at least, what little was visible of it above his tie and collar. The skin there remained unmarked.

"Miss Gray," August said, finally making eye contact with her once more. "None of the facts you've just stated in any way preclude that I must believe in magic. I would argue, these facts might leave one inclined to believe just the opposite." His eyes bore into hers, the veins beneath them darkening further, turning swiftly from purple to black. Spreading, now. Branching, bubbling beneath his skin, as they rose to the surface. "I have experienced nothing close to magic in my lifetime, Miss Gray. I have not had the privilege. But darkness," he said, his voice dropping lower, "suffering, despair. Evil. Depravity. Those, I believe in."

Miss Gray met his stare, her green eyes solemn. "I am sorry to hear that, Mr. Sullivan. Truly, I am."

"I don't need your sympathy, or your pity," August said rather tersely. He regretted it immediately.

"No, I sense that you don't," Miss Gray responded evenly. "You might benefit from your own, though, Mr. Sullivan," she said, her expression calculating.

August had no response to such a statement. The silence felt distinctly uncomfortable, broken only by rise and fall of cicadas humming in the background.

"Right," Jack said, clearing his throat. "Well, Miss Gray was kind enough to reach out to me yesterday to convey her most recent..." he trailed off, making small circles with his hand in the air in her direction as he fumbled for the right word.

"Vision," Miss Gray supplied.

"Yes, vision," Jack continued, "and offered her assistance to us in solving this crime. If her prediction might in any way be accurate, well... surely you must see, August, that we can't take the risk of ignoring it? And if she's wrong, what's the worst that can happen? That we've wasted a pleasant evening, sitting out here in the woods? I'd say it's worth it. Wouldn't you?"

August frowned down at his hands, then up at the treeline that stretched before them. "So, it's going to happen here," he said resignedly. "And the three of us, sitting here, having a picnic at the crime scene, and then waiting in the woods to surprise the killer, that's not going to deter them, in any way?"

"Perhaps that was all going to happen anyway," Miss Gray said pleasantly. "There's no way to know, of course."

"Of course," August said. "But that must mean... that we are unsuccessful, then, correct? In stopping them? Otherwise... wouldn't the murder never take place?" He fumbled over his words. "What I mean is, how could you see it in the first place, if we're able to stop it? Doesn't that mean we fail?"

Miss Gray smiled at him, unmoved by his consternation. "Perhaps, Mr. Sullivan. There is only one way to find out."

4

THE GROUNDSKEEPER. THE STORM CLOUDS.

They waited below the trees, cloaked in shadows. The minutes ticked by with excruciating slowness.

After what seemed to be an unbearable length of time, Jack spoke, breaking the relative silence. "Miss Gray, I'm afraid it's only just now occurred to me to ask what the next victim looks like." He peered in her direction. The light from the nearly full moon overhead barely filtered down to them through the clouds and canopy above. "I pray you're not about to describe your own countenance. I'll have you dragged back to the Cadillac and back to town before you can bat an eyelash."

Miss Gray huffed a laugh at his words, stifling her laughter quickly. "Jack," she said, "of course it's not me. You think I foresaw my own murder and dragged you out here to watch? I am many things, but I am not an exhibitionist."

"Misery loves company, my dear. Besides, I'd like to think that if that were your plan, you'd brought me along to save you, not to merely be a witness to your untimely death."

Miss Gray laughed again, the sound low and husky under her breath. August felt his veins pulse in response and was grateful for the darkness.

"Well, naturally, darling. That would have been my plan all along. And I'm sure you'd have made a valiant savior. But no, the victim looks nothing like me."

Jack fell silent for a moment. "For goodness' sake, Vivienne, it isn't August?"

August sensed them turning to look in his direction.

"Do you mean the victim, or the murderer?" Miss Gray asked in a hushed voice.

Jack thought for a moment. "The victim."

"Lord no," Miss Gray murmured.

Jack made the sign of the cross. August could barely see him in the dark, but he knew from experience that was what he was doing.

August rolled his eyes as Miss Gray continued at a whisper. "The victim is female. A little younger, this time, I'm afraid. A blonde. Tall. Thin. Blue eyes."

Jack sighed, nodding. "The manner of death is the same, I'm assuming?"

"This is ridiculous," August said, unable to keep silent. "I'm sorry," he sputtered, his voice a hoarse whisper. "I'm sorry, Miss Gray, I mean you no offense when I say that this is absolute rubbish."

"I am not offended, Mr. Sullivan," Miss Gray said. "And I won't risk offending *you* further by reminding you that your disbelief only serves to amuse me."

"That's rather prudent of you, Miss Gray," Jack said. "Really, Sully, you do tend to be awfully melodramatic. And often at the worst times."

This elicited another low, husky laugh from Miss Gray, and August felt the blood rushing through the veins beneath his eyes, in his chest, and lower, as a burst of heat coiled through his groin.

"I can't..." August said, shaking his head. He straightened, his knees cracking as he rose from his crouched position.

"Dammit Sully, now's not the time." Jack stood as well, moving over to him. "What have I been telling you all week, you–"

"I can't do this," August said, grabbing Jack by the arm, cutting him off, his voice dropping low. "I'm just going to... to take a walk. Walk for a bit in the woods. I can't sit here any longer."

"This," Jack murmured back. "This is what I'm talking about. You can't keep doing this to yourself. You need to feed. You're wearing yourself too thin. This case has already got you on the edge, you're only making it worse."

August's grip tightened on Jack's arm. "Don't," he hissed. His eyes shifted involuntarily in Miss Gray's direction.

Jack dropped his voice lower, sliding closer to August. "It's not something to be ashamed of, August. How many times do I have to say it?"

August shook his head, released his death grip on Jack's arm, turned, and strode away.

He moved silently through the woods. Passing like just another shadow beneath the trees. The clouds parted above him, allowing slivers of moonlight to pierce the night. August glanced up at the moon a little warily, then back in the direction of the others.

It was nearly a full moon. But not quite. August was well aware that Jack was at his worst at the full moon, and he felt a momentary hesitation. A trickle of guilt. But his pulse was racing now. He could feel the veins standing out, brushing against his shirt, on his chest. She would see. She would have been able to see him clearly now, in the moonlight, if he were still back there. He wasn't fit to be around her. He wasn't fit to be around anyone, when he felt like this. So, August continued, striding silently, further away from them.

He had been walking on his own for perhaps fifteen minutes, maybe more, when he heard it. On the edge of his hearing. Faint; just barely audible. It came from the direction of the church. The graveyard.

August did not hesitate when the sound reached his ears. He took off like a shot, sprinting. Running, ducking, and weaving nearly silently between trees and under branches, the only sound was generated by the rush of air he left swirling in his wake.

He heard it again as he neared the treeline. Miss Gray's voice, crying out. Her words were lost in the wind, but the tone, the urgency, was unmistakable.

August broke through the treeline, slightly winded, panting, and slid to a halt, getting his bearings. They had moved from their hiding spot in the woods. It took several heartbeats for him to locate them. They were out in the open, over by the church.

Miss Gray called out to Jack as August approached at a slower pace, weaving between gravestones as he went, fixated on the dark figures up ahead.

"Jack, I'm telling you, it's not him. Let him go. Please. You *must* let him go." Her voice was slightly unsteady. It was the first time he'd heard any real emotion break through the thick facade of ennui she seemed to wear so well.

August moved to her side instinctively, and he laid a hand on her upper back, near her shoulder. The barest of touches, only so she would know he was there. But still, she gasped and jumped back, startled, her eyes wide, her hand going to her mouth. She had pulled her veil back, as it now lay folded up over her hat.

"Oh, August," she said, "It's– I think he's the caretaker. It's not– I don't think he has anything to do with it. Tell him." She pointed over towards the church, and August moved past her, squinting, heading towards the dark figures that appeared as mere shadows against the white siding.

"Jack," he called out tentatively as he moved closer. But no response came.

When he was just a few feet away, the moon managed to break through the cloud cover above once more, and August was able to get a clearer glimpse of the situation.

Jack stood there, towering over a man who cowered on the ground beneath him. The man's hat had been knocked loose, lying upside down behind him. A pair of gardening gloves was visible, tucked into his front pocket. He had pissed himself, August saw. A dark stain spread over his crotch, as he stared up at Jack in abject terror.

Jack's mouth was open wide. His jaw appeared to be unhinged. Long, sharp teeth glistened in the moonlight. His eyes were pitch black as he stared down at the older man. He held a clump of the man's shirt in his fist, gripping him just below his collar.

"Jack," August said, both hands held out, palms hovering parallel to the ground. "Listen to me. You need to let him go. He's not the one we're after, I promise you. Let go of him, Jack. Come on now."

Jack stilled, his gaping mouth closing slightly. August watched his hand drop a fraction lower and realized he was holding the man several inches off the ground. None of his weight rested on his bent knees; he hung there, suspended, only his feet resting on the grass.

"That's it, Jack, put him down. He's not the one we're looking for."

The man whimpered, and Jack let out a low snarl, tightening his grip and lifting him higher off the ground.

August felt a hand on his arm and turned to see that Miss Gray now stood beside him.

"Jack, please," she called out to him, her expression grim. "Listen to us."

"Miss Gray," August warned, "don't get any closer."

The older man whimpered again, twisting in their direction. "Help me!" he cried out. "Please, this thing came out of nowhere, rushed me in the dark. I'm just the groundskeeper. I haven't done nothing wrong. Please."

"Shh," August held a finger up to his lips, "please, be quiet–"

"Jack, you have to let this man go." Miss Gray moved closer, back erect now, her tone commanding. "Jack, I swear to God, I'll never forgive you. Let. Him. Go." She raised both hands, as she spoke, each word louder, punctuated suddenly by a crack of thunder overhead, that roiled and broke over them, reverberating with raw power.

August stared up at the sky above; swiftly moving clouds loomed, rushing, billowing, and swirling. Blooming, lit from within by an unnatural, greenish light. His jaw dropped open as he watched dark shadows forming within the clouds. A stroke of lightning slashed through the roiling mass, revealing massive, long, sinuous dark shapes, curling and twisting within.

August stared over at Miss Gray in horror, before his focus was torn back to the present struggle.

Jack let out a roar that ended in a growl. He dropped the man to the ground, releasing him completely. He turned, snarling at Miss Gray, before dropping into a low crouch. August felt himself drop into an answering crouch. Miss Gray glared at Jack, apparently unfazed, but August's heart was hammering wildly against his ribcage, and when Jack's muscles coiled, tensing, as though he were readying to spring, August felt himself snap.

He lunged forward, intercepting Jack with outstretched arms, taking him down to the ground beside the church wall. Jack snarled up at him, his unnaturally wide jaw snapping. August practically growled back, shoving him to the ground simultaneously for emphasis. Jack twisted his legs around August, attempting to tip him over as he struggled to gain the upper hand.

August exhaled a great rush of air as Jack twisted his legs, rotating him further. He was slammed on his back against the earth. Jack clambered above him, teeth gnashing. August grabbed him by the throat with one hand and squeezed. Hard.

Jack let out a strangling howling, yelping sound, and the caretaker screamed, his eyes going wide, as he scrambled backwards in a crabwalk, away from them. The world went dark, as another thunderclap shook them, and the moonlight disappeared once more behind the spreading, swirling clouds. Cold rain began to fall on August's upturned face.

August's eyes, he knew, would be nearly as black as Jack's now. The veins on his chest and face stood out, engorged, pulsing, and tight. Jack snarled down at him, and August snarled back, practically roaring. Jack gripped his arm in both hands, pulling, loosening his grip, one centimeter at a time, his unnaturally wide jaw snapping, his eyes black holes in his head. The clouds shifted, and as the moonlight shone down on them once more, Jack paused, seeming to recognize August suddenly. His grip on August's arm loosened, then went slack. August watched as Jack's eyes began to change, and he released his throat.

Jack scrambled off him. He shook himself, shaking his head violently, hunching over, down on all fours. He let loose a garbled growl that shifted into a moan before he collapsed onto the ground. He lay there, panting, as the rain began to fall in earnest.

August's nerves were on fire. Flames of heat licked his chest, his cheeks. He clenched his fists as he peered over at Jack, his chest still heaving. Miss Gray approached them, her tentacled legs curling sinuously, coming to a stop a few feet away. She stared down at Jack.

August continued to pant, to suck in air. He couldn't seem to get enough air into his lungs. He took in great, gulping gasps, willing himself to stand down. The raindrops against his cheeks were a welcome counterpoint to the heat that blossomed there.

Miss Gray raised her gaze from Jack's prone figure. "Thank you, Mr. Sullivan," she said, "that was quite heroic of you, but I assure you, I had the situation well in hand." The ominous banks of swirling clouds overhead were fading now. Dissipating, along with the eldritch horrors concealed within, as they swirled in the wind, and dissolved into nothing but typical grey storm clouds.

August managed to nod, shifting to his side and staggering to his feet. "You should go," he said gruffly.

Miss Gray's brows creased. "I think he's alright now," she began, but he cut her off.

"Miss Gray, I really think it's for the best," August said adamantly.

"He'll be back to his usual self in no time," Miss Gray insisted. "Why would I go? I'm not going to leave you stranded out here; I'm your ride back to town."

"No," he paused, struggling to find the right words. To make her understand. "Miss Gray... *I* need you to go. *Now.*"

Something in her expression shifted. She stared openly at him now. But it wasn't in fear. Curiosity, perhaps. Or something else. She delayed only a moment longer before swallowing and nodding solemnly. Then she turned towards the Cadillac. "I could lock myself in the car. Wait for you to..." she trailed off.

August shook his head. "Just go," he said, his tone more urgent now. "*Please.*"

She studied him, and he held himself back. Waiting. Muscles taut, trembling. Heat bloomed again on his cheeks. She'd seen him, now, at his worst. Nearly.

August felt suddenly ill, as though he might vomit. "Go!" he shouted at her, taking a step forward. "Now!"

Miss Gray didn't flinch. She didn't recoil. She only continued to study him, her expression unreadable, before nodding once more and turning to head towards the car.

5

A SECOND BODY. THE BLOOD THAT DIDN'T SPILL IN THE NIGHT.

They were called to the scene early enough the following morning that the air still held a chill. That was all it was, August told himself. Just a bit of dampness, left over from the rain of the previous evening, which seemed to permeate the world, seeping into August's bones as he stood there. Or perhaps, some miasma, infused into the dead air, outside the small tailor shop on Edgewood Avenue.

August stood outside on the sidewalk, for several minutes before entering the shop. The sign over the door read, in all caps; *'LANGSTON & CO., FINE TAILORS.'* The street outside the little shop, with its red door, was practically empty. Not unusual, necessarily, for this time of day. Although Decatur was likely already bustling by now. Edgewood, however, was not quite as fashionable or prestigious, and it was located slightly off the main drag.

Jack pushed past him, as he stood there, studying the facade of the shop, as though he were nothing but eager to set eyes on the macabre tableau that surely awaited them inside.

And now, August felt he had delayed for as long as possible. By now, his absence had likely been noted and deemed deliberate. Yet another sign of his current predicament, and further evidence that Jack was, once again, and as usual, correct.

So, August dallied no further, taking one last deep breath of the damp air that filled him with dread, he gripped the ornate door handle in his sweaty palm, and pulled open the door to the little shop, forcing himself through the threshold, into the darkness within.

He had hardly moved since. Having entered the shop, August found his forward motion stalled. He stood there, nearly perfectly still, only his chest rising and falling minutely, while Jack ducked and weaved, almost as though he were dancing around the corpse, studying it from every angle, as though in so doing, he would glean even a modicum of rationality from its flagrant, exorbitant blasphemy. All the while, voices rose and fell, drifting from the hidden recesses in the back of the shop. A man's voice, thick with grief.

The young woman–no, girl, really, lay spread-eagle; her arms and legs extended at the extremes of their limits of torsion away from her trunk. She had been carved up the middle. Her ribcage and abdomen were exposed, skin stretched, pierced through with wicked-looking metal hooks, affixed with rough twine that stretched taut; the other end tied to table legs, a drawer handle, a support beam, anything solid and immovable in the vicinity. It was as though her hide was being prepared for tanning, the thin layer of adipose beneath revealed.

The script, scrolling up both arms, branded onto her skin, was red at its core, the edges burned to a black crisp. She had been branded on the forehead as well. Smack in the middle, carved into her flesh, a familiar looking sort of swirl, with curving lines fanned out in a circle from the center. August knew if he counted them, there would be 8 spokes to the gruesome wheel. From beneath the marking, she stared up at him. Her pupils were dilated so wide as to fill the iris, making them appear nearly pitch black. Her veins were engorged, fanning out from beneath both eyes, and across her chest, starting at the base of her neck.

Once more, her heart had been removed. August tried not to look at that gaping cavern; the rough, jagged lines carved into flesh, the scoring marks on the cracked bones of her ribs and sternum.

Jack seemed to be oblivious to the fact that August had joined him. Several officers, the first to arrive on the scene, stood off to the side. Mumbling amongst themselves. One of them turned suddenly, brushing past August and out onto the street. He could hear the man retching before the door slammed shut.

"We must take note, August," Jack said thoughtfully.

"Of what?" August managed to murmur, his voice somewhat hoarse.

"Everything. Absolutely everything. We must compare. Any minute difference may be worth noting. Not just in the body, and it's display, but the scene itself." Jack spun, taking in the shop as though for the first time. "The location is very different, is it not?"

August swallowed. "Yes, it is."

"In what ways?" Jack asked. He took a pack of cigarettes from an inner pocket of his trench coat, removed one, and placed it between his lips.

August sighed deeply. "Well, for one thing, the first body was found outside."

Jack nodded, one hand on his chin, as he paced before the body. "Yes... be more specific..."

August betrayed the tediousness he felt in his tone, as he continued. "On the edge of a field, beneath a tree. *Not* in a shop."

"Yes, that's the most obvious difference. Yes." Jack nodded to himself. He took a turn around the shop. "What else?"

"Really, Jack, must we do this now?" August said. The officers were watching them, listening.

"If not now, when?" Jack quipped. He turned to stare at the officers. "Phillip, did you get close-ups already?" he asked, seeming to follow August's train of thought. "I want every inch of text photographed. Every single inch. And make sure you get a close-up of the mark on her forehead."

The officer holding the large camera snapped to attention and moved forward, holding it aloft.

Jack moved to August's side. The shop door swung open behind them. "The same marking that was carved into the tree..." he spoke as though to himself, his voice pitched low. Then he sighed. "I have to say, I am surprised. I've never known Miss Gray to be wrong before."

August chuckled, unable to keep the derision from his tone.

"There's a first time for everything, isn't there, Jack?" Both men turned abruptly to find Miss Gray standing behind them, her cool green eyes taking them in. "Although *wrong* might be a bit of an exaggeration," Miss Gray continued, moving past them and towards the body. The now familiar scent of magnolias, peaches, and rainclouds, washed over August. He tensed as he caught himself in the act of breathing it in deeply, as one might partake in the scent of a fresh pie cooling on a windowsill.

Miss Gray tilted her head to the side as she stood staring down at the poor girl. "Blonde. Young. Tall. It's hard to tell, of course." She leaned forward. "But I daresay her eyes are, in fact, blue." Miss Gray tutted, shaking her head. "And then there's the name."

"Name?" Jack repeated, frowning. "Maryanne Cole?"

"Langston," August murmured.

"*Langston*?" Jack repeated.

"Above the door," August said, turning towards him with an air of reluctance. "The shop name. Same as on the gravestone."

Miss Gray turned to him with a self-satisfied smile that was nearly a smirk. Once more, August was reminded of a cat. He shuddered slightly as she fixed him with those green eyes.

"Bravo, Mr. Sullivan," Miss Gray said. "You don't miss much, do you?"

Jack's frown only deepened for a moment before his expression cleared. "The name on the headstone matches the name of the shop..."

"Yes. So, I wouldn't say I was entirely *wrong*," Miss Gray said archly. "Thus is the predicament, for those of us who can see into the future. The vision is clouded. Murky. As though one is looking through a window, or perhaps a mirror, thick with layers of dust and grime. One can never be entirely sure of what one gleans. For it is the eye that sees, but the mind, that must interpret." She seemed to stare at August as she spoke, although her expression had a glazed-over aspect to it, as though she wasn't really seeing him.

"An admirable description, Miss Gray," Jack said solemnly. August turned away from them both, resuming his vigil over the body.

They were silent for several moments. "What do you make of the location of the script, August?" Jack said eventually.

When August gave no indication he was inclined to respond, Miss Gray spoke up. "I find it curious that the script is located mostly on her extremities; her hands and arms, and her legs," Miss Gray said, moving to the side of the body. "Although I see there is some text perhaps, along her abdomen, as well. What of the underside of the skin that has been... removed?" She turned to look at Jack, one eyebrow raised.

Jack nodded briskly. "Yes."

"So that was done first," Miss Gray said, "and her chest, and the base of her neck, are left bare..."

"I would think the reason is obvious," August said, his cheeks heating as though he regretted having spoken out loud.

Jack and Miss Gray turned to him, waiting. The officer taking photographs paused and turned as well.

August glanced between them, then sighed. He crossed his arms behind his lower back, clasping his hands together. He strolled around the body, moving between the stands with fabrics and suits on display, careful not to disturb the strands that held her open, until he stood directly behind the body.

"The script is focused on areas of the body where the veins are less prominent. The killers avoided marking the chest, the cheeks... for that reason; to avoid obscuring the veins." He cleared his throat, then fell silent.

Jack was watching him with narrowed eyes. "And why would they want to avoid covering up the veins?"

"*Killers*," Miss Gray said. "Plural. You think there was more than one person involved?"

August remained silent, staring down at the girl's face. Her eyes were fixed on the ceiling above. Her features contorted in pain, even in death. "I do," he said quietly, after a pause, "I think this was done by more than one person, yes."

"Why?" Jack asked.

"The amount of time it would take, for one thing. I would imagine an endeavor of this sort to require at least two people. At least one to complete the..." he trailed off for a moment, "torture, and one to act as a look-out." He paused, thinking. "The detail in the script... if you look here, and here...." he pointed first to the right arm, then the left. "The handwriting– I'm no expert, but it looks slightly different."

Jack frowned, moving closer and squinting. "Perhaps... it's slanted in two different directions, at the very least. Good eye Sully."

August stared down at the girl's right arm, splayed out to the side, her forearm dangling off the display table. His eyes followed the line of text inscribed there. *"In principio erat Verbum, et Verbum erat apud Deum, et Deus erat Verbum."*

"What I can't figure out is how they kept the victims quiet," Jack said. "Imagine how much pain… how she must have screamed… I don't understand how no one heard it."

"Perhaps someone did hear it, and no one came," August retorted swiftly. He was unable to keep the red-hot anger he felt sloshing and swirling beneath his skin from creeping into his voice.

"What a disturbing thought," Miss Gray murmured, staring down at the girl.

Jack stared at August, with a deep frown. "Now what makes you say something like that old boy?"

"She was a vampire, wasn't she? An *upir*," August said thinly. "Are you shocked that no one rushed to her aid?"

"You're making a lot of assumptions there," Jack said carefully.

"That's not the part I find most puzzling," August said, "have either of you noted the distinct lack of blood?"

Miss Gray looked over at August, stilling.

August tore his eyes from the body, from the script burned into the poor girl's flesh. "How did they manage it? They sliced her open, from navel to neck, ripped out her heart…" he swallowed thickly, "and not a drop of blood was spilled."

Jack stood slowly, staring down at the body as though transfixed. "Christ, August, you're right. And I didn't even notice it." He ran a hand through his hair, absentmindedly, then studied it more closely, taking in the long, delicate fingers, the slivers of jagged broken bone that protruded from the wrist. He dropped the severed hand onto the carpet below, jumping back, with a gasp and a visible shudder.

Then Jack knelt once more, studying first the severed hand, then the carpet, then the table above, on which Maryanne Cole lay splayed open. The dark wooden surface beneath her pale flesh gleamed with polish. The cream carpet below was pristine. "How is that possible?" Jack looked at August in consternation, and they stared at each other, expressions grim.

Miss Gray cleared her throat, and they turned to her, heads swiveling. "I can think of only one way to ensure not a drop of blood would be spilled," she said, "and that would be to make sure the poor girl was drained completely, before beginning."

Jack scoffed, a rush of air leaving his throat. "But that's impossible."

Miss Gray met his skepticism with her usual coolness, her features expressionless.

Jack held his hands out to indicate the body. "She was a vampire. Who, or what, on earth could drain a vampire's blood?"

It was August who spoke first. "Another vampire," he said, "it's the only thing that makes sense.

6

KILLING SPREE. GOD IS DEAD.

"I fell asleep in front of the fire, you see." The tailor, Mr. Cole, held his cap in both hands, twisting it tighter as he spoke. "I surely would have noticed that she never came home... but I fell asleep. She wanted to stay late, after we closed for the night. She was going to finish up something for a client. I... I fell asleep..." His voice quavered, then broke. His shoulders shook with silent sobs. "It's because she was a vampire, isn't it? That's what they're doing." He swallowed thickly. "I know what they've been saying in the papers. I know the first one, she was a... a call girl. But this, this is different. Maryanne was a decent girl. This is a killing-spree, isn't it? They're targeting vampires, aren't they?"

Jack cleared his throat. "Now that there has been a second... victim. It is looking that way, yes. We might assume we have a serial killer, who is deliberately targeting vampires, at this point. But at the same time, we're not in the habit of jumping to conclusions prematurely."

Mr. Cole glared at Jack. "My Maryanne was a sweet girl. She never hurt no one. Never got into any trouble. There's no... no one, who knew her personally, that could have done this to her. I don't believe that for a second. This was done out of hatred, for *her* kind." He turned, tone sharp, to August. "And *you* need to do something about it."

August stood off to the side, and slightly behind Jack, struggling to keep his expression, and the skin beneath his eyes, smooth.

Mr. Cole sighed. "What I can't figure out, is how they knew. We kept it a secret, you see." Mr. Cole's cheeks flushed red. He stared down at the floor as he spoke. "Not because I was ashamed of it, mind you– I wasn't." He looked once more at August, his expression defiant. "And I told Maryanne not to be, either. We are a good, God-fearing family. It wasn't our fault she... got sick." He paused; a sob hitched his chest. "But we kept it a secret." His chin jutted forward once more. "I did it for the business; to keep it afloat. There's some people that won't do business with vampires. Maryanne was meant to take over, some day." He sniffed and wiped his hand over his eyes. "So, no one knew. No one besides immediate family... and–" he paused for a moment, his eyes moving back and forth rapidly, "they wouldn't have told anyone– none of them. I just don't understand it..." he shook his head, looking suddenly lost and frightened, "how did they know she was a vampire?"

Silence fell, and August shifted anxiously.

Jack stepped forward. "That's what we're going to find out, Mr. Cole. We'll find who did this, and get you answers." He cleared his throat. "The front door." He pointed towards the front of the shop. "Was it locked, when you left? We didn't notice any signs of a forced entry."

The tailor shook his head, his chest still heaving as he composed himself. "Yes. I'm sure the front door was locked when I left. Same with the back. I double checked them both. Just like always, on nights when Maryanne stays–" he caught himself, a spasm of grief washing over his features, "-*stayed*, late." He wiped his hands over both eyes, head hanging, shoulders beginning to shake.

Miss Gray swept past both of them, wrapping an arm around the tailor and leading him away from the men, over to a pair of armchairs on the far side of the room. "Tell me about her, Mr. Cole," she said. "What was she like?"

August turned away as she sat there with him, trying not to wince at the sobs, the expression of grief that flowed from the poor man. He sighed deeply.

"Come on," Jack whispered to him, "let's leave her to it."

August frowned at him. "Shouldn't we be the ones questioning him?" He turned back to glance at Miss Gray.

"She'll do us justice, Sully, don't you worry about that."

"That's not what I'm worried about, Jack. In what capacity is Miss Gray assisting us, exactly? She's not a member of the force, she's a civilian..."

Jack grabbed him by the arm and led him back to the front of the shop. "Oh hush. I've already told you; she's assisted me before."

"So Chief Waverly knows, then?"

"Don't worry about it, old chap," Jack said, slapping August on the back. "He's right, you know," he segued, his expression grim, "there's no use denying any longer what this is."

August shook his head, his jaw clenched tight.

"A series of murders, targeting vampires," Jack said. "I think we both knew when we saw the first body, that it wouldn't be the last. I'm afraid they're only just getting started."

"It was only a matter of time, I suppose," August ground out, "before someone started killing off vampires. I'm surprised, quite frankly, that it's taken this long."

Jack glanced sideways at him. "Yet, you think it was a vampire, that did it."

August shrugged. "I can't think of any other explanation, can you? How else did they manage not to spill any blood?" He stared at the cream carpet once more. "Unless blood *was* spilled, and they somehow managed to clean it up... but that seems highly unlikely."

"No," Jack said, "there was no blood spilled here. I'd know if there had been." His nostrils flared slightly as he spoke. "No cleaning solutions used recently either." He shook his head. "That theory's out."

August sighed. "Then we're back at another vampire being the most likely solution, aren't we?"

Jack stared over at the body, then out the shop windows, to the street beyond. Activity had picked up now, pedestrians strolling past slowed and eyed the little shopfront suspiciously as they passed by the pair of policemen who stood guard by the door.

"What if that were the point?" Jack said slowly, his expression distant.

"What do you mean?" August asked.

"What if that was the killer's intention? To make it look like the killings must have been done by a vampire? What if they've invented some other method of draining the body? Perhaps they just wanted it to *look* like the killer was a vampire." Jack's expression changed as he spoke, a small smile coming to his lips. "We need to get her back to the morgue; see what Dr. Caudell has to say." Jack paused for a moment. "Drat. It's likely too late to determine whether the same was done with the first victim. Unless we can have her dug up again."

"Jack, let's not start running away with theories, not until we have some evidence. Besides," August frowned, "there was no mention of Dixie's blood being drained in the autopsy report."

Jack moved swiftly, ducking beneath the threads, still connected to Maryanne's corpse. He crouched down, examining her neck closely. "That's odd, isn't it? It's a crucial difference..."

"Unless, her blood *was* drained," August said, "but how could we have missed that?"

"It had rained heavily that morning, remember?" Jack said, glancing over at the window. "Any blood at the scene would have been washed away, right? It makes sense that the absence of blood on the ground beneath her wouldn't have struck us as odd, given the circumstances." Jack shrugged. "Easy enough to miss."

"True," August said slowly, "but the autopsy should have caught it regardless."

Jack had returned to examining the body. "Shouldn't it be easy enough to determine whether she was bitten? I don't see any obvious puncture wounds..." he trailed off, moving to examine the other side of her neck.

"It doesn't just have to be her neck, Jack." August rolled his eyes and sighed, crossing his arms. "It could have been anywhere. Not to mention, her skin is covered with the... script. Easy enough to cover up a puncture wound."

"So, would that mean she was already dead then, when they branded her?" Jack looked up at him, one eyebrow raised. "I should prefer to think that was the case."

August grimaced. "It's hard to say, isn't it?" he said quietly. "If they'd drained her blood, then branded her, then... cut her open." August shrugged. "She may have technically still been alive, albeit likely unconscious, until the final moment." His voice dropped lower, as he scanned her ribcage. "Until they removed her heart." His gaze drifted to her face. He took in her expression.

"Something tells me she wasn't," Jack said, his voice gruff. "Unconscious, I mean."

August swallowed, turning away from the body. He found his hands clenched into fists at his sides and forced them to relax. He moved over to the window, staring out into the street, attempting to ignore the stray passersby craning their necks to peer into the shop.

"We're going to find them, old sport. Don't you doubt it. Whoever is doing this, vampire or no, it's only a matter of time until our shadows darken their doorstep." Jack's voice dropped nearly to a whisper. "And even God won't be able to help them when we do."

"God?" August let out an ironic chuckle. "There is no God, Jack." His teeth ground against each other, and his fists clenched once more.

"You can't mean that, Sully," Jack said gently. "You were a preacher, once. You must have... felt otherwise, at least at one point." The unmistakable sound of Miss Gray approaching reached August's ears, a soft sliding, slithering sort of susurrous.

It was a long while before August responded. When he did, his voice was nearly a whisper. "If there ever was a God, then he's long dead. Or he has abandoned us."

Jack cleared his throat. "What about you, Vivienne? You must believe in a higher power."

When she didn't respond, August turned away from the window to find her studying him closely.

"*My* belief doesn't enter into it, Jack," she said softly. "Besides, that's not the question you should be asking. It isn't whether or not we believe in God, it's whether God believes in us."

7

THE MORGUE. THE PLOT THICKENS.

August was not ashamed to admit, to himself, at least, that he was glad they had missed the autopsy. By the time they arrived in the basement floor that contained the morgue, Dr. Caudell appeared to be tidying up. The smell was bad enough, without any imagery to go along with it.

Jack and August stood off to the side, lingering by the doorway, as he dismissed his assistants with the wave of a hand. Maryanne's body still lay on the examining table, but mercifully, she was no longer splayed open, and a crisp sheet covered her body up to the neck.

"Come in, come in," Dr. Caudell called them over, not bothering to look up from the folder he held open before him. He turned several pages, licking his finger as he did so; to help grip the page, causing August to shudder, and hope he'd washed his hands thoroughly. Then, the doctor nodded to himself, closed the folder, and placed it on the desk in the corner.

"What can I help you with, gentlemen? You know well enough that the official report will be typed up and submitted to you in due time."

"Yes." Jack cleared his throat, moving further into the room. "Of course, of course. We merely wanted to speak with you in person, briefly, to see if you had any first impressions. Anything that stood out to you as different from the first victim?"

Dr. Caudell sighed, folded his arms across his chest, and eyed Jack over the rim of his glasses. "My initial impression, is that the treatment of the body appears to have been nearly identical to the first, in practically every aspect." The doctor walked over to the examining table, as Jack frowned over at August.

"Everything? Hmm," Jack hummed thoughtfully. "Time of death?"

Dr. Caudell sighed once more. "Approximately between midnight and four in the morning. Just like the first." He shook his head. "Really, it will all be in the report. There's nothing significant."

"Really? What about the fact that this victim appears to have been drained of blood?"

Dr. Caudell's head whipped around so fast that August half expected his neck to snap. "What on earth do you mean? This finding is exactly the same as the first victim."

Jack stared Dr. Caudell down, as he slid both hands into his pockets, and seemed to mull over his words before releasing them. "That is *not* what we gathered from the autopsy report."

Dr. Caudell's cheeks turned a particularly bright shade of crimson. "That's not possible. I–I dictated my findings very precisely, the report should have included–"

"So, the first victim *was* drained of blood? By what method?" Jack continued nonchalantly.

His apparent ease only caused Dr. Caudell to appear more flustered. "Wh–why I surmise via oral exsanguination– how else?" Dr. Caudell sputtered. He moved over to his desk and began to shuffle charts and files around, his visage growing more clouded by the second.

"Did you identify teeth marks then, on the first victim? What about this one?" Jack inclined his head towards the body.

"I did indeed." Dr. Caudell stood abruptly and marched over to the table, pulling on a pair of gloves that seemed to have appeared out of nowhere as he went. "Look, here–" he lifted the sheet, and rotating Maryanne's right arm, he indicated a faint mark on the inner wrist. "And here–" he reached across the prone figure, and performed a similar action, revealing a second faint mark on the left wrist. "Two perfectly clear bite marks." August tried to ignore the cross-section of jagged bone at the end of Maryanne's arm, where her left hand had been snapped off.

"And you're sure these markings couldn't have been created by any other method?"

"Such as?" The doctor frowned down at the markings on the left wrist, partially obscured by the branded script.

Jack shrugged. "Something, say, mechanical, in nature? Say a machine, or a syringe, of some type? Something designed to remove blood via other means."

The doctor stared at him for a brief pause, then back down at the wrist he still held in one hand. "I've never heard of such an invention. But yes, I'm quite confident these are bite marks. You can see the nature of the puncture wound, here, if you look closely–

"Were the bite marks in the same spot on the first victim?" Jack cut him off abruptly

"Yes!" Caudell snapped. August stared at Dr. Caudell's bald head. It might have been his imagination, but he thought he saw steam rising from the shiny dome. "I don't understand what you're getting at. All of this was *in* the official report–"

"Who types up your reports, Doctor? Not you, I presume?" Jack's eyes had glazed over now, as he stared down at the body. "Marcy? Up in admin?"

"Well, yes, usually. Sometimes Gladys takes over. But either way–"

"So, you may have spoken the words, during your dictation, as is your usual method, but those words, did not make it into the official report. At least, not in the copy we received." Jack glanced over at August, a grim smile on his face.

"If you'd let me finish," Dr. Caudell said, "regardless of who types up the dictation, I am in the strict habit of reviewing every single autopsy report. Nothing leaves my desk without my explicit approval. I certainly would never allow a dictation I haven't set eyes on to be submitted to the official record."

Jack frowned, staring down at Maryanne's face. His eyes seemed to linger on her forehead, on the many-spoked wheel that reminded August of curling appendages. "And you're sure– you're 100%

sure, that part made it into the final report?" Jack looked up at Dr. Caudell, one eyebrow raised in skepticism.

The doctor seemed to freeze for a moment, his eyes flickering left and right in the air over their heads, as though he would find the answer there. Finally, he let out a deep sigh, the color on his cheeks, which had faded slightly, grew darker once more. "No," he said with a reluctant finality. "No, I cannot be completely sure that sentence specifically made it into the final report. I was not looking for it, specifically. But I read the report through, and did not notice it's absence, which to me, would indicate–"

Jack cut him off once more, pulling a cigarette out of his pocket as the doctor spoke, he grabbed his lighter next, and the flick of his thumb, and the audible click, cut the doctor off as effectively as a slap to the face.

"Good heavens man, you can't smoke in here!" Dr. Caudell's eyes bugged out of his head, and he turned to August with a look that clearly said, *do something*.

August sighed, gritting his teeth. He walked over to Jack, and placed a hand on his fist, careful not to touch the small flame. He shook his head, once, and Jack sighed, rolled his eyes, and snapped the lighter shut once more, dousing the flame. "Fine," he said, with an air of resignation, "I suppose we'll have to check with Marcy."

"And Gladys," August added.

"Yes, *and Gladys*," Jack parroted back to him in a sing-song tone. "The level of incompetence we're surrounded with is honestly exhausting."

"*Incompetence!* Now just a minute, Quinn-" Dr. Caudell started, but he never finished.

Jack moved faster than seemed physically possible, closing the space between him and the doctor before August managed to finish blinking. He had the doctor gripped in one hand, by the neck, and lifted several feet into the air.

"Incompetence, or willful tampering? Which is it? Because if I get even a wiff that it might be the later, I'll have the name of whoever's involved, dragged out of your throat so fast-"

"Jack!" August called out in honest dismay. "Put him down, there's no evidence anyone's tampered with the report."

"Oh, I'll put him down all right," Jack said with a wicked glint in his pitch-black eyes. Dr. Caudell let out a strangled whimper.

"Come now, Jack, that's quite enough." August moved a step closer but stopped there.

Jack didn't glance in his direction. "Who told you to omit that little fact from the report? Hmm? And don't you dare lie to me. Because if you don't give me the answer I'm looking for, I'll be visiting Marcy next." Jack grinned, the corners of his mouth stretching far too wide, curving up to meet his ears. "And perhaps... I'll pay your *wife* a visit, afterward. Does she know about your little... indiscretion?"

Doctor Caudell issued strangled sounds, as he hung from Jack's fist. His eyes were beginning to bulge, and his bright red cheeks were shifting to purple. He kicked his feet back and forth in the air, and swung wildly at Jack with one fist, while the other grasped at the fingers closed around his lower jaw and windpipe.

August sighed, shaking his head. "You know," he said, "it would really be in your best interest to cooperate, Doctor."

Dr. Caudell's form seemed to go limp, as though all the fight left him at August's words. He patted Jack on the arm, weakly, twice, and Jack released the man, over the desk chair.

The doctor's hands rose to his throat, as he gasped in air, gingerly palpating the tender skin, marred by bruises that were already swiftly forming. He eyed Jack warily. "You're fucking insane," he gasped, "just like they've always said."

Jack smirked. "Only when it comes to things like murder, old boy." Jack smoothed his suit jacket and leaned forward. "Now, are you going to start talking, or do we need a repeat performance?"

"I swear," the doctor held both hands up, a look of panic flashing over his suddenly pale features, "I–I completed the autopsy, dictating the findings out loud, like I always do. I th-thought, when I reviewed the report, that it was complete. I swear to you, I didn't tamper with it, and there's no way Marcy did either." His expression hardened as he continued. "And if you plan to hurt one hair on her head, either her, or my wife, you had best just kill me now and be done with it. I don't care what the– the *fuck* you are, I promise you, I will find a way to make you pay."

Jack smiled benevolently at the doctor, and then over at August, as though he found him delightfully amusing. "I am not the monster here, Caudell. I'm not in the business of hurting women. But I will take it upon myself to be honest with your wife, on your behalf, seeing as you find yourself incapable of doing so."

"How did you find out?" Caudell stared up at him, jaw going slightly slack. He looked paler now. Exhausted. Defeated. August knew, in his gut, the man was telling the truth. He hadn't tampered with the report. Not on purpose. But could it have been a mistake, of some sort? A clerical error?

Jack continued to grin, and leaned closer to the doctor, sucking in air audibly, through flared nostrils. The older man pulled away, shrinking back against the chair. "Marcy's perfume..." Jack mused, "it has such a particular scent." His eyes turned cold, all traces of humor vanishing. "You smell as though you bathed in it."

The doctor's lips pressed in a thin line, and he sat up a little straighter. "Fine. So I'm having an affair. I'll admit it. But I don't know anything about that report being altered. If I knew someone had tampered with the autopsy report, I would say so. No one would be able to stop me, if that were the case." His chin jutted forward, despite its proximity to Jack's teeth. "I am a physician. I have been a medical examiner for nearly twenty years now. A man of honor–"

"Enough," Jack barked. "You swear no one approached you? No one suggested you leave that part out?" August stared intently at the doctor's pale visage, now dripping with beads of sweat.

"No!" He practically shouted back, "absolutely not! No one approached me. I can't explain how this happened, but this must be an error. An oversight. Who–" he stopped abruptly, his eyes gleaming suddenly with an inner light, "Why? Who do you suspect?"

Jack stood upright, and began to pace nonchalantly past the desk, and across the room. His shiny black shoes squeaked on the mint green floor tiles as he strolled, hands clasped behind his back. "Suspect? I suspect no one, specifically. But I find it very odd. Very odd indeed. Too oddly specific of an error... to be just an error. Don't you agree, Sully?"

August sighed, thought for a moment, then shook his head. "I don't know, Jack. I don't know what to think."

Jack smiled at the doctor, and he recoiled visibly. "Always the cautious one, my partner." His smile widened. "But me, I'm the opposite. It's not that I don't think with my head, so much as I think with both my head, *and* my gut. And my gut, well, it's not quite so... civilized... as my head tends to be. And it's usually hungry." He moved closer to the doctor, who leaned back once more, trembling slightly. "Right now, my gut is telling me that this was no error."

Dr. Caudell had no response, but stared mutely back at Jack, not taking his eyes off him for a second. The man didn't dare blink.

Jack straightened abruptly, his demeanor shifting. "Anything else, of particular note, in the autopsy this evening, Doctor?" Jack asked, his voice dripping like honey.

The doctor stammered, flustered for a moment, then shook his head. "N-no. Other than the... the symbol, carved into her forehead. There was no such marking, on the first victim."

"Yes." Jack nodded thoughtfully. "But it was still present, at the scene. They carved it into a nearby tree, last time."

"There was nothing else that stood out as significantly different, from the first victim." Dr. Caudell wiped his hand over his face, appearing drained and exhausted. "It will all be detailed in my report..." he trailed off, wincing slightly at his choice of words.

"I'm sure it will be," Jack said. "Just make sure you triple-check it, this time. Hmm?"

The doctor was nodding vigorously before Jack finished the thought.

Jack turned to August and smiled. "Come now, Sully, we don't want to burden the good doctor. Let's see ourselves out."

8

MISS GRAY. COMMUNION.

Jack led August through the streets, cutting through alleyways. As they left the hustle and bustle of downtown behind them, storefronts soon gave way to lawns, and August realized they were heading towards a residential part of town.

"Where are we going, Jack? And why must you insist on walking?" August wiped sweat from his brow as he spoke.

Jack paused, turning to face him. "I like to get a feel for the streets, the city." He breathed in deeply, nostrils flaring, as he scented the air. He continued, walking backward for several paces. "Besides, I think it's good if we're seen out and about, don't you? Let people see us out on foot, stalking the streets at night; it will give them some peace of mind."

August snorted. "If the public actually saw you out stalking the streets at night, they'd be running in the other direction, screaming."

Jack only smirked in response and spun back around.

"I do believe it's a full moon tonight, Jack, or perhaps the next." August scanned the sky above. "We really shouldn't be out past dark. It's too risky." Besides, he thought to himself, that little performance he'd put on earlier, with the doctor, well, he wasn't so sure it was just a performance.

It was the sort of thing he'd seen Jack do many times; pretend to be even more unhinged than he was. Let the person he was questioning think he was going to go feral on them. But there had been a look in his eyes that August didn't like. A faint gleam, akin to the hunger he felt swirling and gnawing inside his own gut. He had been ready to step in, had things gotten out of hand. There was always a chance of that, this close to the full moon.

"That was a little harsh, don't you think? Back there with Caudell?"

"I've never liked that man," Jack called back to him. "He's a pompous bore. Thinks he's better than everyone else. And if there's even a sliver of a chance that someone tampered with that report, you know as well as I do that we have to get to the bottom of it."

"Hmm," August hummed thoughtfully. "No matter who gets hurt along the way?"

Jack paused in his stride, with a half-glance back at August.

"Either way, as I was saying, I don't like the idea of you out past dark tonight."

Jack only laughed. "I've no doubt you'll manage to keep me in check. You always do. Besides, this shouldn't take long."

"I'm being serious. I'll not let you out past nightfall. Remember what happened last time? We must be back by then."

"Are you my fairy godvampire now? Shall I turn into a pumpkin, if I'm out past midnight?

"You'll turn into something a lot more dangerous than a pumpkin, as you very well know," August growled. Jack ignored him. The wind picked up. August frowned, glancing up at the dark storm clouds in the distance. "How much farther?"

"We're nearly there," Jack said.

They continued for several minutes in silence, as August grew increasingly exasperated. "Am I correct in assuming no amount of begging will lead to you telling me where we're going?"

"I've never known you to beg, old boy," Jack said. "Besides, we're here."

Jack came to a stop in the street, at the end of a brick walkway. August nearly ran into him. A black wrought iron gate spanned the entryway, with sharp spikes crowing the newel posts. They stood there, peering over the gate, which sat in the only gap in the thick hedge that bordered the property, nearly hiding it from view.

An elegant, but foreboding house stood at the end of the winding walkway, set far back from the street, most of its peaked roof hidden by a thick canopy of trees. It reminded August of a gothic cathedral. A rounded facade rose to the right, and in the small turret, was a little round window. August glimpsed a figure, standing there, a black shape, backlit against the light that poured from the room within. He stared up at the figure, which seemed to be staring back at him.

"Come," Jack said, as he swung the gate open and strode down the walkway. "We're late."

Late for what? August muttered to himself, still fixated on the dark figure above.

Jack knocked three times, before turning the handle and leading August inside, against his wishes.

August was met with the distinct impression of wealth. Plush carpets and rugs, polished surfaces, dimly lit with warm candle-light. Jack did not pause on the threshold. Rather, he led August on with a purpose, as though he knew exactly where he was going.

Soon enough, August found himself in what appeared to be a large dining room, set in the back of the property. Cathedral style windows looked out upon what August presumed must be the backyard, where trees and shrubs swayed and danced in the wind.

August was startled to realize that they had interrupted what he could only assume to be an elegant dinner party in progress. A crowd of people, perhaps as many as ten, sat around a long table. The room was so dimly lit, and the guests sat so silent and still, that he did not notice them immediately upon entry. He fell back towards the doorway, as though he was hoping to melt into a puddle and ooze himself out of the room and back down the hallway.

But Jack stood erect, pausing for only a moment, before walking confidently further into the room. He moved back towards the wall, taking a relaxed stance next to a sideboard. He folded his hands behind his back, and stared at the head of the table, on the far side of the room.

August watched his partner, mouth gaping open, before following his line of sight. It took him a few seconds to recognize the woman who sat at the head of the table. All eyes were fixed in her direction. So much so, in fact, that no one seemed to be aware of August at all, as he stood awkwardly in the doorway.

A low vibration emanated from Miss Gray's throat. Her eyes were closed, a dream-like, almost blissful, expression on her face. She swayed slightly from side to side. Her lips stretched further, in a self-satisfied, feline grin, before parting. An odd ticking sound left her throat, almost as though she were mimicking the sound of a door creaking open on rusted hinges, and August felt a hot jolt of terror sluice down his neck and through his spine as the hairs there stood on end.

The odd noise turned into a low chuckle, then a laugh. And still, Miss Gray's eyes remained closed. "For you seek, but you do not see. You talk, but you do not listen. For the least among you, I tell you, is the wisest, and the greatest among you, the fool."

The voice that fell from her lips, was not her own. Deep and masculine, with an odd rasp to it. August raised his hand and was halfway through tracing the sign of the cross in the air before he caught himself.

Miss Gray laughed again, her head falling back, her voice moving to her throat, reducing to a low vibration, until she was once more releasing that odd, unnatural ticking sound, which ended in a gasp.

When she spoke again, her voice was once more changed. Now feminine, with an immaturity to it that had been missing mere moments ago.

"I will not fear. For the lord is my shepherd. I shall not fear, for the lord–" She jerked back and forth, as though trying to free herself from invisible restraints.

Then another voice issued from her throat, weaker and trembling. "*Mother Mary, who art in heaven, hallowed be thy name!*"

She cried out suddenly, causing the crowd gathered around the table as well as August, to jump.

She pitched forward, her face contorting with terrible emotion. "*Behold! I have refined thee, but not with silver; I have chosen thee, cast thee in the furnace of affliction!*"

Her head tilted back once more, lolling on her neck, as she spasmed, her chest pumping forward, shoulders jerking. A crack of thunder pealed overhead. The crystal on the sideboard shuddered and tinkled in response. A large candelabra, hanging over the middle of the table, swayed violently, and half the candles shuddered out abruptly.

"*He approaches! He approaches, with the storm in the night. He approaches. The night is dark, and full of screams. Repent! Repent now, or suffer your sins!*"

Miss Gray let out a long, high-pitched scream. A wail, that seemed as though it would never end.

August clapped his hands over his ears momentarily. Then he rushed forward, moving to Jack's side, he grabbed him by the arm. Jack turned to face him, jerking in surprise.

August had to yell to be heard over the wailing. "What on earth Jack? What's happening to her? We need to do something!"

The figures at the table were finally stirring. Turning to look at one another in shock and horror. Those seated closest to Miss Gray were leaning away. A man seated on the far side of the table shoved his chair back and got to his feet, taking several steps across the room, his gaze never leaving Miss Gray, his eyes wide.

"She's alright," Jack had to raise his voice over the cacophony, as he turned to August, laying a hand on top of his. "She'll snap out of it. Eventually."

But Miss Gray seemed to be spasming harder now, shaking and jerking in her chair. As her head tipped to the side, August caught a glimpse of her eyes. They were now open and rolled back so far in her head that only the whites were visible. A foamy substance dripped from her parted lips.

"My god man, she's having some sort of fit. We need to help her." August moved forward, sliding his hand from beneath Jack's as he moved to Miss Gray's side. He was just in time to catch her, as her back arched impossibly further, and her body, still shaking and spasming, catapulted out of her chair.

August held her, cradled in his arms, and watched as the scream on her lips died away. He felt her body, rigid at first, suddenly go limp, as her weight relaxed against him. August lifted his elbow higher, attempting to prop her head upright. Her eyelids closed, fluttered against her pale cheeks, before opening once more.

She stared up at August, appearing fully conscious, her eyes boring into him. *"You,"* she said, her tone sharp. Her voice had returned to the guttural, masculine tones she had first spoken in. She smiled wickedly at him. *"I am coming for you next, Preacher,"* she spat the title at him, as though it were a curse word. *"Can you not smell the flames? The fire calls to you. Cast yourself upon it! Repent! For the fire will claim you either way. Though even that, will not be enough to cleanse your soul."*

"Who's coming for me?" August asked, leaning away from her involuntarily.

Miss Gray smiled again, her features oddly distorted. Her voice shifted again, when she next spoke, once more high and feminine. *"Him,"* she whispered, *"The Many-Legged King."* She began to laugh, either at her own words, or the expression on his face. *"He sees you. Seeks you, in the night. One monster, hunting another. But you cannot hide."* She laughed harder, tipping her head back, *"For he knows... he knows..."*

August was panting now, breathing heavily. He surveyed the room around them, but no one else seemed to have heard. Miss Gray's words were lost in the uproar, in the commotion in the room. One of the guests had apparently fainted, and another was insisting, loudly, that she had seen *something,* in the air, floating behind Miss Gray.

An older woman stood off to the left, pointing at the shadows that fell in the back corner of the room. Her eyes were wide, and her mouth was dropped open into a perfect round 'o'. She trembled and shook, crying out, as an older man, presumably her husband, clasped her on the shoulders and attempted to drag her away. "I saw it! I saw him! There, in the dark, watching us!"

A hand clasped on August's shoulder, and he jerked away, startled, nearly dropping Miss Gray. He turned and found Jack hovering over them.

"Move aside now," Jack's voice called out to the crowd behind him. "Bring her this way, Sully. You got her?"

August shifted his grasp as Miss Gray's body went completely limp, her eyes closing once more, a peaceful expression on her face, as though she were merely sleeping. August managed to nod.

"Good man, steady on," Jack said. He turned, his voice louder now. "I said move aside, let him through, show's over." He parted the guests that had gotten to their feet and moved forward to gape down at Miss Gray's prone figure.

Jack led August out of the dining room, down darkened hallways, and eventually, up a grand, winding staircase. While the house had appeared imposing from the street, August had not guessed at the size or depth of it. They seemed to walk for what felt like an eternity.

August kept his head bowed, his eyes on Miss Gray's upturned face. He was remotely aware of dark passages, lined with unlit gas lamps, and ornate picture frames. Eventually, August realized a maid had joined them. She scurried behind them and slid past August to follow Jack first into a doorway that opened into a large bedroom.

She rushed over to the bed and drew the bedding down. August lay Miss Gray carefully down onto the bed, before stepping back. He watched numbly as the maid covered her mistress, tucking the blankets around her, and scurrying to the windows to draw the curtains closed. Next, she untied the ribbons at the corners of the bedposts as well, allowing sheer, gauzy curtains to fall free. She drew them closed on the far side of the bed.

Jack had taken a seat at a small side table off to the right. He caught August watching him and gestured to the chair that sat opposite. "Have a seat, old boy. Ah-ah," he called out to the maid. She froze, in the act of closing the remaining curtains over her mistress. "Leave those, please. We will stay, and keep watch over her."

The maid's lips pressed tightly for a moment in dissatisfaction, as her gaze flickered over them, taking them both in. "You're him, aren't you?"

Jack raised an eyebrow at her.

"Jack Quinn. That detective. The one who–" the maid flushed slightly and seemed to think better of continuing.

A ghost of a smile twitched the corners of Jack's lips. "The very same." He inclined his head towards her.

She flushed deeper, a bloom of pink spreading over her cheeks, before looking away, and nodding briskly. "Ring for me, when she wakes." She gestured to a thick golden rope that hung against the wall near the bed. "It may be a while."

Jack nodded. "We're used to waiting. Please see that the rest of the guests take their leave, will you?"

They sat in silence for several minutes after the maid departed. August's heart was still racing. He leaned forward, staring at the prone figure of Miss Gray, both arms resting on his knees, hands clasped. "What the hell was that, Jack?" He spoke softly, without looking in Jack's direction.

Jack stared over at August for several seconds, then he pulled a cigarette out of his inner coat pocket and rested it between his lips. He crossed his arms over his chest and leaned back in his seat. "Well, I suppose she would call it a communion."

"Communion?" August repeated.

"With the other side." Jack gestured with one hand, spinning it in circles in the air. "You know, ghosts, spirits, what have you. Miss Gray is known for her ability to commune with the dead."

"So that was supposed to be... what? One of our victims talking, was it?" August asked, his voice thick with anger.

"It may very well have been." Jack shrugged. "I can't say."

"And their spirit just so happened to show up, right as we entered the room?"

"Not everything's a scam, Sully. You have a particularly suspicious nature you know."

August shot him a sideways glance. "As should you, seeing as you're a detective."

"I have a questioning nature." Jack held a finger up. "There's questioning, and there's suspicious. One is decidedly more jaded than the other."

"Call me jaded, or whatever else you like– I don't believe in ghosts, and even if I did, I don't believe we," August gestured between them, "the living, can speak to them."

Jack seemed to deliberate for a moment. "I suppose it's more that she's channeling them, than speaking to them."

A crack of thunder echoed above them. August resisted the urge to move over to a window. He had a guess as to what he might see up in the clouds, if he drew the curtains aside. "Absolute rubbish," he said stiffly. But he had to admit, if only to himself, that he was no longer quite so certain.

"Really?" Jack leaned forward, peering at him, an odd expression on his face. "And what did she say to you there, at the end? I couldn't make everything out, but it sounded deliciously macabre."

August glared back at him, his gaze landing momentarily on the unlit cigarette. "You know, sometimes, I almost think you enjoy seeing me tortured."

Jack chuckled, then shrugged. "It's just that you're so delightfully good at it. It's like watching a skilled artist paint, or a boxer... box. It's quite difficult to look away."

August's eyes darkened slightly, and the veins beneath his eyes, which had remained hidden for the past few hours, shimmered, rising to the surface.

Jack's too-wide lips spread wider in a smile. "You're so practiced at playing the tortured soul. I can't help it if I find you... riveting."

"Don't you dare light that in here, Jack." Miss Gray's voice, weak and shaky, startled both of them. "Or I'll have your head to decorate my gate."

9

THE FACTS THUS FAR. HALLUCINATIONS.

"Why how rude of me," Miss Gray said, as she slid herself to an upright position, "I have not even offered you tea." She nodded to the thick golden rope that hung beside the bed, just out of reach. "Mr. Sullivan, be a dear and ring the bell pull, will you? I'll have Lottie bring us some refreshments."

August stared at Miss Gray in consternation, before moving obediently to his feet. He eyed the golden rope wearily. It ended in a fat tassel, which hung several feet off the ground. The other end disappeared through a hole set high in the wall. He reached up, grasped it in one hand, and tugged, gently, at first, then harder, until he felt a weight shifting somewhere on the other end, and a bell, somewhere far away, tinkled.

Miss Gray nodded up at him. "Thank you," she said. "I don't know how I've found myself here, with the two of you present. I suppose you arrived late to dinner?" She frowned over at Jack.

He bent forward at the waist. "My apologies, Miss Gray. I'm afraid we were tied up elsewhere. We arrived just in time to catch the tail end of your–"

"Performance." August finished for him.

Miss Gray's eyebrows went up, but she apparently chose not to respond to the remark.

August moved back over to take his seat at the small table beneath the window.

The maid, Lottie, entered the room, and curtsied at the door.

"Ah, Lottie, will you be so kind as to bring us some tea and refreshments for the gentlemen?"

"Are you sure, Miss? Perhaps you should rest."

"I am quite rested, and quite well already, Lottie. Thank you. Tea, please."

"Yes miss, right away," Lottie said demurely. She shot Jack and August a warning glare before she slipped away through the doorframe.

Jack chuckled. "She is protective, that one."

Miss Gray smiled at the empty doorway. "Yes, she is," she said. "Unnecessarily so." She sighed and smoothed out the comforter over her lap.

August flushed slightly and stared down at the floor. He felt rather uncomfortable about the entire visit and wished nothing more than to leave.

"Did I say anything that might be helpful to your investigation?"

Jack sighed deeply, seeming to think for a moment. "Perhaps. I think you said something about us all burning in hell. And your voice, at that time, sounded like that of a young lady. But before that, you sounded more like a man. So, perhaps August's theory is correct, and there was more than one person present during Miss Maryanne's unfortunate demise."

August snorted slightly and shook his head. "A theory which Miss Gray herself was well aware of."

Miss Gray stared at him, an icy expression on her face. "Mr. Sullivan, I assure you, nothing you witnessed tonight was in any way a performance. I was not even present during the events. I was elsewhere. And I can confirm that your theory is, in fact, correct. There was more than one person involved in this crime." She closed her eyes as she spoke. "I would say there were at least... three men in the room."

"Men?" Jack leaned forward, eyes sparkling. "What makes you sure they are all men?"

"Their stature," Miss Gray said, her eyes remaining closed. "The width of their shoulders. I cannot see their faces. They are all wearing hoods, long hoods, and cloaks. Some dark color... perhaps crimson. Only dark holes, for eyes." She shuddered visibly.

"Oh goodness," August said, "did they happen to call each other by name? These hooded men?"

"Really, Mr. Sullivan." Miss Gray's eyes flew open. "Your skepticism continues to both astound and amuse me. It is not nearly as fantastic as you think it to be. Why, anyone can learn to channel as I do. All it takes is willingness. An openness, and the right frame of mind. I could show you, you know." She locked eyes with him, her lips curving in a devious sort of smile. "I've done it before. Give me enough time, and I will put you in a state of consciousness so deep, that even *you* will become a believer."

August had stilled, under her gaze, some color rising to his cheeks. "Are you talking about hypnosis?"

"Ah, so you're familiar with the concept?"

"Indeed, I am. And I am well aware that much of what has come out of these, hypnotic episodes, is later proven to be complete fabrication."

"I assure you, what I see is not created by my own mind. For I am not so depraved." A dark shadow passed over her visage as she spoke. "If you are brave enough, I can show you. Then you may decide for yourself." Miss Gray fixed him with an intense stare. "Tonight, should you wish."

August only stared back, unmoving.

"What else did *you* see tonight?" Jack asked solemnly.

Miss Gray thought for a moment, then closed her eyes, and took a deep breath. "I saw the room– the shop. But mainly, the ceiling, as I was lying prone, just as Maryanne was. I was looking out, through her eyes. I felt her pain, her fear. And I saw them. The hooded men, in shadows. The flames they conjured to use in their torture, caused their shadows, flung on the walls, and the ceiling, to twist and distort." Miss Gray's voice faltered. "It was a scene from hell."

August shook his head at her words, swallowing thickly.

"Did they speak? What did they say?" Jack was leaning forward, perched on the edge of his seat.

"I could hear them chanting. In Latin. Many voices. It sounded like more than three men speaking at once. There very likely may have been more, standing outside my line of sight."

"They read the passages from the Bible, in Latin? As they inscribed them?" Jack appeared transfixed.

Miss Gray nodded. "Yes, that may be."

August laughed darkly. "All of which the imagination could surmise, with what you already knew of the crime scene."

Miss Gray's eyes flew open once more, her pupils expanded and shrank as August took her in, her chest rising and falling rapidly, as though she were returning to herself, to the room. "I can only insist, once again, that my mind is not capable of creating the horrors I have seen whilst straying beyond the veil."

"Yet, the unconscious mind, Miss Gray, is surely capable of creating the most elaborate constructs, all without any awareness of the conscious mind, is it not? How else does one explain dreams?" August said quietly.

Miss Gray stared at him silently for a few seconds, before turning to Jack. "Did I say anything else, while in the trance? The rest of it is... blurry."

"You must tell us, August," Jack said archly, "what did Miss Gray say to you, at the end there?" He looked over at Miss Gray. "You spoke directly to August, at the end. He was playing the hero and managed to catch you before you collapsed. I couldn't quite make all of it out."

August appeared flustered, his eyes moving back and forth rapidly, as he recalled Miss Gray's words. "It was nothing to do with the case," he said abruptly, shaking his head. "It doesn't bear repeating."

"Are you certain?" Jack asked. "I thought I heard something about fire, and the cleansing of your soul." Jack's dark eyes seemed to twinkle slightly as he watched August intently.

August flushed deeply. "Then you've already gathered the gist of it, haven't you?" August said. A dark web of veins stood out against his pale cheeks once more.

Miss Gray cleared her throat. "I must clarify, Mr. Sullivan, that anything I utter, during such a state as you found me in, is not of my own invention, nor of my own volition. It is, rather, the expression of those no longer amongst the living, and sometimes, it can be of a rather... unfortunate nature."

"Thus I have already been instructed by Jack, Miss Gray. You need not burden yourself with further explanations." August's cheeks were flushed as he spoke, and he struggled to keep his voice even.

"Similarly, you need not burden yourself with guilt, Mr. Sullivan, although I fear it is already far too late for that." She tilted her head to the side, as she studied him. "Another reason you might consider allowing me to hypnotize you. It can be most enlightening. I have found it to be highly therapeutic, myself. Although, as I mentioned, one must be brave enough to face it. Not just the horrors that await, but oneself. Which is often far more difficult."

August's veins darkened further beneath his eyes, and his breathing became rapid.

Jack watched as August's fist curled tighter around the armrest of the chair. "Perhaps, another time," Jack said cheerfully.

"I beg of you, do not speak to me of guilt, or burdens, Miss Gray." August spoke through gritted teeth, "For I know more on both topics than I should ever care to admit," August snapped. "Now," he rose to his feet, "as much as I would like to stay for tea, and your... hypnosis attempt, I fear, we must be on our way. We have wasted too much time as it is dallying here, and we cannot afford for yet another night to pass with the killers at large, and unchecked."

A crack of thunder sounded over their heads, and the sound of raindrops against the roof and windows permeated the room.

"I dare say, it's pouring out there now, I highly doubt the killers will be cavorting about in the rain," Jack said calmly.

"Don't be a fool, Jack, I hardly think that a little rain will stop them from killing again, if that is their wish."

"I must agree with Jack, Mr. Sullivan, I hardly think they will be eager to stalk their prey in a deluge." Miss Gray waved her hand at the windows. "And I can say with absolute certainty that this will not be clearing up any time soon. Please, have a seat."

August paused in his pacing and peered at Miss Gray through the curtains drawn around the foot of the bed. He sighed deeply, attempting to corral his anger, and slow his breathing. His shoulders slumping in resignation, he moved to take his seat once more at the small table. "If rain is all it takes to stop them, then perhaps you would be so kind as to cause it to rain indefinitely, Miss Gray." August struggled to keep the derision out of his voice. "We would be much obliged."

Miss Gray met his gaze unperturbed. "I shall see what I can do, Mr. Sullivan."

"Look here, we won't be wasting time, regardless," Jack said. "We have the three of us, gathered here together, we shall put the remainder of the evening to good use. Let us go over the facts we've learned most recently and see what we might come up with."

August sighed. "We've hardly learned anything new though, have we?"

"Well, let's start with the autopsy. Miss Gray did not have the pleasure of being present. Shall we first summarize what we were able to glean from the latest autopsy? Then, let us lay out the facts of the case, thus far, as we know them."

August waved his hand dismissively. "Be my guest."

"Very good." Jack stood and began to pace the room as he spoke. "We know there have been two victims thus far. Both female. Both on the younger side, both vampires."

"One, widely known to be a vampire, but not the other," Miss Gray added. "The first victim, was a member of a brothel, was she not, and her services were advertised as such. The other, a respectable girl, from a religious family who kept her identity a secret."

"Ah," Jack said, "very good, Miss Gray." He inclined his head graciously. "We must not forget that. For that may be an important detail." He held up a finger. "Let's not forget a second curious detail we learned at the second crime scene; the doors to the shop, both front and back, were supposedly secured. Both were locked, when Mr. Cole left the shop that night. What does that suggest to us?" He raised an eyebrow, glancing back and forth between August and Miss Gray. "It suggests that Maryanne opened the door herself and let the killers inside. Meaning; either she knew them, or was not suspicious of their appearance. But I am getting ahead of myself, let us start at the beginning."

August sighed deeply, and cradled his head in his hand, one elbow propped on the table beside him.

Jack continued his monologue. "Both victims were found in the early hours of the morning, with the killing having taken place sometime during the night; likely between midnight and four in the morning. The autopsy of the second victim, revealed her body to have been drained of blood." Jack stopped, holding up one finger. "Correction, the same was noted, at the time of the autopsy of the first victim as well, per the medical examiner, Dr. Caudell, at least. However, that little detail somehow did *not* make it into the official autopsy report."

"Curious in and of itself," Miss Gray murmured, her eyes twinkling slightly.

"Indeed," Jack said crisply. "Don't forget," he turned to August, "we still need to question Marcy. As far as that little... slip up."

"And Gladys," August said wearily.

"Yes." Jack snapped his fingers. "*And Gladys.* We must be sure to stop in, next time we're heading to the office." He cleared his throat. "Now, Dr. Caudell has concurred with August's theory that the victims were likely drained by a vampire, rather than by other means. Thus, we know that at least one of the killers involved is highly likely to be a vampire."

"Highly likely?" Miss Gray asked. "Isn't it practically a certainty at this point?"

"Not necessarily," Jack said, a smug sort of grin on his face. "I prefer not to make any unnecessary assumptions, Miss Gray. For example, what if... just humor me for a moment, what if, the killer is *not* in fact a vampire. That would be a reasonable assumption, would it not, given the facts as we know them, but rather than assume a vampire is directly responsible, what if we ask ourselves to imagine the alternatives? If the killers involved in torturing the victims are *not* vampires, what then? What possible explanation can we arrive at? Could it be that they completed their torture, after a vampire has fed? Perhaps, after a vampire has finished feeding, and left the young ladies in a state near expiration, our group of hooded men arrive on the scene, and perform their... eldritch ceremony? This is a plausible alternative, is it not?"

"It's a preposterous explanation," August said, lifting his head from his hand. "You're suggesting that a group of hooded men are following a vampire, who happens to only feed on other vampires, around the city, waiting for him to feed, and then swooping in afterwards to torture the victim? How do they accomplish this exactly? And what could their motive possibly be?"

"I am merely suggesting we explore every possibility, August. We can't afford to make assumptions about anything."

"Either way, this vampire, then, that you're suggesting is going around feeding on other vampires; he's still a murderer. He's draining these girls to a point that they can't possibly recover from and leaving them to die. Alone. It would have been kinder if he had killed them, rather than leaving them to suffer. So, if that is the case, he is still a murderer."

Jack nodded. "Fair enough," he said evenly. "But again, let's not assume. You said *he*, twice. For all we know, the vampire is a female." August's eyes narrowed as he stared back at Jack.

"I agree we shouldn't fall into the trap of making assumptions, Jack. And it's a fine theory, but unfortunately, I don't believe it to be correct. You're forgetting one thing," Miss Gray said smoothly.

"What's that?" Jack asked, turning back to Miss Gray.

"I saw through the second victim's eyes tonight. I spoke, with her mouth. She was very much alive, and able to talk to her killers, as they tortured her. I think we must be assured that the vampire was in fact, an accomplice, and present in the room throughout the ceremony."

"And we're back to taking your *hallucinations* as facts, are we?" August asked sharply, rising to his feet. "I cannot stand this another moment."

"Your tea, Miss Gray." Lottie stood in the doorway, blocking August's escape, glaring at him through narrowed eyes.

"Very good, Lottie, you may place it on the table please." Lottie moved to the little table and began to lay out the tea.

Jack spoke up from the window across the bed chamber. He held the curtains back with one hand, as he peered up at the night sky. "I daresay you were right, Sully. The full moon is on the rise. It's pitch black and pouring out there. We shall have quite a time of it making it back home tonight."

"Oh for the love of God, Jack. I told you we shouldn't have come. It isn't safe for you to be out." August ran his hands through his hair. He glanced sideways at Lottie, but she seemed to have chosen to ignore his outburst, turning to take her leave of them.

"And Lottie," Miss Gray called after her, "please, if you would be so good as to prepare rooms for our guests. They will be staying the night."

10

THE BELL PULL, THE VEIL.

No amount of protesting could have saved him. At least, that was what August told himself, as he stared sullenly out the window in the library.

Miss Gray had dismissed them to the library, after a volley of words that solidified their fate as overnight guests, with the promise of joining them soon.

Jack sat in front of a roaring fire, seemingly lost in thought, while August made the rounds from window to window, peering at the large full moon, bright and rotund, whenever he was able to catch a glimpse of it between the storm clouds that swirled overhead.

August turned to Jack. "You seem to be blissfully unaffected, for once. May we not just take our leave? I'll escort you home. Let's sleep soundly in our own beds tonight, Jack."

"That's because I'm so focused on the case," Jack said, his eyes retaining their glazed over look even as he spoke. "There is something nagging at me... I can't quite make out what it is. It's distracting enough that I find myself unable to think of anything else. Besides," he added, "there has been nothing to provoke me tonight. Were we to take to the streets, that may not remain the case."

August sighed to himself and turned back to the window.

Jack continued. "Regardless, I am sure I shall sleep soundly tonight, whether in my own bed or no. It is *you* who seems troubled."

"That's because I am," August said. "I'd much rather be on my own, thank you very much, than trapped here."

"I think we both know what you would rather be doing, and it's not something you can do alone."

August whirled back to Jack, with a sharp retort on his tongue, and a practically feral expression on his face, but he was cut short by the appearance of Miss Gray, in the doorway of the library.

"My my," she said. "I should say you would certainly benefit from hypnosis tonight. If not that, then at least a stiff drink."

"I don't drink," August said, visibly calming himself.

Jack laughed loudly. "Not spirits, at least. August here prefers a more iron-rich vintage." He shook his head and laughed again. "Oh, sometimes I find myself to be quite witty."

"Yes, you're hilarious, Jack," August said sardonically. "I can't get enough of the vampire jokes. Do tell us another."

"Okay..." he thought for a moment. "Why don't Southern vampires bite just anyone?"

There was a protracted pause, as August glared at Jack.

"Why?" Miss Gray asked in a deadpan voice.

"Because, mama always said," he waved a finger at August, "*'you don't put your mouth on folks you didn't court proper.'*" August rolled his eyes and stalked away across the library.

"Words to live by old boy," Jack called after him. His voice dropped low. "Even if they do smell like magnolias and bad decisions."

August's back stiffened, and he paused imperceptibly in his pacing, although he gave no other indication he had heard. He strayed across the room, stopping to examine a stack of books left out on a table. One of the books lay open, its pages yellowed with age. August's breath hitched in his chest as he took in the symbols inscribed there. He turned slowly to face the duo by the fire, to find Miss Gray watching him intently.

"This symbol–" he pointed at the page, "how did you manage to come across it?" August peered down at the script that lined the top and bottom of the open pages, but it remained Greek to him. "What does it mean?"

Jack stood abruptly, marching over to join him.

Miss Gray remained seated. "Your first question is much more easily answered than your second," she said.

"Good lord, Vivienne," Jack said, as he leaned over August's shoulder to peer at the symbol.

"The short answer is, I recognized it," Miss Gray said.

August's gaze snapped back to her with narrowed eyes. "When?"

She was staring into the fireplace now. "The moment I first saw it. I thought perhaps it meant something simple, like 'fire'. It's a pagan symbol... I think. Although now, I'm not so sure..."

August frowned down at the page. The swirling eight spoke wheel-like shape with its curling appendages stoked something akin to fear deep in his gut. "It seems oddly familiar... " he shook his head. "I mean, aside from seeing it at the crime scenes."

Jack clapped a hand on his shoulder. "Perhaps you've seen it before, somewhere else. It will come to you." He moved across the room and took his seat once more.

"You know, hypnosis can be highly effective at recovering repressed memories," Miss Gray said, "bringing them back to the surface."

August sighed. "We're back to that again, are we?"

Miss Gray crossed her arms. "Really, August, I wish you would let me attempt to broaden your mind, at least. If you don't believe it's possible, then I don't see what your objection can be."

Jack raised an eyebrow and twisted to peer at August. "She has a point, you know."

August sighed deeply, glancing between the two of them. "You know what? Fine." He shrugged, moving over towards the fire. "You're right, Miss Gray. I don't believe it's possible. So go ahead; do your best. Or your worst."

"You couldn't handle my worst, Mr. Sullivan," Miss Gray said.

August cheeks flushed bright red, and he glared fixedly back at Miss Gray, the veins below his eyes hot and shimmering, as Jack laughed. "Try me," August snapped.

Even Jack fell silent, at the look on August's face, and Miss Gray's throat bobbed slightly, as she swallowed. She remained perfectly still for several seconds. Then she slid forward, until she was perched on the edge of her chair. She gestured to the chair beside her. "Have a seat then, Mr. Sullivan."

August sat in the chair beside her as Jack watched, an amused grin on his face.

"Let's see it, then," August said. "How does this work?"

Miss Gray smiled, her eyes flickering over his features. "Jack, dear, would you be so kind as to bring me my harp? It's just over there." She lifted her arm and pointed across the room. "It's quite heavy, but it has wheels on the one side."

"Certainly!" Jack wheeled the large, ornate harp over to Miss Gray, tilting it upright once it rested before her.

"Thank you." She smiled up at Jack, turning the harp, and tilting it back, until it rested against her shoulder. "Just try to relax, Mr. Sullivan, and keep your mind open, as much as possible."

August snorted. "I can assure you, I will try, but I have heard a harp played before, Miss Gray, and I did not see spirits afterward."

"Not by me, Mr. Sullivan," she replied evenly. She gave him a small smile. "Will you, try? Actually? Please?"

August swallowed. Then he nodded briskly. "Fine. Yes," he said. "I'll try."

Her smile broadened, and she lifted both hands to the harp, along with at least six of her tentacles, and began to play.

August watched her, and he kept his promise. He really did try. The music was beautiful. Achingly so. Filled with a deep sort of melancholy that spoke to him directly. He watched Miss Gray's face, her expression shifting, peaceful at times, and others distraught, heavy with emotion. He watched as the shadows cast by the flames in the grate flickered and danced over her features. Her dark hair shone with strands of red and gold spun through dark curls. His eyes strayed again and again to her blood red lips, to the curve of her neck. And while he struggled at first, to ignore Jack's presence in the room, he eventually forgot that he was there.

He forgot about the full moon. The storm that raged outside. The case. He forgot about the hunger, that ate away at him slowly, from the inside. The guilt. He forgot about the pain. The shame. He forgot everything, but the sound of the harp, and the woman who played it.

When at last the song ended, August shook himself. He blinked rapidly, then ran his hand down his face, with a deep inhale of air.

"Well?" Miss Gray was smiling over at him.

The harp was gone. August turned, to find it sitting on the other side of the room, where it had been before Jack retrieved it. And Jack himself was nowhere in sight. His chair sat before the fireplace, now empty. The logs that had been stacked in the grate were now nothing but white-hot coals.

"I–I–" August stammered. "I must have fallen asleep," he said, getting to his feet abruptly, he bowed slightly to his hostess. "My apologies, Miss Gray. I fear I have kept you up far too late. I shall check on Jack and then retire to my room. Goodnight."

He turned to leave the room, and he heard Miss Gray, although her voice was oddly faint, murmuring from somewhere behind him. "Goodnight, Mr. Sullivan, I hope you sleep well and dream of pleasant things."

It wasn't until August had made it all the way upstairs that he realized he had no idea where he was going. He did not know which rooms Lottie had prepared for him and Jack. He was quite certain he had been told, at one point, but he could no longer recall the details, and he must find Jack. He must check and make sure he was asleep. Especially tonight, of all nights.

August found himself in a long, dark corridor. He could hear thunder still, faintly, in the distance somewhere outside. The corridor was lined with gilded frames. He moved closer to the next one. The image he found waiting there left him feeling somewhat unsettled. A silver tray lay on a table, piled with fruit, and a woman's head. Her eyes were open, staring. Two crows sat atop her head. August peered closer and saw that her scalp had been cut open. The skin over her brain, and half of her forehead, had been peeled back. The crows feasted on the exposed lumpy grey matter.

August pulled back, away from the painting, and glanced up and down the corridor once more, unsure which direction he had come from, or which direction might bring him back to the library, to Miss Gray. He decided to follow the corridor to his right and took off in that direction.

August walked, and walked. He passed more paintings, each one more disturbing than the last. He came to one which depicted a gleaming tabletop. A woman, naked, splayed out on the table before him. She was curvy, a line of red ran up her abdomen, from just above the dark patch of hair between her legs, up between both breasts. Her hair was dark, falling in ringlets over her shoulders. August gasped and jumped back. Miss Gray's face looked out at him from the painting, contorted in agony.

August rushed down the corridor, his breathing rapid, his heart pounding in his chest. He turned right, at the end of the hallway, and there, hanging before him, suspended in the very middle of the hallway, was a long, golden rope.

It ended in a fat tassel, the other end disappeared into shadows, somewhere high above.

August rushed to the rope. He hesitated for only a moment, before grasping it with both hands, and pulling downwards. He heard a loud bell chiming, somewhere far above him. Then, he waited.

She appeared, after an indeterminable amount of time. She approached from the hallway ahead of him. He stared past the golden rope, watching her approach with ice cold terror coursing through his veins.

Her hair had been worn loose, when he had seen her last, her features contorted. But still. He would recognize her anywhere.

She was clothed, this time. She walked with an easy languidness to her movements that struck him at once as both sensual, and mocking, somehow. His jaw tightened, and his fists clenched. His heart leapt into his throat.

"It's not possible," he said through gritted teeth.

"Now now, Mr. Sullivan," the young woman tilted her head to the side. "You said you would try."

"You aren't real," August insisted.

"Real or not, here I am," she said sweetly, holding her hands out to either side. She curtsied a little. "Our time is limited, Mr. Sullivan. I can feel you resisting. Attempting to wake already."

"But I am awake," August said, staring down at his body.

"No." She shook head, smiling sadly at him. "You aren't."

"I'm telling you, I am."

"Do you want to waste our time arguing? Or shall we spend it doing something more, provoking?" She smiled suggestively at him, and August felt the veins beneath his eyes, in his chest, swell, and expand slightly. He watched in fascination as dark lines appeared beneath her eyes, as if in answer.

"You're the first victim. Dixie," he said despite himself. He moved a step closer, as she nodded, smiling still. "How... but how..." he moved past the golden rope, coming closer, his eyes wide.

"Never mind how." Her expression darkened, and her smile fell away, as her full, red lips curled up in a snarl. "Concern yourself with why. Why did they do this to me?" Her demeanor shifted suddenly. She stared off into the distance, over August's shoulder. "He tricked me. Made me think he cared." She shook her head. "He brought me flowers..." her voice trailed off, then came out guttural, thick with anger and grief. "They used me. Tortured me. Drained me. He had the audacity to cry, afterward. I won't rest until I see him, see all of them, torn from this earth."

"Who!" August cried out, taking a step closer to her. "Who did this to you?"

Her veins darkened, bulging now. She lunged forward, grabbing him by the collar of his shirt, she pulled him to her, and suddenly she was naked, pressed against him. He moved to push her gently away, but froze, as a red line appeared, parting her smooth, velvet skin, running up her chest, between her breasts.

"No," August murmured in horror, gripping her by the shoulders. "No, no…"

She cried out, her mouth dropping open in a scream, her features distorting, twisting in agony.

"No, not yet! Tell me who did this! Tell me your real name!" August pulled back involuntarily, as she screamed, her mouth yawning open. He watched in horror as curling script began to appear, across her hands, and down her arms, etching itself, branding itself, onto her skin with invisible flames. The scent of sulfur, and something cooking, filled his nostrils, just as it had at the crime scenes.

"No! Please!" August raised both arms, over his face, as he pulled further back, his eyes squeezed shut.

"August! Come on now, Sully! Wake up! What's happening to him?" Jack's voice drifted to him now, in place of the young woman's. August opened his eyes, peering through his arms, and saw only Jack, leaning over him, both hands gripping his shirt. August swatted at Jack's hands and arms, and he let go abruptly.

"August?" Jack was panting, his chest rising and falling rapidly. "Are you alright?"

August peered up at Jack, blinking rapidly, shaking himself. He took in the room around them. He was back in the library, in the chair beside Miss Gray. She sat there, with the harp still before her. The fire had burned down some, but the logs were still there, crackling away.

August looked up at Jack. His unnaturally black eyes, and the too-wide curve of his mouth brought him sharply back to reality.

"I'm alright, Jack. Calm down." He held his hands up, palms facing Jack. "I'm okay, it's alright."

Jack seemed to shrink slightly, his shoulders relaxing. He took a step back, turning away from August. He moved over to the chair beside the fire and took a seat. By that time, his features had returned to normal. He reached into the pocket of his jacket and removed a cigarette. He placed it between his lips and gave them both a small smile, his mouth no longer appearing disproportionately large. "Well, then, go ahead. Tell us what you saw. Don't keep us in suspense."

August turned to Miss Gray with wide eyes. "How did you do that?" His chest began to rise more rapidly, as he recalled all he had seen. The young woman had been solid. Real. When she had gripped him, he felt her, pressed against his chest. But no, he reminded himself; that had been only Jack. He must have been semi-conscious. Aware enough to feel what was happening to his body, as his mind walked elsewhere. "Was it a dream? I– I thought I woke up, here in the chair, but then, I woke up again, just now, a second time. I was only dreaming."

Miss Gray watched him solemnly. "What happened, August?"

August sighed and leaned back in his chair. "I told you goodnight. The fire was burnt low, in the grate. I thought I had fallen asleep, and you had sat up with me. I went upstairs. I wanted to check on Jack."

Jack nodded as he spoke. He was staring into the fireplace, at the flames that still roared there.

"I went up the stairs and followed the corridors. I was looking for our rooms, although... I realized I didn't know where they were, exactly. I was hoping to find my way back down to you, or to run into Lottie, to ask her. And as I was thinking that I found a rope."

"A rope?" Miss Gray said. "What sort of rope?"

"Like the one there." August gestured to the golden rope that hung by the fireplace. "To call for Lottie."

"You mean a bell pull?" Miss Gray frowned.

"Yes. It was a bit odd, though. It was hanging right in the middle of the corridor. And I couldn't see the other end of it. It disappeared into... blackness. I pulled it." Miss Gray's eyebrows lifted slightly as he spoke. "I only waited a few seconds, before she appeared."

"Lottie?" Jack asked.

"No." August shook his head. "It was the first victim. Dixie LaRue."

"You're sure?"

"Yes. I'd recognize her face anywhere."

"You summoned her to you?" Miss Gray was watching him intently now; her eyebrows still lifted in surprise.

"What? No, I didn't–" August frowned, shaking his head.

"You did. When you pulled the rope."

"But–"

"Did she speak to you?" Jack demanded.

"Yes," August said slowly.

"What did she say?" Jack rose to his feet. "You must try to recall her exact words."

"I..." August began, then stopped abruptly. "It's already fading. I can't recall exactly."

"Just try!" Jack exclaimed.

"I *am* trying," August spat back. "She said something– something about them torturing her. About how they... they used her. She said she would see them ripped from this earth. She said–" August paused, standing, as he recounted her words, her face, already fading from his mind.

"What?" Jack moved closer to him. "What did she say?"

"She said he cried, afterward. That he brought her flowers... I think maybe she meant the vampire. She said something about him draining her, and that he cried. No..." August shook his head. "I think I have that wrong. She mentioned someone else as well, a man. She said 'he', but did she mean the vampire, or someone else?" August stomped his foot in frustration. "Dammit. I can't remember for sure."

"It's okay, Mr. Sullivan. It's not easy to recall the details. They will only fade more, with time. Fortunately, or unfortunately, as it may be," Miss Gray said softly.

"I saw... you," August said slowly, "in a painting. In the corridor, upstairs. You were... you looked like you were about to be... splayed open. Just like the victims. It was..." August trailed off, his cheeks heating slightly.

Miss Gray stared back at him, unblinkingly. "I think, I am safe, Mr. Sullivan. Knowing what we know about the killers, I doubt they will target me. Some things that you see, beyond the veil, are likely products of your own imagination, as you suggested earlier.

Not all, mind you, but some. I suspect that is the case, with this painting."

August's cheeks burned hotter at her words, and he turned away from them both, walking over to the far bank of windows. He peered out into the storm. "It was horrible," he said softly.

"Well, it's over, old boy. You don't have to go through it again," Jack said cheerfully.

"For now," Miss Gray said.

"What do you mean?"

August turned away from the window, as Jack echoed his inner dialogue out loud.

Miss Gray was staring at the flames dancing in the grate. They threw odd shadows over her face. "Once you've pulled back the veil, it can be difficult to keep it closed."

11

THE SPEECH.

Jack fell into line behind August, sullen and silent, as they marched through the streets, the first hint of the heat that would soon become unbearable in the air.

"It's already getting hot," August muttered.

"You're the one who refused Miss Gray's offer to give us a ride," Jack responded crisply.

August frowned at his words. A handmade sign caught his attention, fixed at eye level on a shop window; *'Upirs and Coloreds not welcome.'*

"Oh, pardon me, if I'd prefer to arrive in one piece," August snapped back.

Jack chuckled darkly. "Are you sure it's not too late for that?"

"Piss off," August said, pausing and turning to Jack. "What's gotten into you lately?"

"I could ask you the same," Jack said.

August turned away and glanced up the street ahead. He nodded. "Looks like we're in for a show today."

A large crowd had gathered, spilling into the street outside the courthouse. Several reporters, some holding cameras aloft, some holding notebooks, pushed and jostled, for a closer view. August heard the squawk of feedback, and then an all too familiar voice rang out over the din of the crowd.

"*Fuck*," Jack swore under his breath. "Should we duck around through the alley?"

"Wait a minute," August said, "I want to hear this." He moved closer, spying Merritt Colfax, the district attorney, holding up a hand as he spoke into a megaphone.

"Now, now, I know you must have a lot of questions for Chief Waverly, and we'll get to them next. But first, I'd like to take a moment to speak on behalf of Fulton County, when I say, we will prosecute the perpetrators of these violent crimes to the fullest extent of the law."

The reporters in the crowd surged forward, all clamoring and asking questions at once. Merritt attempted to quiet them, then held the megaphone further away from his mouth, covering the end with one hand, as he turned aside to speak in Chief Waverly's ear.

"I'm surprised he doesn't have us standing up there with him," Jack said. "Come on, we should go before they notice us."

"Probably tried and couldn't find us," August said. He thought for a moment. "Then again, maybe he didn't try very hard. No one wants to see me behind a podium."

"Rubbish," Jack said.

"It's not, and you know it." August eyed him sideways. "You, on the other hand, the crowd loves."

Jack grinned rather smugly and shrugged. He removed a cigarette from his pocket and placed it between his lips. "Well, that can't be helped, can it?" August's eyes narrowed. "What?" Jack shrugged again, pulling out his lighter. "We're outside."

Chief Waverly stepped forward. "Thank you, thank you." He waited, one hand raised, palm out, until the crowd quieted once more. More pedestrians were drifting over to join the mass at the base of the stairs. "As DA Colfax has just stated, we will put an end to this violence, and the perpetrators will be held accountable. We have our best men... our best team, on this case. And they will not stop until the murderer is found and brought to justice."

The crowd surged forward once more as he paused for a breath. August moved a little closer, weaving between bodies to catch a glimpse of the third person, who stood a little lower on the courthouse steps.

"Mayor Dorsey," Jack said over his shoulder. He stood at least a head taller than August. "Can't pass up a photo op, can he? Not when he's up for re-election." He flicked his thumb down on his lighter and lit the cigarette.

August frowned slightly. "I can't say I'm a huge fan of his, but given the alternative..."

Jack snorted and glanced around at the growing crowd. "You mean Boone Radcliff? I hear he's amassed quite a following, with his... unorthodox platform."

"He's a bigot," August snapped, turning back to Jack. "Plain and simple. He makes no effort to hide his hatred for vampires. I'm betting he flies a confederate flag at home, too, when no one's watching."

"I don't know whether he truly is, or whether he's just trying to make himself more appealing to the unwashed masses." Jack shrugged. "Either way, I've met him before," he sniffed, "I can't stand the man myself."

"A man who spouts evil, for the sake of political gain, *is* evil. Whether he believes in the hatred he spews or not," August said coldly.

"There it is. Deep down, you're still full of fire and brimstone..." Jack grinned at him and blew a ring of smoke. "Once a preacher, always a preacher."

August shook his head, and opened his mouth to retort, but Jack was no longer paying attention. He had turned back to the hubbub at the courthouse as a new voice rang out.

Mayor Dorsey stood behind the small podium. He wore a sharp navy-blue suit, and a grey tie that complimented his salt and pepper hair. His brown eyes were kind and full of warmth. "I want to personally thank each and every one of you, for your concerns for your fellow citizens. It is no secret that the victims of these heinous crimes have been members of our vampire community, and it would appear, at this time, as though vampires are being specifically targeted. I want to take a moment to remind you that I despise hate and bigotry in all forms. We will not allow these abhorrent acts to continue."

A light scatter of applause rang out. "Not only that," Mayor Dorsey continued, "but we will continue to stamp out any anti-vampire graffiti throughout the city. I will remind you, those of you who need reminding, that we will not stand for it. All members of our community are welcome here and should feel safe to walk the streets. Unlike my opponent, I will not tolerate hateful discrimination, whether it is based on the color of a man's skin, or his affliction, with a most unfortunate disease."

The applause was louder this time. Although not everyone present clapped and cheered. More than a few were booing. August scanned the crowd with narrowed eyes.

"See," Jack said, "what an opportunity. He can play the hero and get a dig in at Boone Radcliff at the same time."

"He's a politician, Jack. What do you expect?" August sighed, surveying the crowd once more.

"Come on, let's get going, duck through the alley and around to the station. I want to go over the autopsy reports. Maryanne's better be ready." Jack threw his cigarette butt on the street and ground it beneath his shoe.

"I have a better idea," August said thoughtfully. "Let's go back to Madam Beaufrey's."

"The cathouse, *again*? Why?" Jack groaned and rolled his eyes, glancing up at the sky.

"Because, I have an idea," August said firmly.

"Well," Jack smirked, "there's no better place to try out whatever fantasy you've conjured up. I suppose we have our visit to Miss Gray to thank for this?"

August's fist connected briefly with his gut, and Jack pitched forward with an "Oof." He grinned up at August, releasing a low chuckle. "Looks like I hit a nerve."

"Let's go." August took off down the street, heading away from the courthouse.

Jack followed him a moment later, still laughing to himself.

12

THE CATHOUSE, MADAM BEAUFREY, REDEMPTION.

Madam Beaufrey herself answered the door. August heard a shuffle, followed by a squeak of a hinge, then a pause, before the door to the cathouse was flung wide.

"Gentlemen." Madam Beaufrey struck a pose in the open doorway, one hand draped on the frame. "I did not expect to see you back so soon." She gave them a wicked sort of smile. "What can I do for you, on such a fine afternoon?" She squinted out at the bright sun, now halfway through its climb through the sky to its apex. Despite what must feel like an early hour to her, she was dressed to the nines, draped in fine-looking silk, her blond hair styled in fat juicy curls. Her lips were painted deep crimson.

Jack bowed slightly at the waist. "We're here on business, Madam Beaufrey, not pleasure, I'm afraid."

"Again?" She pouted, her bottom lip coming out in a slight pout. "You've questioned my girls half to death as it is Jack. I'm confident they've told you everything they know already."

"Which is nothing, apparently," August said dryly.

Jack shot him a warning glance. "Now, Madam Beaufrey, I'm sure the ladies have done their best to be helpful, but we have a new line of inquiry that has opened up, and we simply need to ask a few questions, and be on our way."

Madam Beaufrey's pout only deepened, despite Jack's attempt to smooth things over with his habitual charm. "They're supposed to be resting, at the moment. Getting some sleep. Not being agitated–"

"No one wants them agitated," Jack held up his hands, "but it can't be helped."

"Maybe you can ask me your questions first." She frowned slightly at them then sighed and turned her back, walking languidly into the dimness of the entryway. "Follow me, boys," she called over her shoulder.

August found himself seated in her office once more. She offered them coffee or tea, which they politely declined.

"Well then, best get on with it," she said calmly, leaning back in her chair. "But I'll say it again; we aren't hiding anything. We want the murderer found just as much as you do. If not more," she said. As though she read their skepticism on their features, she snorted, and folded her arms over her chest. "You might think otherwise, given Dixie's... affliction. But I treat every one of my girls like they are one of my own, detectives. Dixie was no different."

She sighed deeply, glancing over at the window across the room. Thick velvet curtains were drawn tight, blocking out the sunlight. "In fact, she was one of my favorites. She had something special, Dixie did. Not just because she was an upir– that was only part of it." Madam Beaufrey laughed wryly. "I won't lie; she brought in a significant portion of our proceeds... gentlemen of a certain... predilection, found her services to be invaluable."

August cleared his throat and shifted somewhat uncomfortably in his seat.

"You'd be surprised, how many were interested in partaking..." she smiled fondly, "and not just men. Dixie appealed to all persuasions. It wasn't only sexual, you know. Although I'm told the experience can be... incredibly erotic..."

"So I've been told," Jack said, "although, I've never experienced it myself."

Madam Beaufrey's focus flicked to August briefly, then she nodded, somewhat absentmindedly. "You should have heard them..." she trailed off, sighing, and glancing over at the window again, "how they would scream... sometimes I could hear it from here. Sitting here, at my desk. Even though her room was all the way across the house. She had so many returning clients. Once they had a taste, they couldn't stop. They were fanatics, some of them. It did make one... curious... They used to follow her down the hallway, practically salivating." She smirked. "The poor fools. Half of them thought they were in love with her, of course."

August flashed back to his vision of Dixie, in the hallway at Miss Gray's. How she had smiled at him, her lips curling, the tips of her teeth just visible. Her bare breasts pressed against his chest. He imagined her, hips swaying as she walked down the hallway, some poor fool brought to his knees in her wake. August could feel the familiar tightening in his veins, as he tried to push the images away.

He flashed back to the present to find Madam Beaufrey smiling at him, a hungry sort of glint in her eyes, as though she were seeing him for the first time. August cleared his throat and willed his pulse to slow.

"You could make a killing, you know," Madam Beaufrey said, sweeping him up and down. "You would be... very popular..."

Before he could react, August felt Jack's hand on his arm, his grip tight. "Now now, Madam Beaufrey, I can't allow you to poach my partner; he's an invaluable resource to the Atlanta PD."

Madam Beaufrey leaned back in her chair, the glint of greed fading from her bright eyes. "I'm sure," she said kindly. "Although, I have to admit, I am surprised they've allowed you to continue in your role, Mr. Sullivan. Chief Waverly must be more of a softy than he lets on. How many palms did he have to grease to keep you on the payroll?"

August cleared his throat. "I was already... turned, before I was hired," he said, finding his voice. "They knew exactly what I was."

She raised an eyebrow at August. "Really? What did you do before?"

August sighed internally. "I was a preacher," he said stiffly.

He had expected Madam Beaufrey to laugh. He was surprised at the brief flicker of emotion that passed over her features. Grief? Pitty? August's hands curled, his nails digging into the armrest of the plush armchair.

Madam Beaufrey was silent for a moment, then she nodded, glancing down at his hands, before meeting his gaze. "I see," she said evenly. "The universe has a cruel sense of humor, does it not?" She slid a cigarette case to the center of the desk, removed a cigarette with a long, slender cigarette holder, and had it halfway to her lips, as Jack leaned forward, clicking his lighter, one palm cupped around the flickering flame. August shuddered slightly, as he watched the end of the cigarette catch.

She drew in a deep breath. "Thank you, Jack dear," she breathed out. "Now then," she smiled over at August, a too bright smile that didn't reach her eyes. "Ask me what you came to ask."

"You mentioned Dixie had amassed quite a following, did she have any particular returning clients who came to see her in the week or so before her death?"

Madam Beaufrey sighed, took another deep pull from her cigarette, and glanced up at the ceiling. "You asked a similar question last time," she said quietly, "and the time before that."

"Anyone who brought her flowers?"

Madam Beaufrey paused, frowning for a moment. "Flowers..." she said slowly, her eyes shifted up and to the right, as though she were remembering. August resisted the urge to lean forward eagerly.

Madam Beaufrey shook her head a moment later and shrugged nonchalantly. "Not that I can recall. But Adelaide might know."

"Who's Adelaide?" August asked, frowning over at Jack. He didn't recall the name from their previous visits.

"Her roommate," Madam Beaufrey said.

"Her roommate?" August repeated, moving to his feet. "We didn't know she had a roommate. Where is she now?"

Madam Beaufrey frowned up at him. "I really would rather not have her disturbed. She's been having a hard enough time as it is. This will only bring it all back up again." She leaned forward though, as she spoke, and stabbed the end of her cigarette into a small ashtray that sat on the desk and got hastily to her feet. "Come along, then. I'll take you to her."

They hung back discreetly, while Madam Beaufrey roused Adelaide. Jack eyed August wearily as they leaned against the walls of a dimly lit corridor. The hallway was windowless. There was no sense of the time of day in the warren of winding hallways that made up the cathouse. A lone candle sat on a side table at the far end of the hallway. August supposed the house was kept dark on purpose, the better to hide the identity of patrons who slunk through the door.

"You alright old boy?" Jack asked without looking at him, busy plucking stray hair off his coat.

"I'm fine," August replied gruffly. "Stop worrying about me."

Jack let out a low, rough guffaw. "Easier said than done, my friend."

August only shook his head, his jaw clenched tight.

"You should think on it, you know," Jack said smoothly, now removing invisible hair and lint from his shirt.

"Think on what?" August asked through clenched teeth.

"Madam Beaufrey's offer." Jack grinned over at him. "Not full time, of course, I couldn't stand to give you up. But part time? On the side? I'd say that could work out just swell."

August snorted, shaking his head at Jack in disbelief. "Are you serious right now? What are you suggesting? That I whore myself out?" August held his arms out to his side. "Because I haven't hit rock bottom just yet, huh? Let's add prostitution to the list. Give me a fucking break Jack."

"What?" Jack shrugged. "I'm being serious, Sully. I'm not saying you have to... you know... just, the feeding part. Why the hell not?"

"It's illegal, Jack." August cringed as his voice rose in volume.

"Yeah, it is. But you're going to do it anyway, aren't you?" He met August's gaze as he took a step forward, his expression suddenly intensely serious. "That's the thing you can't seem to wrap your brain around, August. You're going to do it anyway. You're going to have to feed. It's inevitable. The longer you put it off, the more dangerous you become. Why do you do this to yourself? I'll never understand it." He shook his head. "You're going to feed anyway. You might as well feed off willing participants, and get paid for it."

"You want to know why you don't understand? Because you have no idea what it's like, Jack, you can't possibly understand–"

"Oh please," Jack waved his hand, "spare me the theatrics. I'm not a vampire, I get it. But do you really think I have no clue what it feels like?" Jack laid a hand on his chest. "I'm a goddamn monster, August. You've seen me." August shook his head. "No. Don't deny it. You know exactly what I am. What I am capable of. So you can spare me the speech, okay? If anyone knows how you feel, besides another vampire, it's me."

August's jaw clenched tighter, and he snapped suddenly, unable to stop himself. "You *don't* know, Jack. You can't possibly. *You* can control it. *You* can hide it. Aside from one night, every four weeks, you can turn it on and off, like that." He snapped his fingers in Jack's face. "You don't have to walk around, all day, in public, waiting for your face to betray your goddam emotions, your every fucking, inner thought, your... desires, aren't visible to strangers. You don't know what it's like to live that way; you turn it on whenever it suits you. When you need to take someone down, you let the... monster, take control for a few minutes. And people love it." August held his arms out wide. "To them, you're a goddamn hero. *I* let the monster inside *me* take control, and people die. Innocent people."

August paused, his chest rising and falling rapidly, and Jack glared back at him. "You have no idea what it's like, Jack. To devote your whole life to the church. To God. And to wake up one day and find you've become the one thing you promised you'd never be." August shook his head, and he hated the way his voice crumbled as he spoke, but he continued anyway. "I'm an abomination, Jack. Against God, against life, against–"

"No, you aren't, August. You're a good person, actually. One of the best I know, in fact." Jack shook his head. "You can't help what you are. Any more than anyone else can." Jack scoffed. "So you need to drink a little blood every once in a while," he shrugged, "so what. Didn't you eat meat, before? Do you really think it's that different? We're all just animals, at the end of the day. That's all we are. We all need to eat, to consume, in order to survive. Something else needs to die, to keep us alive, every goddamn day. How is this any different?"

August stared silently back at Jack, unable to formulate a response for a moment. "A steak is different than a person, Jack. That's how."

Jack laughed. "Fine. Fair enough. But you don't have to kill, in order to feed, August. Self-control–"

"Yes, self-control. That's it. That's all that stands between me, having a drink, and someone dying. Forgive me if that makes me nervous."

"So, you're scared," Jack said swiftly, "good. Admitting that is the first step."

"Fuck off," August said sharply. "You're not my goddamn shrink."

"No, I'm not. But clearly you need to see one."

August rolled his eyes. "I told you, I'm fine. Mind your own business, and don't worry about it."

"You are my business," Jack said glibly. He seemed to let it go, as he strolled a few paces away, but then he turned back. "You're scared. That's part of it. But there's more to it than that. You don't think you're worth it."

"Oh for Christ's sake..." August muttered.

"Think of all the good you've done, since you joined the PD. Think of all the criminals, truly evil people, that are no longer out on the streets, thanks to you. Think of how many lives you've probably saved, August. You've used your... strength, for good. If that isn't redemption, then, fuck... I don't know what is."

August turned away, scowling, his eyes burning suddenly.

Jack took a deep breath, his features relaxing, his shoulders falling. "Look, I don't know man, I'm just trying to tell you; you can't keep punishing yourself. The only person who has a problem with it is you. You're the one who can't accept it."

"Really? What about all the assholes out there, like Boone Radcliff? Hmm? What about the people who were out booing in the street today, during Mayor Dorsey's little kumbaya speech? You know, I passed a shop, on the street this morning, with a sign, saying *'Upirs and Coloreds not welcome.'*" August pointed up the hallway as he spoke, his voice rising again. "You want me to believe everyone's okay with who, or what, I am?" August shook his head. "That's a lie. A fairytale."

"You said it yourself, August," Jack said calmly, "they're assholes. All of them. Plain and simple. There have always been assholes, and there always will be. You can't let them get to you. You can't let them win."

"There is no winning, Jack," August said. "And there's no redemption. Not anymore. Not for me. It's too late for that. I've accepted my fate. You don't need to try to save me from it. It's not possible."

"That's where you're wrong, old boy." Jack shook his head and smiled at August. "It's never too late."

August still stood there, silently, his chest rising and falling rapidly, when Madam Beaufrey stepped back into the hallway.

"She's ready for you, gentlemen." She approached the men where they stood halfway down the hall, her voice pitched low.

"Please, be gentle with her. She's always been a fragile little thing, and she's still grieving."

She placed a hand on August's shoulder, as he passed, gave him a sad smile, and disappeared down the hallway.

13

THE BEAU. THE ROSES. THE OFFER.

When they entered the bedroom, August found himself gazing around the room in surprise.

During their last two visits, Madam Beaufrey had loaned them the use of her personal office, and a sitting room to conduct their interviews. They chose to divide and conquer, given the number of women they had to interview, and they had ventured no further into the cathouse. They certainly had not been permitted to see the bedrooms. Madam Beaufrey had insisted that all of Dixie's things had already been collected, and her room had been cleaned. She had brought them a cardboard box, containing her meager personal belongings. They had gleaned nothing from studying them.

August was taken aback by the size and grandeur of the bedroom. One large bed, sat as the centerpiece, draped in silk curtains. A fire crackled and roared in the hearth across from the bed, framed by a low coffee table and two comfortable looking armchairs. The room was so large, in fact, that August at first struggled to locate Adelaide inside it.

He eventually found her, where she sat perched beneath the window, on a small window seat. Several layers of gauzy, sheer

114

curtains covered the window behind her. She sat framed in a warm, golden glow, from rays of the sun that penetrated through the layers.

She wore her hair loose, her long brown strands falling in shining waves, highlighted with crimson and gold. She was dressed in a fine-looking lavender silk robe, tied loosely around her slim figure. The deep V at the neck dipped far too low for decency, past the curve of her breasts, splayed naturally to the side. August swallowed thickly. Her features were bathed in shadow, as she sat backlit, crowned in a halo of golden light.

"Come in," she said, her voice high and lilting. "Please, make yourself at home." She raised her hand to gesture towards the only chairs in the room, where they sat in front of the fire.

"Thank you," Jack said warmly, "Miss Adelaide, isn't it?" His voice was gentle, none of the emotion from their conversation in the hallway leaking through. But August found himself oddly shaken by the exchange. He shivered slightly, though whether it was from cold, or nerves, he wasn't sure. The room certainly wasn't warm. The elegant old house seemed to have managed to retain the coolness of the night before, and August had a feeling that the fire had only recently been lit, likely by Madam Beaufrey, upon entry.

Jack moved over to one of the armchairs. "May I?" He asked magnanimously. Adelaide dipped her head, and August watched as he effortlessly lifted both solid-looking armchairs, one in each hand, and carried them over to the window. "Come now, August, don't be shy." He waved August over to the second chair.

Jack waited until August joined them, having given Adelaide a brief bow and a nod, and settled into the chair beside him. "Now, Miss Adelaide, you may remember me from a previous visit. Seeing you now, I'm sure I've spoken with you before, but I confess, I did not realize at the time that you were Miss Dixie's roommate."

Adelaide gave Jack a brief, small smile. Her wide brown eyes remained solemn, and flickered nervously in August's direction, before falling to her hands, where they lay in her lap.

August's cheeks burned, as he realized the likely cause of her anxiety. He was still rattled from his confrontation with Jack, and the veins beneath his eyes were taut and engorged. No doubt his eyes were the color of coal above them. He clenched his jaw and resisted the urge to sink his nails into the armchair. The woman's innocent gaze swept him once more, as though she sensed his discomfort. August hated himself, in that moment, as he watched her swallow, her throat bobbing slightly.

"If you don't mind," Jack continued gently, "we'd like to ask you just a few more questions. We shall be quick."

"Yes," she said, her voice faltering a little, "I–I remember you. You're Jack Quinn; I know who you are." She gained confidence as she spoke. "You're the detective... the one who..." she trailed off, as she studied him more closely, her curiosity getting the best of her. She cleared her throat. "I heard you only take the cases you're interested in. Is that true?"

Jack failed to suppress a wry grin. "That's not inaccurate." He shrugged one shoulder. "They give me quite a bit of free rein."

"Thank you, then. For taking her case. Dixie," Adelaide said, her chin lifting, "it's not something we'd expect. None of us. Not if it were us." August watched as tears filled her eyes, but her chin remained lifted, her voice steady. "She'd be touched, you know. Being what she was. It would have meant a lot to her, to know that someone cared."

August felt his heart crack a little at her words. He took a deep breath and found himself blinking rapidly.

"They do care," Jack said, his eyes fixed on hers. "A lot of people care."

Adelaide uttered a small sound, half-laugh, half-sob. "Dixie was black, Mr. Quinn. A prostitute, and an upir. I think you might be exaggerating."

Jack's eyes darkened as he shook his head. "None of that matters. What happened to her... it wasn't right. It wasn't..." he trailed off, glancing at the floor for a moment. When he spoke again, his voice was different, lower. Rougher. "We're going to find the people who did this. I promise you. We won't let them get away with it."

August glanced sideways at Jack. He knew that look. That tone. Jack meant it. And for a moment, August felt his heart quicken. It felt as though something had changed. Shifted. They'd always been committed to finding the killers. What could have possibly changed, August couldn't have said. He knew it was irrational, but he felt a twisting, and then a pounding, low in his gut. The feeling he got before a fight. Before he let himself loose. He stared over at Jack, and he knew then, with an odd certainty, that they would find whoever was doing this. And when they did, there would be bloodshed.

August felt himself shiver slightly, once more, as Adelaide sniffed, nodding at Jack's words. "She was beautiful, you know." She laughed, somewhat wryly. "I mean, of course she was. But... she was different. There was something about her. You should have seen the way men fawned over her." An odd smile twisted Adelaide's smooth features. "And it wasn't just because of what she could do. Although there were many that worshipped her for it. It wasn't just that. It was *her*. She was special. She was kind. She didn't have a mean bone in her body. She–" Adelaide cut herself off, shaking her head, swallowing roughly.

August felt the sudden urge to grab hold of her hand, but he forced himself to stay still.

"I'm sorry," Jack said numbly. "I'm sorry that she was taken from you."

Adelaide nodded, her gaze on her fingers in her lap, as they worked at the hem of her robe. She took a deep breath. "Do you have any clues?" She looked up at them. "Any idea who did this to her? It wasn't... random, was it?" Her attention shifted to August as she spoke. "I heard..."

"What did you hear?" Jack asked, leaning forward slightly.

"I heard there was another girl. That they found a second body. I heard she was a vampire, too. They're saying this wasn't random. At first, we all thought it was because she was a working girl... that it could have happened to any one of us. That maybe she was just unlucky. In the wrong place, at the wrong time. But now, now they're saying it's because she was a vampire." Her eyes shifted over August's features, studying him once more.

"This is my partner, by the way, Adelaide; August Sullivan," Jack interjected.

August nodded and bowed forward slightly. "It's a pleasure to meet you, Miss." The corner of Adelaide's lips quirked to the side as he spoke.

Jack continued, his voice pitched in a low, soothing tone. "Speaking of being in the wrong place, do you have any idea why she was out there that night?" He paused, but Adelaide didn't respond. She remained fixed on August. August did his best to look non-threatening, shifting uncomfortably in his seat.

Jack cleared his throat, attempting to regain her attention. "We still can't figure out why she was out there, all alone, on the edge of the woods like that, at night. So far from the city. How did she get out there?" Jack paused, then went on, his tone shifting as though he were reluctant to continue. "There was no sign of... ligature marks. On her wrists. Or ankles. Nothing to indicate she had been restrained. We're inclined to think that she went to that field willingly, on her own accord." Adelaide only grimaced slightly as Jack spoke. "There were no drugs in her system, either," Jack added. "No signs she might have been drugged or knocked unconscious. So, the question is, why was she there? And how did she get there?"

Adelaide shook her head slowly. "I have no idea."

August picked up the thread. "We were told she never came back here, that night. That she had been booked for the early evening, supposedly by a new, unknown client. But only for an evening out on the town, as an escort. It seems that while that was a bit unusual, it wasn't anything that raised any suspicions."

Adelaide nodded. "It doesn't happen often, but yes, it wasn't uncommon for one of us to be booked as an escort." She smiled, a real, true smile. "I went on a date like that once. He took me to the theater." Her eyes sparkled at the memory. August couldn't help but wonder briefly how she had ended up here.

"What did Dixie herself have to say about it? Did she talk to you about it, before she left that night? Did she say anything that might help us figure who did this?" Jack paused, waiting.

August held his breath. This was the farthest they'd gotten so far. None of the other girls had been willing to give them the time of day, during their last two visits. August suspected they had been warned to stay silent, but Jack insisted that it wasn't like Madam Beaufrey. He thought the girls were just afraid. Said they had come too soon, in the aftermath of the murder. They had been shaken. Scared to talk. They weren't the type to open up to cops normally, much less after something like that had happened. But August wasn't so sure.

None of the women he'd questioned had *seemed* afraid. They had been stone-faced. Unmoving. But today, Adelaide was different. She was allowing herself to grieve. And she wanted Dixie's killers to be brought to justice. There had to be something she could give them. Anything.

Adelaide looked off to her right, staring up at the ceiling, lost in thought for a moment. "I remember her chatting about it. She seemed excited to go out that night. They were going to a restaurant... The Black Sheep." Adelaide smiled, somewhat forlornly. "A fancy restaurant. Do you know it?" She turned to Jack, her expression changing.

He nodded swiftly. "I do know it."

"I've never been there..." the wistful expression returned, and her eyes glazed over. "Neither had Dixie. She wore one of her best dresses. I helped her with her hair."

"She didn't wear it loose?" Jack asked, watching the girl intently.

She shook her head. "No, not at all. Was it... was that how they found her?" Her eyes had taken on that wet look again.

"What else did she say? What did you talk about? Did she tell you anything about the client she was meeting?" Jack prompted gently.

Adelaide sighed, swallowing and gazing over towards the fire. "She didn't know him. The client. Didn't recognize the name. None of us did. Or he used a fake one."

August and Jack glanced at each other.

Adelaide shrugged. "Men do that, sometimes. Maybe he wanted to surprise her... was trying to be discreet... who knows." She sighed. "But I'm sure she was telling the truth. She didn't know who she was meeting that night."

"Do you recall the name he used?"

Adelaide paused and then shook her head. "No, I'm sorry. I don't. It was odd sounding."

Jack's chest deflated a little, as she spoke. He sighed and stared down at the floor.

"Did she have anyone special, who had been coming to see her recently?" August spoke up, he kept his tone nonchalant.

Adelaide swiveled to him, studying him for a moment before she spoke. "You're talking about *him*." Her eyes narrowed as she uttered the last word.

August felt Jack still beside him. He nodded, keeping his expression neutral. "Yes. Tell us about him."

Adelaide sighed, her lips pressed together in a thin line. "He wasn't good enough for her, if you want to know my opinion. I don't know what she saw in him. I really don't." She glanced at the doorway. The door to the bedroom remained open a crack. She leaned forward, towards August, and he leaned closer as well, as Jack turned to glance back at the door. "He didn't *pay*," she said, her eyebrows rising, placing significance on that last word.

August slid closer, until he was perched on the edge of his chair. "She didn't know; Madam Beaufrey, but he didn't pay. He wasn't one of her clients. He was her beau. I think she snuck him in the back." Adelaide's voice had dropped to a whisper. August leaned closer still, as she spoke. So did she, her robe falling slightly wider, further revealing the rounded curves of her perky breasts.

August struggled to keep his gaze on her face. He stared into her wide brown eyes. "What was his name again?" He asked, frowning, as though he already knew who she was talking about.

Adelaide shook her head, propping her chin on her hand, her elbow resting on her knee. "I don't know. She never told me. She always kicked me out when he came around. She didn't like to talk about him. I think she wanted to keep him a secret. I could have pried, I suppose. Now I wish I had." She frowned suddenly. "But, you don't think he– you think he had something to do with this?"

August kept his expression neutral and shrugged. "We have to look into all angles, Adelaide. We can't assume anything at this point."

Adelaide seemed satisfied with his answer. She nodded and took a deep breath. "Well, I never caught his name, but I suspect she had been seeing him for a few months. He came around here a couple times, that week before *it* happened. And I always thought there was something slightly odd about him, now that I think about it."

"Odd how?" August asked, not daring to move from his precarious perch on the edge of his chair.

Adelaide had that glazed over look again. "There was just something about him." She frowned to herself. "I never liked him. He wouldn't let her feed off him. I found that strange. Don't you?" She snapped back to the present, locking eyes with August. "Why on earth was he with her, if he didn't care enough about her to let her feed when she needed to?" Adelaide's frown deepened. "I mean, she had plenty of clients who liked that sort of thing. It's not like she was ever starving. But still..." she trailed off for a moment, her eyes met August's once more, taking in the veins that had quieted slightly, pulsing now just below the surface.

She smiled, almost wistfully, as she spoke, her voice barely a whisper now. "I let her feed from me, you know. Not often. But sometimes, at night. When she needed it. Once... it was after he left. He'd just been here, and she was hungry." Adelaide's eyes traced the veins beneath August's, before falling lower, to the tips of his canines, just visible between his parted lips. "She was always so gentle. She'd never really hurt me. I knew I was safe, with her."

August swallowed nervously, feeling his veins throbbing harder. She was so close to him now, her breath warm against his cheeks. He slid back in his chair, forcing himself to move away from her. August cleared his throat, wiping a hand over his upper lip, folding it over his teeth, as he did so. "So that's how you knew, that um, he didn't let her feed from him, that is?"

"That's right," Adelaide said, leaning back against the window seat. "And I don't think he ever did. I think she made him nervous, a little." She frowned, staring over at the fire. "I wondered why he was with her."

"Would any of the other girls know his name?" Jack asked, glancing between Adelaide and August with an eyebrow raised. "Anyone else we can talk to?"

Adelaide seemed to shrink in a bit on herself. "I think I was the closest to her... I doubt any of the other girls would know anything I don't."

Jack nodded briskly. "Of course, of course." He waved a hand, seemed to think for a moment.

"Did he ever bring her flowers?" August asked.

Adelaide thought for a moment before nodding slowly. "Yes. He did. More than once, actually."

August sat up a little straighter. "When was the last time? Recently?"

Adelaide stared over at the mantle for a moment. "Yes. Just a few days before she died. He brought her roses, that time." She cocked her head to the side. "Yellow roses. I remember, because I thought it was odd, that they weren't red. I said, 'doesn't that mean friendship, or something like that?' And Dixie just laughed. She told me they were yellow because that was her favorite." Adelaide smiled, her lips wobbling slightly. "She said when she was little, her father would bring her mother a dozen red roses, once a year, on their anniversary. And he always brought home one yellow rose, just for her." Tears filled her eyes once more. She reached up this time, wiping them away as they began to stream down her cheeks.

August moved without thinking, reaching forward and placing a hand on her knee. He hadn't meant to. And he froze in place there, but she seemed not to notice. She continued to cry silently, wiping her tears away as swiftly as they fell.

Jack was leaning forward in his seat, eyes bright. "Did the flowers have a card? Any sort of card with a symbol or name of a shop you might recognize?"

After a moment, Adelaide managed to slow her tears. "I–I don't know, there might have been a card. Yes. I think there probably was. But I can't remember what it looked like." She shook her head, and a fresh volley of tears rolled down her cheeks.

August slid his hand away from Adelaide's knee, hoping it had remained unnoticed.

"Would she have kept the card? Madam Beaufrey had a box of her things, what happened to it?" The question was more rhetorical, as it fell from Jack's lips, but Adelaide nodded through her tears.

She pointed over at the closet in the corner. "There. I kept it. I don't think she had any family left. She never did tell me her real name, so I don't know how I'd find them, anyway. But I told Madam Beaufrey I wanted to keep it, just in case."

Jack moved over to the closet, pulled the door open, and returned a few seconds later with the cardboard box. He set it on the chair and rifled through the items inside. "Ah ha!" He pulled a small pink card from the box and held it aloft. Then he flipped it open. "*To DL, with love,*" he read out loud. He frowned slightly. "It's signed only '*-H*'." His shoulders slumped forward. "That's it. Not much to go on." He held the card out to August, who scanned it quickly.

"Dammit," August muttered to himself.

"That's too bad," Adelaide said quietly. "Well," she sighed, "I don't know his name, but I know where you might be able to find him."

Jack and August froze, heads swiveling to stare at the young woman. She had pulled a handkerchief from a pocket of her robe and was dabbing at her eyes.

"You do?" Jack said sharply.

Adelaide nodded swiftly. "Yes." Her voice dropped to a whisper once more, and she glanced at the doorway. "He hangs around with *Red,* and his crew." Her eyes went slightly wide as she spoke. "Another reason he wasn't any good for her." Adelaide shivered slightly, drawing her arms around herself.

Jack and August looked at each other, expressions grim, then Jack turned to Adelaide. "What did "H" look like? Can you describe him for us?"

Adelaide thought for a moment. "He was tall. Dark hair: he kept it cut short. He was black." She frowned, staring into the fire for a moment. "He had a scar, on the back of his neck," she said, "it was an odd shape... almost like a, a swirl or something. I remember he caught me staring at it once, when I'd walked in on him dressing to leave..." Adelaide stopped, looking up at Jack. "He seemed angry, at the time. I thought he was just flustered... it was an odd sort of scar. Looked like it had been done on purpose."

Jack nodded, his expression grim, then he leaned forward, holding his hand out to her. She placed her hand in his, and he kissed the back of it briefly. "Thank you. I think you may have just helped us more than you know."

"You didn't hear anything from me," Adelaide said swiftly, a small smile on her lips, and a flush of pink splashed across her cheeks.

Jack nodded and winked at her. "We are nothing if not discreet. Don't worry my dear." Jack held up the card, with an eyebrow raised.

"Keep it," Adelaide said.

Jack bowed and turned to go.

August stood and nodded at Adelaide in thanks. "Thank you for all your help, we appreciate it."

She didn't respond, watching him carefully, until he turned to follow Jack out of the room.

August stopped midstride, as a hand gripped his wrist and pulled him back with surprising strength. Adelaide stood behind him. She had moved past the armchairs, and stood there, framed by the window, once more silhouetted in a golden haze. August's breath caught in his throat, as he studied her features.

"What I did for Dixie," she said, her voice pitched so low, that August moved closer instinctively. "I'd do it for you, if you ever need me to." She peered up at him, resting her hand on his chest. "You're different, too," she smiled sadly at him, "aren't you?"

August remained silent, perfectly still, but his heart hammered away beneath the palm of her hand. He didn't bother attempting to hide the bloom of color that rushed to his cheeks, or the dark veins that swelled to the surface. Adelaide did not seem fazed by it. Her sad smile only widened. August couldn't look away from her big brown eyes, wide and innocent, taking him in.

"You wouldn't hurt me, either. I can feel it." She took a step back, away from him, and the spell she held him in broke.

He moved sideways to the door, still looking back over his shoulder at her.

"If you need me, you know where to find me," she called softly to him. And he thought, in his haste to leave, that he might have nodded before fleeing through the door.

14

THE BLACK SHEEP.

The manager of The Black Sheep seemed to have materialized out of nowhere. No sooner had Jack and August entered the half-empty restaurant, and stood there, blinking, as their eyes adjusted to the dim interior, did they find themselves swept magnanimously through the swinging double doors into the kitchen by a small, frantically polite Frenchman.

"Why, Mr. Quinn, I am so pleased, no-no; *delighted*, to see you in my fine establishment. But please, tell me you do me the honor of paying me a personal visit. Please, tell me this is not a business matter, for that would be most unfortunate, most unfortunate. And in front of paying customers, no less."

The short man swept a hand down his face, removing a faint sheen of sweat that was quickly replaced. A shock of black hair, standing oddly on end, seemingly for the sole purpose of adding several inches to his height, bobbed and swayed. He reminded August of a small bird. Never still, eyeing them nervously, all with an uneasy grin plastered over his features.

"Antoine." Jack gave the man a gracious half-bow, "It is certainly a pleasure to see you again. But tell me, is this the new fashion? Are you in the habit of showing all your guests the kitchen before they indulge in your fine cuisine?"

Antoine's dark eyes seemed to widen slightly as he laughed nervously and glanced in August's direction, before swiftly looking away. "Mon Dieu, no, mon amie, of course not! But I was merely bringing you to my office, I assumed, perhaps incorrectly, that you may wish to speak with me, and perhaps, in a more private location." He bowed as he spoke, in Jack's direction, and swept both arms towards the hallway that ran down the middle of the kitchen. "Please, please, this way, this way."

He took off down the hallway, Jack and August trailed after him, the kitchen staff watching warily as they passed.

"Ah," Jack said, "so you do have some notion of why we're here."

The Frenchman paused, and turned to stare up at them. "Well, I can only assume, it is in fact business that brings you here today. At this hour."

It was early, not yet time for the dinner rush. But August felt an uncomfortable prickle, as the man seemed to avoid meeting his eyes, before he turned and continued to scurry forward. Jack shot August a look as they fell in line once more.

Once inside the small back office, Antoine located a second chair, sweeping his arm to gesture towards it and stepping back, to allow August to take a seat. He hurried around the desk and plopped into the chair facing them.

"Now, how may I be of assistance, gentlemen?"

Once again, August felt that this statement, despite being in the plural, was addressed only to Jack. He stiffened, and his gaze hardened on the small Frenchman as Jack leaned forward.

"Let's cut to the chase, Antoine, I think you know why we're here. Just over one week ago, one of your patrons dined here, and was found dead several hours later. Care to enlighten us?"

Jack's choice of words had been deliberate, for effect, and he could not have chosen them any better.

The man's face blanched, turning as white as a sheet, before going crimson. "Mon Dieu." He crossed himself as he spoke. "You, Jack, you, of all people, who have dined here, on many occasions," August glanced sharply at his partner, "cannot believe that *my* fine, French cuisine, had anything to do with that abomination."

"Antoine," Jack continued, smiling magnanimously, "do not put words in my mouth, old friend. I am merely wondering why you have not come forward, up to this point. Surely, you were aware the victim had dined here that very evening. Did you not feel a sense of obligation to make the police aware of this fact?"

Antoine's eyebrows rose nearly to his hairline. "*I–I* make the police aware?" He placed both hands on his chest, "But my friend, how was *I* to know the police were not aware? I knew no such thing. And if I did know, why surely, I would not have thought it to be of any significance, and this would be the reason, the only reason, that I would not come forward, and make such a thing known."

August frowned at the man's flowery speech and leaned back in his chair. As he shifted his weight, Antoine glanced at him once more, and he swallowed, his Adam's apple bobbing. "But you cannot think I, or my staff had anything to do with this. This is *encroyable*! The fact that the- the- young lady, that she dined here, that night, it is a mere coincidence. Of what import could it possibly be to the police?" Now Antoine pulled a white handkerchief from somewhere and dabbed his glistening forehead as he waited for Jack to respond.

"Well, you see, the importance cannot be overstated, my friend. We were not aware of the victim's movements that night, not until today. And in fact, this information may be vital to tracing her movements throughout the remainder of the evening. Now, we know that she dined here, but we do not know, for example, who she dined with." Jack leaned forward, eyes piercing. "And that information, my friend, I am relying on you, to provide us with."

Antoine seemed to be at a loss for words for once and could only stammer as he processed Jack's request. "My dear friend, we have so many guests, so many guests, fortunate as we are, to have the reputation that we have earned, that you cannot possibly expect me to recall-"

"Oh, but I do, Antoine, I do." Jack leaned closer. "Because I know you, you see. I know exactly," he leaned even closer, and tapped the man's forehead as he spoke, causing him to flinch, "how, your little mind works. And I know for a fact, that you would have noted, and remembered *exactly* who Miss LaRue dined with that evening. And not only that evening, but every other previous evening, she may have graced your fine establishment."

Antoine's eyes had widened, at the tapping on his shiny dome, but his eyes just as quickly narrowed, and his voice came out low and gruff. "Previous evening? Never. Never had she dined here on any previous evening. Nor would she have been welcome if she had." His eyes hardened to ice chips as he spoke. "The day I see my life's work, overrun by such *filth*–"

"And there it is." Jack cut him off, his voice rising over the smaller man's as he slammed his fist down on the desk. "The real reason you did not come forward. You didn't want it splashed across the papers that Miss LaRue dined at The Black Sheep. Not on the night of her murder, or on any other night. And not just because of her... profession, but because of *what* she *was*."

Antoine's face flashed white, to red, to purple with shocking alacrity. August dug his nails into the armrest of his chair before he had the chance to be consciously aware of the action. He pulled them loose with a tearing sound that brought a look of complete shock to the Frenchman's face.

August stared at Antoine's slack-jawed visage. "Oops," he said.

"Oh, that's nothing." Jack grinned between August and Antoine, with a look of pure glee. "You think I'm bad when I get angry, you should see what happens when–"

"Non, non, non." Antoine stood, holding both hands up, fingers splayed. "This is not necessary, my friends, this is not..." he trailed off, smoothed his crisp white shirt, and took a seat once more. "I will tell you. I will tell you everything you want to know. Everything I can. Please, I have poured my life into this restaurant." The exterior of unflappable charm was gone, stripped away, and only a tired, forlorn little man, sat before them. "I only wished to protect what I have built. I bear your... your kind," he eyed August nervously, "no ill will. Truly, I do not. I do not involve myself with these matters, with politics."

August squirmed in his seat, struggling to stay silent. He thought he knew exactly what the Frenchman thought of *his kind*. He kept his mouth clamped shut, but for once, he did nothing to suppress the hot lines of rushing blood that bubbled to the surface beneath his narrowed eyes.

Antoine looked as though he might pass out, as he took in August's ill-concealed ire.

Jack leaned back into his seat, and placed both feet on the man's desk, propping one foot on top of the other. "You're right, Antoine, old boy. You've put quite a lot into this old pile, haven't you." He gestured vaguely around them. "What is it they say? Blood, sweat and tears?" He grinned, placing one finger over his lips, as he studied Antoine. "Now the sweat part, I believe. The tears... sure." Jack shrugged. "But the blood..." he glanced at his partner, and August couldn't help the small smile that rose to his lips in response. "What do you think, Sully? Has enough blood been spilled in this restaurant?"

"I did not know the man!" Antoine blurted out, his face crimson. "I tell you the truth. I did not know this man, that sat with–with–"

"With Miss LaRue," Jack supplied, his tone icy.

"Yes, Miss LaRue." Antoine dabbed at his brow once more. "I have never seen this man before, who escorted her that night.

He was very well-dressed. His suit, the cut, it was impeccable. He was tall. Brown hair, blue eyes. Very handsome. Very striking. It was not a face you forget. I asked several people, I tell you, several people, who he was. Discreetly, mind you. And no one could tell me this man's name." He held both palms up, facing out, once more.

"How did Dixie appear, to you, that evening. Did she seem to be in any distress?"

"No, no, mon amie, not at all. She appeared happy. They seemed as though they were having fun. Enjoying their meal. I saw her laughing, several times, at something the man said." Antoine shrugged. "I noticed nothing out of the ordinary."

"And I imagine you kept a close eye on her," Jack said. "I imagine you attempted to have them seated in the back, hidden from view. Yes, but you would have kept a close eye on her. What, with her being a vampire, and a whore, I'm guessing you never took your eyes off her. Did you check the silverware, after they left?"

Antoine swallowed and let out an audible little moan as Jack's eyes darkened.

"How was she, when they left?" August asked. "Which direction did they go?"

Antoine looked anxiously back and forth between the two men. "She was unharmed, when she left. Absolutely unharmed." He thought for a moment. "Right! They turned right, when they left. Headed up the street, towards the bank." His exclamation was met with silent, cold stares. "It is the truth; I swear it to you." He crossed himself hastily. His gaze dropped to the floor, as August continued to stare him down.

Jack turned aside to August. "Do you believe him, old boy?" he asked, just loud enough for Antoine to hear.

"I swear it! Everything I've told you is true! On all that is holy!"

Jack grinned over at Antoine. "I'm afraid we've rather fallen in with the *unholy* crowd, these days, my friend."

The man stammered. "I–I meant no disrespect!" His focus shifted back and forth from August to Jack, his face pale as milk.

August allowed the man to squirm under his gaze for several seconds, before he nodded once to Jack.

Jack stood, patting August on the back. "Good. Good then." He leaned over the desk, holding his hand out to Antoine. The man took it reluctantly, as though afraid it might bite him, and he was practically trembling as Jack's grip tightened on his. Jack leaned forward, his voice dropping low. "Where did they go after they left?"

"I do not know!" Antoine squeaked. "No idea! I did not speak to them, I did not..." his eyes went wide. "Terrence, the man who waited on them that evening, he did not learn anything– anything of value. I spoke with him after they left. The man paid, in large bills. He left a good tip. Terrence– he did not get a name!"

"Terrence..." Jack repeated thoughtfully, still shaking Antoine's hand. "Is he working tonight?"

"No! No! But I– I will tell you where he lives!" The man was sweating profusely now. "His address! I have it! Allow me to get it for you!"

Jack smiled. "Why, that would be ever so thoughtful of you. Thank you, Antoine." He turned to August. "Looks like we'll have more than one stop to make tonight."

15

RED. BEDLAM.

The sandwich shop that sat on the street level was located across town from The Black Sheep. It had been a decent hike to walk there. A little bell tinkled above the door as they entered. The burly looking men behind the counter sported tattoos and little white aprons. They took one look at the detectives, and eyed each other surreptitiously, but they did not attempt to stall their forward progress.

Jack continued strolling confidently, whistling under his breath. He marched past them without a second glance, and down a narrow hallway that led to the back of the shop. August trailed behind, his hands in his pockets. The weight of his Colt Officer's Model was comforting against his right hip as they descended a murky narrow stairwell.

The walls of the stairwell itself, and the corridor it emptied into were painted pitch black. Hundreds of names, dates, vulgarities, and sentimentalities were scrawled on the walls to either side. Otherwise, the hallway was bare, and the scuffmarks from their shoes joined a multitude of others on the dirty floor below.

August was assaulted by the scent of beer mixed with spirits and smoke, with brazen laughter, and the cacophony of conversation before he even crossed over the threshold into the dimly lit lounge.

When they stepped into the lounge, the general raucous cut off abruptly for several seconds, as heads turned in their direction, before surging once more.

Jack glanced back at August and made his way over to the bar across the large space. The floor in the lounge was a noticeable upgrade from the flooring out in the corridor.

August took in the joint with his head on a swivel. Low velvet couches and lounge chairs were scattered throughout the room. Dark, gleaming tables, polished to reflect the flickering candlelight above. The room was packed. An open area in the middle was cleared of any furniture, and a small group of people danced to the rhythm emanating from a booming jukebox. A cloud of cigarette smoke hung like a miasma, giving the very air a hazy quality, that led to a feeling of surrealness that seemed to envelop August with each step he took into foreign territory.

He sat beside Jack at the bar, sliding onto a comfortable worn leather stool. Jack ordered for them, holding up two fingers. "Two shots of whiskey."

"How many times have I told you? I don't drink," August said, glancing behind them. He took in the group at the pool tables across the room. Young. Most of them. Muscular. With a griminess to them that was at odds with their elegant surroundings. They weren't looking at the bar. Not a one.

Jack grinned, as the bartender plunked two shot glasses onto the bar in front of them, and poured the spirits. "Who said one of them was for you?" He picked up the first shot glass and tossed it back, slamming it down on the bar upside down. He downed the second just as quickly.

"Good heavens," August moaned.

"Calm down." Jack clapped him on the back. "The night is young."

The night is dark and full of screams. Those were her words. August flashed back to Miss Gray. To the whites of her eyes. The evil smile that spread across her familiar features as she stared up at him. Dixie. In the hallway upstairs. The way the light had left her eyes, as she screamed, at the end.

"You see anyone that looks like he might be our mysterious Mr. H?" Jack asked in hushed tones.

August glanced once more around the lounge. "No one obvious." There were a few black men, lounging about. A few couples. All of them seemed to be ignoring the pair at the bar. Just like everyone else in the room.

"Keep an eye out for that scar," Jack murmured back.

August shivered involuntarily. "I don't like the looks of that group, over by the pool table. Let's talk to Red... get the heck out of here."

"Ah." Jack shook his head. "I doubt it will be that simple." He caught the bartender's eye and held up two fingers. "In my experience, Red doesn't like to be found. Not any more than he likes to be talked to."

August sighed, turning to stare at Jack momentarily, before attempting once more to peer casually behind them, surveying the room. "He isn't here, is he?"

"No. Indeed he is not," Jack said cheerfully.

"Then why are we still here?" Jack shook his head, as August continued. "Did you see how they all froze, when we walked in?"

"There's nothing for it, old boy. The only way we're going to find Red, is Red wanting to find us. That's the long and short of it."

"What on earth are you on about?" August leaned back, distracted for a moment by the lilting laughter of a young woman who appeared to be a call girl. Perhaps even a colleague of Dixie's, who threw her head back towards the ceiling, as she sank into a man's arms. He sat lounging in a low chair, his shirt sleeves rolled up to reveal biceps the size of pistons, covered in tattoos. He wrapped one arm around her, pulled his cigar from his mouth, and blew a plume of smoke into the air. He caught August watching him and stared icily back until August looked away.

"I meant exactly what I said, Sully," Jack said. "The only way we're talking to Red, is if he decides he wants to talk to us."

"So, what's your plan then? How is sitting at a bar, drinking whiskey going to conjure Red?"

Jack only chuckled in response, shaking his head, as though August had said something funny.

August's cheeks flushed. "Enough with the games. I know how much it amuses you to see me left in the dark, but I'm not in the mood tonight. Let's just ask someone." He surveyed the lounge once more. "Let's just tell someone we want to talk to Red."

August felt his impatience growing as Jack appeared to ignore him. The bartender approached, filling two fresh shot glasses. He waited this time, while Jack tossed them both back.

August leaned forward. "Hey, look," he said in a conspiratorial whisper. "We want to talk to Red." August slid his jacket to the side, over his chest, displaying the badge hidden beneath. "Nothing to worry about. Just a conversation."

The bartender displayed no reaction at the sight of his badge. He looked August up and down. At least, what he could see of him above the bar, and flashed him a tight smile. "Yeah. Right. You can fuck right off." He turned to Jack, one eyebrow raised, bottle poised over the nearest shot glass, and he began to refill them at Jack's nod.

"For fuck's sake." August dropped his head in his hands.

Jack's laughter issued from low in his throat, close to August's ear. "Don't worry, Sully. Haven't I always got a plan?"

"Yes," August uttered, through gritted teeth. "That's why I'm worried."

It wasn't long before Jack's plan became apparent. They spent the next half hour or so at the bar. Jack grew louder and louder, as though he was making a point of being as obnoxious as possible. Eventually, he managed to break through the facade of ambivalence displayed by the others in the lounge. August began to catch furtive glances in their direction. He caught people whispering to each other as they began to glare. Muttered sentiments floated their way. Like, *'Filthy upir pig, and his fucking dog.'* None of which seemed to penetrate Jack's consciousness. And while Jack slowed his pace considerably, he continued to throw back shots of whiskey as though he were drinking water.

August didn't understand it. He had never seen the man hungover. Not once. It was inhuman. He supposed Jack must have a different sort of metabolism. While the man seemed to exhibit none of the negative effects of heavy drinking the next day, he began to exhibit all the typical immediate effects of imbibing.

Jack became looser, louder. More garrulous, as the minutes ticked by. He began to show interest in the poker game that the group of thugs in the back were slowly, but steadily, playing to completion.

One of them, sporting similar tattoos to the large beast of a man that still lounged directly behind them, minus the whopping biceps, seemed to be attempting to discreetly keep a close eye on Jack. He appeared to be the leader of the gang playing pool, from what August could tell. He chalked his cue, for what felt like the tenth time, his eyes narrowed and fixed on Jack as he spun on the barstool, singing tunelessly. He was thin. Wirey. With lanky blonde hair. A wisp of a man, really. But somehow, with the appearance of strength in his sinewed arms. August didn't like the cold, calculating look in his eyes.

Jack was becoming boisterous now. He'd gotten to his feet and sauntered over to the jukebox across from the bar, a full shot glass held aloft in one hand. He seemed to be slightly unsteady on his feet. Whiskey sloshed, landing on the floor below.

August watched as he passed the burly man with the tattoos, noting how his eyes never left Jack. August shifted slowly forward, until he was perched on the edge of his stool.

Jack made a show of perusing the records and making a selection. He dropped several coins into the slot, and turned, grinning widely at August. As he made his way back towards the bar, the call girl, blonde curls and tits bouncing, jumped to her feet, and crossed his path. Jack stopped her, one arm held out. She paused, her gaze trailed up his arm until she met his eyes. August felt his gut tighten at the small, secretive sort of smile that curled her lips.

Jack smiled back. The smile of a fisherman, when he's got a fish on the hook. He tossed the shot down his throat. Leaning over the burly man, he threw him a wink, as he set the empty shot glass down on the table beside him. He grabbed the call girl, one hand grasping hers, the other sliding around her waist. He pulled her into his arms and led her out on the dance floor, joining the other couples, most of whom had stopped dancing, to watch the scene unfolding.

"Here we fucking go," August murmured. He glanced over at the gang hanging around the pool table. Sure enough, they'd paused and were now watching Jack intently. He'd counted ten of them. Plus, the big man in the rolled-up sleeves, and his friends. That made another three, at least. At least 13 men. Plus however many others here that were part of Red's crew. August willed himself to stay calm, but adrenaline was already pumping through his veins, and he felt a tingling that only came when he knew he was faced with imminent bloodshed.

Jack seemed blissfully unaware of all of it. He spoke to the pretty call girl, spun her in a circle, as she laughed. When the big burly man whom August had come to think of as Sleeves, got to his feet, August grit his teeth, watching in anticipation.

Sleeves wasn't looking at Jack. He was staring down at the shot glass that he'd discarded on his table. Sleeves picked up the shot glass, tossed it lightly in the air, as though he were testing its weight, then he slung his arm back, and whipped it directly at Jack's head.

August didn't flinch. He watched, waited. Jack's hand shot up. He snatched the shot glass out of the air inches before it slammed into his face. August watched as Jack smiled over at Sleeves. And he watched, as Sleeves paused in his lumbering gait. He noted with grim satisfaction, the momentary look of hesitation that flashed over his features.

But it was too late, at that point. The shot glass flew like it had been shot out of a cannon. It hit Sleeves in the throat with a resounding crunch. The sound he made was strangled, as he crumpled forward, gagging and clawing at his neck. That was when all hell broke loose.

It was an art, in a way. August leaned back against the bar, as he watched, but he kept one hand on his right thigh, close to his Colt Officer's Model revolver. He found himself regretting, for a split second, their decision to walk that night. A getaway vehicle, one of the department's Ford V8s, would have been particularly useful. It would have been a comfort, to know they had it waiting outside. But it was only a split second. A fleeting thought. He watched, as Jack did what he did best. Other than solving crimes, that was. Create chaos.

The blonde wiry man over by the pool table, was the first one to come at him. He ran at Jack's back; a wicked-looking knife held aloft in one hand. Jack heard him coming. He dropped low to the ground, at the last second, moving with his inhuman speed. The blonde fellow, meanwhile, had swung forward, bringing the knife in an arc, aiming for Jack's chest.

The knife sliced through nothing but air. August thought Jack may have slid an arm behind the man's legs, but he was moving too fast for him to be certain. Either way, the fellow's legs went out from under him, and he landed on his back on the hard floor.

The air rushed out of him with an "Oof", and the knife went flying in August's direction. Jack grinned over at him and nodded at the knife. August rolled his eyes, got to his feet, and picked up the knife. He threw it, aiming for the air in front of Jack.

He caught it by the hilt, just in time to shove it into the next man that rushed at him, stabbing him in the upper thigh.

The man let out a howl of pain, and Jack laughed. He flicked his head side to side, like a dog might shake itself after getting wet. When he stilled, his eyes were pitch black– two dark holes in his head, black as night, black as sin. His mouth had transformed, morphed into a gaping maw lined with sharp teeth. Jack tilted his head back, lifting his face towards the ceiling overhead, he let out a howl of his own.

It was unearthly. Otherworldly. August had heard it before, how many times? But regardless, he felt the hair on the back of his neck stand on end. People were screaming now. Running for the only exit, pushing and shoving their way to the door.

The blonde fellow on the ground was recovering now. As was Sleeves. August pointed at Sleeves, opening his mouth to warn Jack.

Jack opened his arms wide, as Sleeves rushed him, line-backer-style, and seemed to embrace and absorb the blow of the impact. Arching his back, he turned and tossed the man across the lounge. He went flying, a blur of limbs and a rush of color. The gang from the pool table ducked, as he flew overhead, and landed with a crash on the pool table. The table creaked and groaned, then buckling under his weight, it sagged down in the middle.

The pool table gang paused, glancing at each other with fur-rowed brows, and then back at Jack. But their leader, the thin blonde, was staggering to his feet off to the side, just out of Jack's view. One of the gang members lifted his pool cue, holding it like a javelin, and let out a roar. The others followed, spurred to action by their brave comrade, as their leader groped for the closest weapon he could find.

His hand grasped the neck of a wine bottle that sat on a nearby table. He lifted it aloft, wine sloshing and pouring down his back.

"Wine bottle," August called out, in an almost bored sort of voice.

Jack spun, catching the bottle before it crashed down on his head. He crushed the bottle in his fist, opening his hand a moment later, as bloody shards of broken glass fell with a tinkle to the floor.

"Pool cue," August said, and watched as Jack spun in time to grab hold of the cue with his other hand. The cue stopped in mid-air, but the man holding it didn't. His feet continued running beneath him, and he was jerked to a stop, his feet flying out from underneath him, as he let go of the cue and fell on his back. August let out a snorting laugh.

"Oh, you think that's fucking funny?" The blonde fellow sneered over at August. "Upir prick." He grabbed hold of the nearest chair, and flung it in August's direction.

Jack's fist connected with the man's gut, as August ducked to the side, knocking his stool over as he went. The chair crashed against the bar where his stool had been.

"You're going to have to try harder than that, asshole," August shot back at the blonde.

The scrappy blonde grit his teeth, dropping into a fighting stance, his fists raised. "Look at you, big man. All bark and no bite," he sneered.

August's gaze flickered from the little blonde man to Jack. Jack spun, still holding the pool cue, as a knot of men rushed him. The cue connected with three or four of them, knocking them backward, as it snapped in half.

Jack glanced at the now sharpened end of the cue he still held in one hand. He dropped to the floor as the next man rushed him with a fist lined with brass knuckles, stabbing the pool cue through the top of the man's foot. The man yelped in pain, arms flailing in a circular motion as he fell back onto his rear.

August returned his focus to the blonde man, who seemed unwilling to take a step closer, preferring to taunt him from a distance. He had grabbed hold of another chair, and staggered forward, grunting with the effort, and tossed it in his direction once more. August moved faster this time, spinning out of the way, he lunged at the blonde, managing to grab a fistful of the man's shirt as he attempted to dodge his grasp. He dragged him close, and the man's fist connected with August's jaw, stunning him for a second.

August shook it off, and flexed his neck, in a wave of motion that rippled, rolling down his shoulder. He felt the veins beneath his eyes, across his chest, swelling and pulsing. His eyes were pitch black, as he grinned down at the blonde. August watched as his expression shifted from disdain to stark fear. His canine teeth elongated, pushing their way between his parted lips.

"Oh shit," the blonde managed to murmur. August lifted him, raising him high off the ground, before tossing him over his shoulder. The blonde man hit the wall of fancy glass bottles behind the bar with a loud crash, bringing the shelves down with him as he slid to the floor. August leaned over the bar to watch as he flailed and writhed in pain on his back on the floor below.

"Now it's a real party," Jack called out.

August turned, watching as Jack lifted one arm, holding it parallel to the ground. One of the remaining pool crew ran into his open palm. Jack's hand closed around the man's throat, and he looked down, letting out a grunt of surprise.

Jack laughed, as the man's arm swung in an arc. A knife handle appeared, sticking out of Jack's gut.

Jack froze for a moment, still holding Red's goon aloft, wide-eyed, and gasping for breath. The man's fingers searched, splayed, landing on the handle of the knife once more. He pulled it from Jack's gut and raised his arm to stab him again.

Jack grabbed his wrist with his other hand, and lunged forward in a blur of teeth. His jaws clamped down on the man's arm with a sickening crunch. Jack released his grip on his neck as the man howled in pain. The man's severed arm fell to the floor, along with the knife.

Jack let the man go, as he screamed, falling to his knees. Jack staggered backwards, blood dripping from his open mouth, a dark red stain blooming on his white shirt.

"Jack!" August cried out, but Jack only laughed, staggering back another step.

He shook his head once more, spraying blood, as he sputtered. "I'm fine; it's just a flesh wound."

August shuddered as the scent of fresh blood hit him. He breathed in deeply, nostrils flaring, scenting the air. He struggled to hold himself back. He could feel his will slipping, as Jack watched his internal struggle with a look of pure glee.

August glanced down at the man on the floor at Jack's feet. His blue eyes were wide in terror as he stared up at August. He lifted one hand in the air, outstretched in August's direction. "Please. Don't." The man looked at the severed arm he held up in the air, jagged shards of bone gleamed stark white. *"Fuck,"* he hissed, dropping it. It fell to the floor once more with a sickening thud.

Jack turned to the group of men who stood huddled together across the dance floor. The man in front looked at the pool cue in his hands and dropped it like it was a hot poker. He held his hands up in supplication. "Red," the man gasped, "he won't like this."

"No," a voice called out from the other side of the lounge. "He won't."

August turned, as a bear of a man stepped through the doorway. He was so tall, he had to stoop to fit through the frame.

He wore his bright red hair slicked back, off his forehead. Green eyes blinked at them from above a full mustache and bushy beard. He took in the mess they had made in the lounge, his gaze landing first on the ruined bar, then the severed arm, then on Sleeves, where he still lay unconscious, or possibly dead, on the cracked pool table.

Red glared at Jack, shaking his head. "Really Jack? *Again?*"

16

HANK, A WARNING.

"Maybe you'll have the foresight to instruct your people to let you know, the next time I show up asking to talk to you."

Red let out a sound that was practically a growl. "Maybe next time, you'll have the foresight not to destroy my personal property."

"It's the only way to get through to you."

"And the only way'a getting through to you, is a boot up your ass," Red scowled, his cheeks flushing. "I oughta–"

"What?" Jack asked mildly, one eyebrow raised.

"I swear to God, if it were anyone else..."

The door to the office swung open, and a young woman poked her head in. Strawberry blonde hair fell in thick, frizzy waves, and sparkling green eyes peered at the trio, shoved inside the cramped office. "Jack!" She seemed to float through the doorway, moving to stand at Red's side. "I heard it was you! We haven't seen you in ages!"

"Rose, get yerself back downstairs and help tend to the men," Red growled, his scowl deepening.

"Oh nonsense." Rose waved her hand. "I've already had a look at them. They'll all keep. No one's in critical condition." Her focus wandered to the red stain on Jack's white shirt. It had grown larger, as they sat there. He still had dried blood coating his chin, and spatters all over his chest. "Can't be so sure about this one." She lifted her chin in Jack's direction.

"He's fine," Red insisted. "If it'd hit anything major, he would've bled out by now. You know that as well as I do."

"No harm in taking a look now, is there?" Rose pushed her sleeves up. "Jack?"

Jack sighed and stood, gesturing to August. "Trade seats with me, old chap." They shuffled awkwardly past each other, and August watched, bemused, as Rose helped Jack to unbutton his shirt, pulling some bandages and disinfectant from a pocket in her dress. Red, shockingly, allowed this to happen, albeit with a deep scowl on his face.

The group fell silent as Rose tended to Jack's wound. August watched, controlling the rise and fall of his chest, willing his engorged veins to stand down. His gaze strayed from Rose's face, the smattering of freckles, on her upturned little nose, the slight frown on her plump lips, down to her cleavage, just peeking out of the top of her dress as she leaned forward. That wasn't helping matters. He felt on edge, about to snap, ever since the fight, and the intoxicating scent of blood that still lingered in the room only made it worse. He needed to get himself back under control. August tore his eyes away from Rose.

Jack winced as she applied the disinfectant. "He's right, you know. If I was going to die, I would have by now," Jack said.

Rose gave him a disapproving glance. "The wound is quite deep, Jack."

"I'll be fine. I'll see a doctor in the morning. It's not worth worrying over."

Red leaned back in his chair, crossing his arms over his chest. "She won't be worrying over you, I can promise you that, you great lout. Now, tell me what is it that you needed to talk to me about so desperately, that ye had to take out half of my best men to do so. I'm losing my patience."

Jack sighed resignedly. "It's a small matter, really. We're looking for someone, known to us only by the initial *'H'*. A tall black man, with an odd scar on the back of his neck." Jack watched Red closely as he spoke, although he gave off an air of nonchalance. "And it wasn't as though we used lethal force, Red. We're both fully armed, you know. And not just with firepower."

"Speaking of arms, you left a severed one downstairs," Red growled. "Was that really necessary, Jack?"

"I'm only pointing out," Jack continued, "that the damage could have been much worse, should we have wished it."

"And ye don't think the same is true fer my men? What the hell do ye think they carry? Every one of 'em's packing heat. They're not accustomed to fighting with pool cues, do ya ken? But, no one wants the blood of the famous Jack Quinn on their hands, now do they?" Red leaned forward sneering, then he turned his focus onto August for the first time. "And this, I suppose, is yer new minder."

Red eyed August up and down, and August suspected he took in the barely concealed rapid rise and fall of his chest, along with his too-dark eyes, and those God-damned veins. Rose allowed herself to be distracted long enough to study August briefly as well as her father spoke. "Is yer boy going to be alright, Jack?" Red asked thoughtfully. "I would hate for more blood to be... spilled, tonight."

Jack frowned over at August, taking in his dark eyes, and the veins that still throbbed beneath them, then he seemed to perk up suddenly. He gestured to August. "This is my partner, August Sullivan. We've been working together for, what, Sully? Nearly a year now?" Jack beamed at August, before turning to Red. "And, yes, he'll be just fine. Lucky for you, he has more self-control than your entire pack of idiots combined."

"Watch yer tone with me, Jack." Red pointed at him.

"August, this is Jasper Roth. More widely known, as Red." Jack turned to smile affectionately at Rose, as she continued to patch up his wound. "And this lovely creature, is Rose Roth. Jasper's only daughter."

Red's eyes flashed dangerously, and August turned his gaze once more on the young woman who knelt beside Jack. She smiled over at him, twin dimples forming on her cheeks. His heart pounded painfully in his chest, in response.

"It's a pleasure, Mr. Sullivan."

August inclined his head in her direction, not trusting himself to speak.

"Enough with the pleasantries," Red snapped. "What do ya want with this 'H', and what makes you think I know a thing about 'im?"

Jack sighed, straightening, as Rose completed her task.

"There," she said. "That should hold for now." She gave him a serious look. "I want you to be seen by a doctor, Jack. Tonight. I'm not kidding."

"I'm not planning on keeling over anytime soon, Rose. Not when such beauty still exists in the world."

Even August had to roll his eyes, and Red's head looked like it might pop off his body. "You cheeky son of a bitch, I'll gut you if you even think–"

Rose laughed and made her way to the door. "This 'H'," she said briskly, "I think I've seen him around. He's tall, and he's got a funny sort of marking, on the back of his neck. A spiral shape, almost. He hangs out around the lounge sometimes, with the boys. Although," she frowned, "I haven't seen him as much lately. Maybe, in the last three months, or so. Goes by the name of Hank."

"Hank," Red scoffed. "There ain't no one on my payroll that goes by the name of Hank." Red glared coldly at Jack. "Yer wasting yer time here, Jack. *Barking* up the wrong tree. As usual."

Jack's eyes darkened almost imperceptibly. But August knew it for the warning sign that it was. August doubted that anyone other than Red, or perhaps Chief Waverly, could have gotten Jack to back down tonight. Even August himself, normally would have had a time of it. It was no easy task. Especially not once blood had been spilled.

Rose cleared her throat, drawing their attention to where she still lingered in the doorway. "No, Pa, he's not one of yours." She looked at him with wide, innocent eyes.

"I know it, girl," Red scoffed. "Hank," he seemed to think for a moment, running a hand down his beard. "I think I have seen him around, now that ye mention it. An' I only have one thing to say on the matter." He paused, seeming to think over his words. "I'd be careful. I'd be very careful, if I were you. See," Red leaned forward, placing two meaty arms on the desk, "this Hank, he ain't on my payroll, but you can bet your ass he's on someone's. And if I were you, I'd leave it well enough alone."

"Not an option," Jack said, leaning forward. "I need to know what you know. Who does he work for?"

Red shook his head, lips in a thin line. "I don't mess around with politics, lad." He pointed at Jack. "You know that about me. I keep outta all of it. I never did nothing, but try to mind my own business."

"His business was bootlegging, by the way," Jack said, leaning towards August, "amongst other things."

Red leaned back, spreading his arms wide. "And the end'a prohibition put an end to all that, now didn' it? These days, I'm just a family man." Jack laughed darkly as Red continued. "I keep a few small business interests, here and there. A man can't leave his family destitute, after all." Red glanced over at Rose, who stood half in the room, half out. "My wee lass here, she's all I have left."

Rose smiled patiently at her father. "He's right, Jack," she said, turning to him. "It's best you leave well enough alone." Her tone sharpened, her expression shifting. "You don't want to find this 'H'. If it *is* Hank, you're looking for. Best let sleeping dogs lie, as the saying goes." She shot Jack one last dark glance. "And see a doctor, Jack. I'll know, if you don't." And with that, she was gone.

$$17$$

THE CLIENT LIST. ADELAIDE.

"What the hell was that about?" August could barely contain himself. He waited until they reached the sidewalk before the question burst out of him. He scanned the street afterward, dimly illuminating streetlamps sat few and far between, separated by pockets of void. There seemed to be no pedestrians in sight, although a low fog hung over the city. The air felt dense. Cloying. August's chest was heaving, as he sucked in the night air, humid still, somehow, despite the edge of a chill that it held.

His nerves were frayed to the core. Like a rope, left hanging on by only a few threads. He could feel it. All that pressure, building. Ready to explode.

Jack just shook his head, at August's question, not breaking his stride, practically stalking down the street ahead of him.

"Jack? Seriously? What was she talking about? We need to go back there. Clearly, they know something. They're hiding something." August held both hands out, staring at Jack's back in consternation as they walked through the dark streets.

"You don't mess with Red, Sully," Jack called back to him. "Going back there now will do us no good."

"Red? *Christ.*" August ran his hands through his hair. "I don't know who was scarier; Red, or his daughter."

"Rose?" Jack snorted, finally easing his pace slightly. "Rose is a bloody saint, Sully." He paused briefly. "But I have to agree; she is somehow terrifying." Jack sighed, coming to an abrupt stop. He glanced up and down the street, then planted both hands on his hips. "You know what's really ticking me off about this whole thing?"

"What? The canine jokes?" August couldn't help but grin, despite himself. And it felt good. It cut slightly through the panicked energy that simmered beneath his skin.

Jack didn't respond, his eyes locked on August in the gloom.

"They did get a couple good ones in, didn't they?" August continued. Jack continued to glare at him. "What?" August shrugged. "It's usually nothing but vampire jokes. It's refreshing."

Jack's expression was deadpan.

"Oh, come off it, where's your sense of humor? Suddenly missing, when the jokes aren't at my expense for once?"

"No, August," Jack sighed resignedly. "It's not the canine jokes that are ticking me off. It's Madam Beaufrey."

"Madam Beaufrey?" August frowned.

"She may very well be at the crux of all this." Jack took a step forward. "Don't you see it?"

August frowned back at him, brows furrowed.

"Think about it, man! How did Dixie LaRue know where to meet her client that night? Hmm?" Jack lowered his voice, eyeing the other side of the street, as a couple walked briskly past, rushing between the comforting glow of streetlamps. "Dixie told Adelaide that she was meeting someone at The Black Sheep: she was excited to be dining there. But how did she know where to go that night? Who must have told her?"

"Madam Beaufrey," August said flatly.

"Exactly. Madam Beaufrey. Presumably, Dixie only knew, because *she* knew. Madam Beaufrey would have been the one to book the client, right? And she would have been the one to inform Dixie of the plan. Yet, we visited the cathouse twice, in that first week, after Dixie was found, and not once, not *once*, did Madam Beaufrey think to mention the fact that she knew where Dixie had gone that night." Jack shrugged. "Well, her first stop, at the very least."

"You're right," August said. "You're absolutely right. She was vague and evasive. And we were so focused on questioning the girls... I'm not sure I ever explicitly asked her if she knew where Dixie was going that night. Did you?" Jack shook his head. August sighed. "Maybe she didn't lie, but she clearly withheld information."

"She most certainly did," Jack said sharply. "We need to go back there. We need to find out what else she knows. No more games. I want a full list of Dixie's clients."

"I thought she claimed there wasn't one?" August retorted.

"Oh, she did. But I don't believe that for a second, do you? I bet you that woman has records accounting for every single penny that moves in and out of that place. You think she doesn't know who her girls' clients are? At least the repeat ones?"

August frowned. "Well, why were we so nice to her then?" he sputtered. "You were all... charming, and magnanimous, and I followed your lead."

"You collect more flies with honey, my friend. You know that better than anyone." Jack shook his head. "But I'll tell you, I have half a mind to march there right now and drag her out into the street and down to the station." Jack's eyes shone in the moonlight that filtered through the clouds overhead.

"Jack, you know that's not a good idea. Not tonight."

"We're wasting time, August. She could be the key to this whole thing. I want answers. Tonight."

"You don't really think she's behind this?" August asked. "What has Madam Beaufrey got to do with politics? You heard Red just now. He implied that Hank had something to do with politics. That whoever's payroll he's on, does, at least. That can't be Madam Beaufrey."

"No." Jack frowned. "You're right. And besides, Hank obviously doesn't work for Madam Beaufrey. Dixie was sneaking him in the back door... keeping him a secret." Jack swiped a hand through his hair, then paused, staring down at it. He jumped back with a little yelp, and the severed hand landed on the pavement below with a dull, wet thud. *"What the fuck?"* Jack murmured to himself. He glanced up at August in consternation, but he was busy, gazing off into the gloom of the foggy street.

Pale clouds swirled above, grey shadows, passing over the full moon, carried by a night breeze that whispered of dangers unseen.

August shuddered with that sudden feeling, of a goose, walking over his grave.

"No. None of it makes sense…" August murmured. "It feels like we're so close, but I can't put my finger on it."

"Well, I'm going back there," Jack said briskly. "Now. I'll confront her, demand the client list."

"Jack, I'm not letting you get within a half mile of that brothel. Not tonight."

Jack stilled for a moment, fighting his irritation. Then he sucked in a deep breath. "Fine. You'll have to go by yourself."

"What?" August frowned. "No, Jack, I can't–"

"Just go, Sully. Do this, okay? For me. We can't afford to waste any more time. We need to track down Terrence, the waiter, from The Black Sheep. And we're really no closer to finding Hank. The clock is ticking, August. Time's running out. How long until the next victim is found?" August sighed, and Jack moved closer to him. "Look, I know you're used to being the good guy, but you can play the bad guy, just this once, can't you? Just make it clear you're not leaving without that list."

"Jack," August insisted, his voice low.

"Come on, Sully. Christ, look at you. You look like shit. You're wound tighter than a drum." Jack studied him for a moment. "You need to release some of that tension." He grinned. A slow, oddly wolfish smile. "I think you can manage it, old boy. Just flash a little tooth, let those veins really pop, and be done with it, okay?" Jack patted him on the shoulder, and took off down the street, walking backward. "I'll catch up with you tomorrow."

"Jack," August called out hoarsely, attempting to keep his voice down. "Just where are you going then? It's a full moon, Jack, I can't just let you wander off on your own." August said the words, but deep down, he doubted he'd have the strength to stop him, should he lose control. Not tonight.

"I'm going to see a doctor, Sully," Jack called back, "If there's one thing I can't afford right now, it's having Rose after me." He shot a grin in August's direction, and the last thing he saw, before Jack disappeared in the gloom, was a flash of white teeth.

August had made it about a block, muttering to himself, attempting to get his nerves under control, when he spied an unsettlingly familiar symbol. It was painted by hand on the brick wall to his left. He nearly walked past it, head down. If it hadn't been for the pool of light from the nearest streetlamp falling just so, it would have been obscured in darkness.

August froze, mouth agape. The eight curving lines were emblazoned in bright orange, standing out from the brick wall; drip marks, bleeding down, made the eldritch symbol appear as though it were melting. August lifted his hand and gingerly dabbed at the paint with one finger. He felt it squish beneath the pressure of his fingertip, and he swiped to the side. A daub of orange paint lifted away. It was fairly fresh.

As August studied it more closely, he noticed a line of text, much smaller, scrawled in red, hastily, beneath. He had to squint, moving closer, to make out the handwriting. Whoever had done this, had clearly been in a hurry. *'From blood, hast thou been begotten, by blood, thou shall be cleansed. For his fire will sweep over and through you, and leave nothing in its wake." Verse 44, -The Many-Legged King.'*

August stumbled back, his stomach churning. To the side of the strange inscription, half-hidden in shadows, he could make out more writing, different in size and style from the quotation below the symbol. His eyes flickered over the strokes of paint. *'Blood filth,'* scrawled sideways, and below that, *'Death to all upirs.'*

August made his way to Madam Beaufrey's in a daze. His pulse was hammering so hard he could hear it in his ears. A steady, rapid tattoo against the pounding of his feet on the pavement. He had never understood the real depths of hatred people held in their hearts. Not until he'd been turned. As a white male, of moderate means, and then a man of the cloth, he'd always been treated with respect. Until he wasn't. That was the definition of privilege, he now knew. A life lived in comfort, completely oblivious to the full depth of human depravity.

His hands were shaking, fingers numb with pins and needles, he sucked breath after breath into his airway as though through a straw, forced into panic-stricken lungs. He raised his fist. He hadn't intended to break the door. But he was running on pure adrenaline now. He had taken the stairs of the cathouse two and three at a time, and when his knuckles connected with the aged wooden door, his fist shot straight through it on the second of the intended three knocks.

He heard a gasp, on the other side, a rapid intake of breath, caught in a throat. And there was something so feminine, and arousing about that small sound, that August felt an answering swelling in his loins that mirrored the pulsing in his veins. The points of his canines lengthened in response.

He should have left then, he told himself afterward. But in reality, it was already too late.

Madam Beaufrey had the temerity to attempt to smile at August when she opened the damaged door. Her smile was gone in a matter of seconds.

She led him through a maze of dim corridors to her office. When August refused to sit, she pursed her lips shut and waited.

"You've been holding out on us," August sneered, as he paced back and forth behind the pair of empty chairs opposite Madam Beaufrey.

"I've been more than willing to cooperate–"

"Twice!" August growled, his chest heaving. "We visited twice. Three times, counting today. And it never occurred to you to mention you knew where Dixie was going that night? If we hadn't found out from her roommate, we would still be in the dark," August scoffed. "And there's another point!" He held a finger up, wagging it in the air, "You neglected to mention that Dixie had a roommate, didn't you? What are you hiding, *Madam* Beaufrey?

And I don't want to hear any lies, or protestations about protecting your girls, or their clients."

August shoved the chairs to the side. Madam Beaufrey managed not to jump as they slammed against the walls of her office. He planted both hands on Madam Beaufrey's desk and leaned forward. She was barely able to hide her involuntary flinch. August's voice dropped to a dangerous whisper. "We want a full client list. The names, of every single one of the assholes, who ever visited her. Do I make myself clear?"

Madam Beaufrey's eyes hardened, and her expression shifted, her features going oddly flat, as though the face she usually wore, was just a mask, now removed.

"Confidentiality is the only thing standing between this business, and complete ruin. What do you think happens if my guests find out their identities are no longer protected? I can't just hand over a list to the police. I'm not a fool, detective."

"So, there is, in fact, a list." August punctuated every syllable.

"Of course there is," Madam Beaufrey sneered.

"I'll tear this entire house apart, room by room, until I find it. I will drag every single one of your *girls*, and their *guests*, out into the street. And then I'll drag you down to the station, for a little interrogation. But I won't do that at night. In the dark. No. I'll wait until broad daylight, until the streets are full. Until there are as many witnesses as possible."

Madam Beaufrey laughed. "Oh, you'd enjoy that, would you? Go ahead, make a mockery of me. I provide a much needed, and much utilized service to this community. The revenue this establishment brings in, alone–”

“I’ll have you brought up on prostitution and money laundering charges so fast your head will spin, and trust me, the district attorney, Merritt Colfax, doesn’t give a shit about the *services* you provide. You, and this cathouse, have been a thorn in his side for quite some time, and he has been itching to take you down. I promise you; Chief Waverly will have my back as well.”

“Chief Waverly?” Madam Beaufrey smiled wickedly up at August. “Ask yourself, dear, if Merritt Colfax, and Chief Waverly both want me out of business, then why am I still here?” She spread her hands out in an elegant gesture, indicating the room. “Has that thought occurred to you, Detective Sullivan?”

August stilled, then leaned over the desk once more. “I want the client list. I’m not leaving without it.”

“Come back with a warrant,” Madam Beaufrey snapped.

August straightened, looked around the office, and then turned and headed for the door. He paused, looked back, and peered over at the window, behind Madam Beaufrey’s desk. “Oh, I’ll be back. But not with a warrant. It’s a full moon, tonight, you know.” August sighed. “And Jack… well, he wanted to come with me, but I told him I could handle it myself.” August turned away once more, and took another few steps, shrugging as he went. “I’ll have to tell him I was unsuccessful.” He paused, one hand on the doorframe, and turned to smile over at Madam Beaufrey. “I’ll see you soon, Madam. And I won’t be alone.” He inclined his head, tipped his hat, and stepped through the door.

August made it a few paces down the hallway when he heard her cry out. "Wait!" He smiled to himself as retraced his steps back into the office.

He had been pacing in the small sitting room, for about ten minutes. Madam Beaufrey insisted she needed time to put together a list of Dixie LaRue's clients. She had brought him a cup of coffee, which sat losing heat, on the coffee table. August waited. Whenever he felt his blood begin to boil, he focused his energy on pacing.

He was once more circling the small space when the door swung open on creaky hinges. "Finally," he growled, spinning towards the door.

Adelaide stood there, her big brown eyes wide and solemn. August raised an eyebrow, his shoulders dropping slightly from where they were hiked close to his ears. She watched him, with the frozen, wide-eyed stillness of a doe, or perhaps a rabbit, when it encounters a predator.

"Oh," August said, "it's you."

She remained still, for another few jagged heartbeats, and August didn't move a muscle, as though sensing her potential to bolt.

Then Adelaide smiled, a hopeful, yet wistful sort of smile. "You came back."

August felt the hot, bubbling tide of rage, fueled by despair and hunger, ease slightly in his chest. But he was too far gone to stop himself from replying, rather too gruffly. "I'm not here to see you."

Adelaide's smile faltered, then wilted like a lily, left too long in the hot Georgia sun. She nodded briskly, as she swallowed. "No, I suppose not." She attempted to smile again and failed. "Why would you be?" Then she turned and left.

August stood there, frozen, for several seconds, listening as her light footfalls pattered up the corridor, towards the grand staircase in the foyer. He heaved a deep breath, then released it back into the air. "*Fuck.*"

He tracked the sound of her footsteps up ahead as she climbed the stairs, down the first corridor, then to the right. He could hear her still, memorizing the cadence of her steps. He could even hear her heart pounding, growing fainter and fainter, as she increased her speed, and the distance between them. Despite the murmurs, the cries of passion, the moans, and, yes, the unmistakable crack of a whip, behind closed doors.

August swept past them all, his trench coat flying loose behind him. He paused, listening, at the next juncture. There she was, to his right, then a left, and down a shorter hallway. The footsteps stopped. He slowed his pace, eyes on the door at the end of the hall, on the left. He was sure he had the right door.

August lifted his fist and knocked. Making sure to do so gently, this time. There was a long, expectant pause, before a faint voice called out. *"Come in."*

He found her where she had been seated before; perched on the window seat, like a fragile little bird, high in a nest. This time, the window was open wide to the night air, and Adelaide's hair lifted slightly, as she sat with her eyes closed, breathing deeply. The lights were off, no fire in the grate this time, the room was illuminated only by moonlight.

August allowed himself to move several paces into the room. He left the door open behind him. When she didn't turn, didn't acknowledge his presence, he cleared his throat. Her eyes remained closed. Her heartbeat had steadied. A deep, pounding, jagged rhythm, that called to him.

"I'm sorry, Adelaide, I– I didn't mean to sound..." August trailed off. *Sound what? Cruel? Callous?*

"It's fine," she said flatly, opening her eyes, and turning to face him. "It's not your fault. It was foolish of me to be..." she paused, shook her head, gaze dropping to the floor. Her heart pounded faster now. "Hopeful."

She watched him once more and seemed to study his features in the moonlight. August could only imagine how he looked. His eyes were coal black, he knew, and his veins, a dark purple-black web. His fangs forced him to keep his mouth open. He was practically panting like a dog. Salivating, as his eyes strayed involuntarily to the curve of her pale, delicate neck.

She was dressed in a plain white, cotton nightdress. It reminded him of the crisp white shirt Jack had worn, only this evening, marred by the red plume of blood as it spread. Adelaide stared at him. Her eyes narrowed, almost imperceptibly. But he saw it. Took it for barely concealed contempt.

August turned away from her and stepped further into the shadows that lined the room, but not before the spasm of shame and disgust swept over his features. He cursed himself for following her. For coming here at all. And he willed himself to walk away. To leave.

Adelaide was moving, once more. He tracked her once more, by the sound of her footsteps, and her beating heart, as she moved slowly towards him.

She moved closer, until she stood just behind him. He flinched, when she placed a hand on his arm. And still, he avoided her gaze. Her pulse was rapid now. Picking up speed. He felt his own answering, his heart racing in response. She slid her hand up his arm, around to his chest. She grasped his lapel and began to remove his coat. She tossed it on one of the chairs by the fireplace, and returned to him, making her way slowly to face him.

She slid one hand up, tentatively, until she was cupping the side of his face in her palm. She ran the tip of her finger, lightly, gently, over the veins beneath his eye. He finally allowed himself to meet her eyes. She was smiling. A satisfied, knowing, smile. "I never admitted it, you know, to Dixie," she murmured, her voice low, and husky, "but I always enjoyed it." She moved even closer, pressing herself against him, until her lips hovered just under his. "I like the pain," she whispered.

And somehow, then, he was kissing her. He pulled her closer, both arms around her. He moved to her neck, pulled there, by a force stronger than himself. Her heart was hammering, pounding, as he kissed that curve, the hollow, at the base of her throat. And when he finally pierced her skin, she let out a small moan. His last somewhat coherent thought was to remember, ruefully, that he'd left the door open.

18

THE CHIEF. THE TURN. THE REMINGTON.

August had been sitting at his desk at the station for about an hour before Jack finally showed up. The list remained sealed in the envelope he had taken, rather hastily, from Madam Beaufrey's outstretched hand, as he avoided her smug gaze when he left the cathouse early that morning.

He busied himself reading once more through the original autopsy report for Dixie LaRue, along with the report for Maryanne, and took handwritten notes of the facts they had gathered so far. Several officers had filtered in and out of the station, as August sat there waiting. He prepared himself to fix his face, for when Jack finally made his appearance, for he had the distinct impression, as those with guilty consciences often do, that Jack would take one look at him and know exactly what he had done last night.

As it turned out, he needn't have worried about his face. The bell chimed several times in a row, and a mess of officers and fellow detectives filed into the station. August scanned them briefly and went back to his notes. Jack must have slipped in behind them, because August didn't see him, until he was standing by the coat rack, hanging up his trench coat.

"Jack," August called out to his back. "Glad you finally decided to show up."

August's carefully crafted expression of innocence fell immediately into one of shock as Jack turned to face him.

Jack was covered in blood. Splatters splashed across his white shirt, now more red than white. But more shocking than that was the large amount of blood that coated his mouth and chin and ran down his throat.

August shot to his feet. "What the hell Jack?"

"What?" Jack asked, seemingly nonplused. He reached into a pocket of his trench coat, came up empty, and tried the next. He patted an inner pocket, sighed, then fumbled for the other side of the jacket.

"What do you mean, what? Where'd all that blood come from?"

Jack pulled out a cigarette from his coat and placed it between his lips. His lighter was in his hand, and flicked on, before August could protest. He lit the cigarette, inhaled, and glanced down at his shirt. "Oh," he said dryly, "don't worry. It isn't mine."

"That is hardly reassuring," August snapped.

Jack shrugged and moved to his desk, plopping down into the seat. He slung both legs up and settled in with his feet on his desk.

"Well?" August asked expectantly. "Whose blood is it then?" Jack sighed, and opened his mouth to answer, but before he could get a word out, August continued, his eyes narrowing suspiciously. "Where did you go last night?"

Jack gave him a look. "I told you; I went to see a doctor. Although," he peered down at his side, examining his shirt, "I have a feeling I may have torn the stitches just now."

"Doing what?"

"Well," Jack said, "after I went and got stitched up, I decided to pay Terrence a little visit."

"I knew I should have taken the card with his address from you."

"Wouldn't have made a difference, I had it memorized."

"Of course you did," August said wearily, "go on."

"It was the strangest thing, Sully. Terrence, did not come home last night."

August frowned at him. "And you know this how?"

"I know this," Jack replied glibly, "because I spent the entire night curled up on the sofa, in his front room."

"So," August lifted a finger, "so far, we have breaking and entering... I'm going to go ahead and add assault," he lifted another finger, "I think that's a safe bet at this point. Shall I add an illegal search without a warrant, to the list, or did you only touch the couch?"

Jack laughed, took another drag from his cigarette, and sighed. "Oh Sully... Well, I'm glad to see you're back." Jack laughed again at his expression. "What? You're back to being your typical, slightly grumpy, sarcastic self, and I'm so glad to see it! And to what, or should I say, to *whom*, do I owe my thanks?" Jack grinned wickedly at him, as he waited for a response.

"Don't try to change the subject," August said. "Whose jugular did you rip out, Jack?"

"I could ask you the same, old boy. I reckon."

August's glare turned icy as they stared each other down for a moment, then he lifted the large, sealed envelope in the air. "I have the client list you requested."

Jack was on his feet and reaching for the list before August realized he was no longer sitting.

He snatched it back just in time. "Ah, ah, nice try. I want to know how much damage you've done first. I appreciate a fair warning, before I get called into Chief Waverly's office."

Jack's eyes lingered on the envelope. "Calm down. No one's going to come barging in here to file a complaint with Waverly." Jack shrugged. "Well, besides, possibly, one small, upirist Frenchman."

August's voice dropped lower. "What did you do?"

"Well, like I said, I found it odd that Terrence never came home last night. Almost like someone might have tipped him off, maybe. So naturally, when I woke up this morning, and found myself still on his couch, and Terrence nowhere in sight, I took a little stroll down to The Black Sheep, to speak with my good friend, Antoine."

The corner of August's mouth twitched. "I assume he's still alive?"

"He was when I left him," Jack replied smoothly.

"And did he squeal like a pig?" August leaned back in his chair, able to relax slightly, now that he was fairly certain Jack hadn't killed anyone.

"For the most part," Jack said. "I still suspect he's holding out on us. He admitted he warned Terrence we were planning to pay him a visit. What I'm not clear on, still, is why."

August nodded thoughtfully. "I can't believe you walked all the way here looking like that."

Jack grinned, taking a seat once more at his desk. "Waverly might hear about that part."

"You think?" August asked, one eyebrow raised. "Well." He held up the envelope once more. "Shall we?"

They sat side by side at Jack's desk, scanning through the list of handwritten entries.

"This is going to take a while," August said after a few moments.

"It certainly is," Jack concurred. "I have to say, I'm impressed, Sully." August glanced at Jack in confusion. "You must have made quite an impression on Madam Beaufrey. She's included the dates and everything. The list is very thorough. Much more so than I expected."

August shrugged. "Yeah, well, I was particularly irate last night. I may have accidentally punched a hole through the front door."

Jack laughed, and hit August in the shoulder. "No kidding?"

August snorted. "I can't take all the credit. I threatened her with Merritt Colfax, and Chief Waverly, neither of which swayed her. It was only when I threatened to bring you back there, that she decided to hand it over."

Jack smiled broadly at him. "Awe, I'm touched."

August's brow crinkled slightly, as they stared back down at the list. "You know, there was something she said that bothered me. She sort of suggested that the brothel was being protected by someone higher up. She asked if I ever wondered why DA Colfax and Waverly haven't come down on her." August searched Jack's profile as he spoke. "Why do you think that is? I just assumed they'd let it go because for the most part, the brothel causes so few problems. Things tend to stay quiet, and–"

"Sully," Jack murmured, holding up the list, one finger pressed against the page. "Look."

August grabbed the bundle of pages and peered closely where Jack's finger still pointed. "'*Boone Radcliff*,'" he read in a hushed voice.

"Yes," Jack said. "There, and here, and again... here," he flipped to the next page. "Sully, these dates go back, at least the past six months." He continued to shuffle pages, scanning, running his finger down each line.

"*Christ.*" August leaned back in his chair, running both hands through his hair, pushing it back off his face. "Is he the most recent entry?" He asked, sitting upright.

Jack flipped to the very last page and let out a rush of air. "No. Unfortunately. It's some bloke I don't recognize. Says it was an '*Earnest Bunbury*'. Jesus, what a name."

August frowned. "Wait, that's a fake name. It must be. Isn't it obvious?"

Jack's brow furrowed, and he shook his head. "Not to me."

"Earnest... Bunbury... it's someone Bunburying!" August waited for a flash of recognition that never came. He sighed. "It's from Oscar Wilde's play, '*The Importance of Being Earnest*'."

Jack shook his head. "Never heard of it."

"Really? But..." August trailed off. "Never mind. It's obviously a fake name."

Jack frowned. "You're sure? What if this Earnest is the killer?"

"It can't be, Jack. Or– well, maybe it is, but that's not his real name. Someone's being clever. In the play, 'Bunbury' is a fake friend that one of the characters makes up. He uses the friend for all sorts of excuses; to get out of doing things he doesn't want to do, or, going places, he *does* want to go."

Jack sighed. "I'll have to take your word for it, old boy." He continued to scan the list.

August leaned back in his chair with a deep sigh. "Anyone else you recognize on there?"

"Not yet," Jack muttered back. The pair sat in silence for a few seconds.

"But why?" August sat up straight, turning to Jack.

"Why what?" Jack asked

"Why on earth would he use his real name?" August said. "Boone Radcliff, I mean? Mr. Bunbury used a fake name, why didn't Boone?"

Jack paused. "Maybe he did," he said slowly.

"What do you mean?" August frowned.

"Say Boone Radcliff shows up at the cathouse one day. Or maybe he calls, asks for Dixie to be sent to him... how long can he hide his identity? Maybe he did give Madam Beaufrey a fake name," Jack shrugged, "doesn't mean she didn't know his real one."

August mulled this over. "Still. Why'd she give it to us then?" He said thoughtfully. "If it's Boone who's been protecting her, why would Madam Beaufrey hand him to us on a silver platter?"

Jack removed the cigarette from between his lips and stamped it out in the ashtray. "Just 'cus he's on the list, doesn't mean he's guilty, August. We need to be careful here. We can't afford to be wrong."

"No," August said, "of course not. We don't know that he was involved... I'm not going to go storming after him without proof. My point is, why didn't Madam Beaufrey cover for him? She could have easily given him a fake name on this list, or, better yet, omitted him completely."

"Was this not the original?" Jack frowned down at the list. "Where does she keep it then? Some sort of ledger book?"

"I... um, I don't know," August admitted, "I didn't see. She said she needed some time to gather the list together. She had me wait in the sitting room."

Jack raised an eyebrow at him. "Alone?" August remained silent. "For how long?"

"I..." August trailed off, his cheeks growing warm.

"How long did it take her to 'gather' the list, Sully?"

"I'm not sure," August said flatly.

The ghost of a smile parted Jack's lips. "Oh, you're not sure how long it took? And why's that, Sully? Hmm?" Jack laughed at his obvious discomfort. "*Where were you last night?*" He parroted, mimicking August's mannerisms and tone. "Where were you— you lying sack of shit?"

Jack laughed, as August scowled, blushing furiously. "It's your goddamn fault for sending me there in the first place. You saw what sort of... *state* I was in. What did you think would happen?"

Jack just continued to grin and shook his head. "I'm proud of you, Sully. Really, I am."

"Oh, fuck off." August stood and pushed his chair back over to his desk. He wiped the embarrassment from his face as he did so. "What's our next move?"

Jack glanced around the office, thinking for a moment. "Come on." He stood abruptly. "We'll copy out the dates, and double check each entry later." He began shuffling folders around on his desk. "Where's Dixie's file?"

"I've got it here, on my desk." August leaned over and grabbed it. "Why?"

"Is the autopsy report in there?"

"Yes. I was reading through it earlier."

"Good. Bring it with you. We're going to talk to Marcy."

"For fuck's sake Jack." Chief Waverly glared at them through an open doorway. They'd made their way over to city hall. Marcy and Gladys were tucked away in a warren of desks, back in admin. It was just their luck that the Chief happened to be in the building. "Get in here," he barked.

Jack and August exchanged a glance and shuffled into the room. Chief Waverly turned to the man who sat behind a large desk across from them. "Jim, can I borrow your office for a few minutes?"

Jim nodded briskly, wide eyes fixed on Jack, as he practically scurried out of the office, closing the door behind him.

Chief Waverly turned to Jack. "Just what in the hell do you think you're doing walking around like that? And in City Hall, of all places?"

Jack sighed, taking a seat in front of the desk, as the Chief claimed Jim's vacant chair. "Look, Chief, it wasn't part of the plan, but–"

"There's always a but, with you, isn't there? But nothing," Chief Waverly said. "I swear to God, Jack, you're going to get us all fired one day. It's either that, or you'll be the reason I keel over. Maybe both! I've had it with the escapades."

"I'm sorry, Chief," Jack mumbled.

"Oh, you're sorry? You know, a few people called in complaints to the station this morning, about a man, walking around covered in blood. Claimed it looked like he'd just been feeding on someone. One of them insisted they'd seen the murderer. I've had two patrol cars out there, combing the streets, looking for the guy!" Chief Waverly's face was now the color of a tomato. "Jesus Christ! This is the last goddamn thing this city needs right now!"

Jack had the grace to hang his head slightly. "It won't happen again, Chief. Really. I'm sorry. I just–" he placed the list down on the desk and slid it over towards the Chief. "Look. It's a list of Dixie LaRue's clients. Guess whose name is on it?"

"Who?" The Chief asked, picking up the list and glancing down at it with a look of disdain.

"Boone Radcliff," Jack said, a look of triumph on his face. The Chief froze at his words. "Now," Jack shifted forward in his seat, "we don't have a case yet, but this is it, Chief. I can feel it. We're going to chase this down, wherever it leads. And if that son of a bitch is involved, we're going to do whatever it takes to nail him."

Chief Waverly appeared to have recovered his composure. He looked down at the list, then back up at Jack and August, in turn. "If Boone Radcliff is involved, I'll tie the noose for him myself," he said grimly, "but we have to be sure. We have to be 100% sure. The case will need to be airtight."

"We know, Chief, we know." Jack nodded.

The Chief sighed. "Boone's planning on holding a rally; giving a campaign speech, out at the carnival, on Friday night. It'd be an opportunity to speak with him. Discreetly." He added with a pointed look.

"Got it," August replied.

Jack leaned forward. "Chief, there's something else." Chief Waverly heaved a sigh, then nodded for Jack to continue. "There was a key piece of evidence missing in the official autopsy report for Dixie. We're here to speak with Marcy—"

"And Gladys," August interjected.

Jack nodded, rolling his eyes slightly, "Yes, *and Gladys.* But it's our understanding that it was Marcy who typed out the dictation."

Chief Waverly's frown deepened. "What are you suggesting exactly?" He asked sharply. Jack hesitated, glancing over at August.

August cleared his throat. "We spoke with Dr. Caudell at length, and we're confident he's not aware of any possibility of the report being... tampered with. He swears the information that's missing, about her body being drained of blood, was included in his dictation. He *thought,* it was also included in the report, when he read it over."

Chief Waverly sighed, and looked away, glancing out the window. "What makes you boys think it was tampered with? Couldn't it have been a mistake?"

"That's what we're here to find out," August said.

The Chief nodded briskly and handed the list back over to Jack. "Fine. Just be careful, boys. Keep your findings to yourself. Report back to me, when you have more. I want verbal reports, for now. Nothing in writing, you understand?"

"Yes," they uttered in unison. August shifted uncomfortably in his chair, his heart rate rising.

"I mean it." The Chief raised his finger and pointed at each of them. "You be *fucking* careful. Keep your eyes open."

"We understand," August said thickly.

"Good." Chief Waverly stood. "You're dismissed. Keep that list somewhere safe." He pulled the door open, and paused in the doorway, turning back to glare one more time at Jack. "And clean up that goddamn blood."

Marcy Davis was pretty, in a faded overdone sort of way. She wore her dark hair cropped short, in a wavy bob that reminded August of the style flappers used to wear. He wondered briefly, if the hairstyle was a holdover from a youth spent chasing less respectable pursuits. Her eye makeup and rouge were applied rather too liberally. When they entered the backroom, seeking her out in the maze of desks, she seemed to be anticipating that they were headed her way.

Her head popped up, and she watched them approaching from across the room with a pleasant smile plastered on her face. Jack glanced back at August with a brief eye roll. Of course, there was also the blood. More than one set of eyes watched them as they wove between desks to the back of the room.

"Jack!" Marcy said, as she stood to greet them. "You haven't visited in ages." She smiled warmly. "But, um, did you know, you've got... you've got a bit of blood on you, dear."

"Marcy," Jack said, grinning broadly. "It's always a pleasure." He turned, gesturing to August. "You remember my partner, August Sullivan?"

"Why yes," she said, turning her attention to him. "I've heard so much about you."

August reached out and shook her hand, pondering her choice of words. But Marcy's smile never faltered, he had to give her credit for that. "Well," she said, glancing around them. "I'd offer you both a seat, but..." she shrugged. There were no available chairs in sight. They chuckled politely, as she laughed at her own joke a little too long.

"There's no need," Jack said, "I don't expect this will take very long. But you know what, how do you fancy a quick stroll?"

"A stroll?" Marcy asked, her smile wobbling.

"Yes, a stroll. Why, there aren't even any windows down here, are there? I imagine you might enjoy taking a little walk." His grin widened, and he held an elbow out to the side. "Let's take a turn outside, shall we?"

"A turn?" Marcy asked, now her voice wobbled as well.

"A turn," Jack repeated. His elbow remained offered.

Marcy shrugged, and giggled a little, then went over to Jack, and slipped her arm through his.

August walked behind them, the case file still in his hands, now with the client list tucked inside as well. He listened as Jack and Marcy chatted. They spoke about the weather first, then moved on to discussing several mutual acquaintances who worked elsewhere in City Hall.

Marcy seemed to be at ease, from what August could tell. They strolled around the block, and August tried not to look at the graffiti that littered the expanse of bricks to their left. The day was already heating up. He found himself longing for the cool dimness and fog of the previous evening. From there, his thoughts strayed naturally to the way he had spent the evening. He pushed the thoughts away abruptly, as he felt the veins beneath his eyes begin to pulse. They retreated almost instantly. It still struck him, after all this time, how much easier it was to control when he had fed recently.

August was pulled from his reverie by a sudden shift in the tone of Marcy and Jack's conversation. She had pulled away from him, and was standing with both hands on her hips, her mouth framed by deep frown lines. "How dare you," she hissed, leaning forward. "If you weren't covered in blood, I'd slap you across the face."

Jack shrugged. "To each their own. But really, Marcy dear, enough with the theatrics." He turned to indicate August. "You have an audience of one, and I can tell you with certainty, that he does not care." Marcy now included August in her look of wrath.

"Now, I did you a courtesy, suggesting this little stroll. I could have asked these questions down in the office, in front of every-one." Marcy's fake eyebrows floated several inches above her eyes. "But–" Jack held up a finger, "I didn't. Now, are you going to tell me what I need to know? Or do I need to play dirty?" He moved a step closer to Marcy. "Because let me tell you, I have no problem paying Mrs. Caudell a little visit. And I have zero qualms, about a little blood." Jack's tongue darted out of his mouth, and he licked his lips in slow motion, his tongue left a wet swath in its wake in the dried blood.

Marcy's expression was unreadable, as she stared at Jack, her mouth gaping open. After several seconds of stasis, she turned and looked at August, her cheeks blazing. "Well. I would appeal to *you*, but I doubt you'll be any more civil than your partner here." She turned back to Jack. *"Animal,"* she hissed. Then she smoothed her suit jacket and seemed to take a few seconds to compose herself. "I'll tell you what I told Richard."

"Who?" August asked, brows wrinkled.

"Dr. Caudell," Jack said.

"Ah," August said, "please, continue."

Marcy shot him a look. "Richard warned me you would be coming to speak with me. I told him that as far as I can remember, I recall that part of the dictation, and I recall having transcribed it. I have every confidence that I did not leave out the part about the– the blood." She added, as though she was now reluctant to say the word.

"What about after?" Jack asked crisply. "After you finished the transcription, what did you do with it?"

"Why I submitted it to Rich– Dr. Caudell, of course." Marcy puffed up her chest.

"Immediately?" Jack asked, eyes narrowing.

Marcy stilled, seemed to think for a moment. Her chest deflated slightly. "No, not immediately." She wiped a hand across the beads of sweat gathering on her forehead. Her eyes went wide, and she stared down at the severed hand she inexplicably held in her own. She dropped it to the ground with a screech, as she jumped back, arms flapping.

"Where on earth did that come from?" Jack muttered, glancing about them, then up at the sky. August just shrugged.

Marcy swallowed, still staring at the hand, then continued, regaining her composure. "I set the report down on my desk, just for a few minutes."

Jack crossed his arms over his chest. "Are you in the habit of leaving autopsy reports that are part of high-profile cases just lying around on your desk, for anyone to read?"

"Of course not!" Marcy snapped. "It was Gladys' birthday. Everyone was there. They'd brought out the cake. We were all singing to her."

"So, how long were you away from your desk, with the report left sitting out?"

Marcy sighed, looking away once more. "It can't have been more than 20 minutes, maybe... maybe half an hour or so."

"I see," Jack said sharply. "And would that be enough time for someone to swap out the report?"

"Swap it out?" Marcy frowned.

"Yes. Say they borrowed it, from your desk, typed it up, just as you had, but omitted that one line? How quickly could someone duplicate the report? Could it have been done in the time it took you to sing happy birthday to Gladys, and have cake? I really hope, for your sake, that the answer is yes," Jack said. "Because if the answer is no, I'm really going to have a hard time believing you told me the truth when you claimed no one approached you and asked you to tamper with that report. Especially given that we know they would have had the perfect weapon they needed to ensure your cooperation. Blackmail, is a powerful tool, my dear."

Marcy seemed to lose all her stamina as she frowned, her eyes welling with tears. "Yes!" She blurted out. "Yes, there would have been enough time. If the person were a decent typist, then yes."

"August, do you have the report?" August moved over to them, sliding the autopsy report out of the folder and handing it to Jack.

"And is this, the report you transcribed?" Jack held it out to Marcy with a flourish, like a lawyer at trial.

Marcy took it from him, her shoulders slumping forward. She blinked rapidly, staring down at the report. She seemed to pause, straighten a bit, and looked up at Jack with damp lashes, an eager expression on her face. "This proves it," she said triumphantly. "There's no way this report was typed on *my* machine. You see, I've been complaining for some time about the faint line next to the letter 'x' that shows up on my Remington. It's even on record, that I complained!" Marcy smiled up at Jack. "But they told me the letter 'x' was used so infrequently, that it hardly mattered. And look here, at the victim's name, *'Dixie'*, with an 'x', and there's no line."

Marcy handed the report back to Jack, a faint, satisfied smile on her lips. "This report wasn't typed on my Remington, Jack. It's definitely not the copy I transcribed."

19

THE DREAM. MARYANNE. VIVIENNE.

August lay in bed, dimly aware of his position in space. His mouth was open, his head tossed back, both arms stretched over his head. He had gone to bed early, and swiftly fallen into a deep, dreamless sleep. Still satiated in a way he hadn't been in months, he slept like the dead.

But now, that paralysis was starting to break. Slowly. His eyelashes fluttered. A toe twitched. He was able to blink. But his limbs remained frozen. Spread and held, muscles sore, unable to contract. Unable to move. He had experienced true, lasting sleep paralysis on only a handful of occasions. Each experience had left him feeling deeply unsettled. And now, as the particles that made him August Sullivan returned, slowly, he began to recall who, and what he was. Where he was. The murders. He was supposed to be finding the murderers.

He heard it then, as reality came flooding back to him. An agonizing, trickling return of his consciousness. She was mumbling. Murmuring. Chanting, perhaps. Her voice was low. Too low for even his keen ears to make out the words. And still, he couldn't move. But he sensed she was there, somewhere near the foot of his bed.

He used the part of himself, he supposed later on, that hadn't yet returned, to look down. And there he was, lying prone on his back. Arms stretched over his head. Mouth hanging open like a fish. And Miss Gray sat to his left, in the little chair beside the window.

She must be the one mumbling, he realized. Although, that didn't seem quite right. Because her head was tipped back, and her eyes were closed. And her chest, appeared to be still. So still. Too still to be drawing breath. Then she jerked, as August watched. An arching spasm, as though there was a string tied to the center of her chest. A gasping intake of air. August continued to fight the paralysis, willing his arms to tense and lower, his legs to move. He thought he saw himself twitch, a hand shifting slightly. But then he was distracted.

A pale figure. Thin and wasted. Waif-like. She sat crouched at the foot of the bed. In the very middle of the room, half in shadow, arms slung around her legs, head down. A swath of hair visible, flowing down her back. She was naked. A jumble of pale limbs and jutting bones, ribs and scapula under taut skin. She was chanting. Under her breath, steadily. Unfaltering. Miss Gray jerked once more, spasming harder. She moaned, weakly. *"No!"* Then she cried out. *"No... please! Make it stop!"* Her eyelids opened, and August, floating somewhere above, saw only the whites of her eyes.

Then he was back in his bed, and his limbs were finally obeying. Muscles contracting. He lowered his arms, painfully sore, and he grabbed his pillow as he sat. He bolted out of bed, clumsily, still wrapped in his sheet, he stumbled towards the middle of the room, throwing the pillow at the form shrouded in shadows.

But there was nothing there. Nothing at all. His pillow slid several feet across the wooden floor before coming to a stop. August turned to the small armchair by the window, heart pounding with residual fear, and found it just as empty.

He stood there for several seconds, processing, then shook his head, and stumbled to the bathroom. He fumbled for the light switch and glanced at his reflection in the mirror over the sink. He saw himself, standing there, skin carved and split. Ribs cracked open. His heart, oddly engorged and blood-red, pumping, spasming frantically away, with a mechanical mindlessness that practically sickened him.

August turned at the low husky laughter that drifted to him from the bedroom. Miss Gray stood there, in the middle of the room. She held both hands in front of her chest, a small flame cupped in her palms, flickering in the dark, throwing her features into irregular planes. Her hair was worn loose, falling nearly to her waist. She was soaked. Water dripped onto the wooden floor to pool beneath her feet. August watched in horror as she laughed, his exposed heart pounding in his chest.

Tentacles rose and curled behind Miss Gray, rising behind her head, as though sprouting from her back. Thick and black and writhing. Blood red eyes peered out at him on the underside of each slick member.

August heard a low chuckle coming from directly before him and turned back to the mirror with a start. He was smiling. An oddly seductive smile, beneath lids half-drawn, as though he were drugged, or in a stupor. Blood trickled from the corner of his mouth. His smile widened, and he began to laugh in earnest, throwing his head back as flames licked up the side of his face. One half of his visage turned black, skin cracking and peeling as he watched. August lifted his hand to his face and saw that it was covered in script; curving lines of Latin text, interspersed with odd symbols.

August staggered back, with a gasping intake of air. He turned to Miss Gray once more, and found her floating in mid-air, head tilted back, both arms extended to the side, palms raised towards the heavens. Flames rose, sputtering, from her hands and the top of her head, rising higher, as her laughter echoed, growing ever louder. Her head snapped forward suddenly, her eyes meeting his, and she spoke in a voice that was not of this world. *"Give yourself to me, preacher. For all evil things must burn."*

August's lungs could no longer suck in air. It felt as though all the oxygen had been drained from the room. The image of Miss Gray tilted and swayed before him, and his vision went black.

He was in his bed, blinking up at the ceiling. He lowered his arms to his sides, wincing. He struggled to sit, almost afraid of what he might find. But he knew there would be nothing. Nothing in the armchair. Nothing at the foot of the bed. It was just a dream. Just an odd series of dreams, that wouldn't end.

He sat. And there, at the foot of the bed, hanging from the shadows that lined the ceiling above, hung a long, thick, golden rope.

He waited as long as possible. Steeling himself. He was certain, nearly, completely certain now, that he was truly awake. He thought perhaps the rope would disappear, with that certainty, but still, it hung there. Oddly accusatory. Waiting for him.

When he pulled it, August heard a sound, like a chime, ringing somewhere in the distance. Then he waited.

He hadn't expected her to use the door. It creaked open slowly, on rusty hinges, and he chastised himself for forgetting to oil them. It wasn't Dixie, who walked through it.

It took August a moment to recognize Maryanne. A swath of pale, straight blonde hair swung loose behind her back. She was dressed in what he realized must be her shop uniform. A simple, plain dress, with a crisp white apron worn over it. She had no smiles for him.

They stared at one another, for what seemed an insufferable length of time. Finally, August spoke. "M-Maryanne Cole?" He took a step forward. "I'm August Sullivan. I'm trying to catch whoever did this to you."

"I know who you are." Her voice came out as dull and flat as her expression. "What do you want?"

"What do *I* want?" August stammered. "Wh-why, well... why are you here?"

Maryanne's eyes narrowed, her expression shifted, as she took in their surroundings. "You summoned me here. I don't want anything from you."

August frowned slightly, trying to catch up. "Well, I– the bell pull appeared, so I pulled it. I thought that meant...." he trailed off. "Did you want to tell me something?" He shook his head, correcting himself. "Is there something you can tell me, that will help me find the murderers?"

"Murderers?" Maryanne repeated, as though the word felt foreign on her tongue.

"Yes." August took a reluctant step closer. "You were found, in your shop. You had been..." he cleared his throat. "They tortured you. Hurt you. Killed you." She didn't react visibly to his words. "Help me, Maryanne. Help me find who did this. Did you see their faces?"

Maryanne looked at him in what he could only interpret as barely concealed disgust. "You're one of them, aren't you?" She sneered. "A vampire. *Upir...*" it came out as an insult. A slur.

"But..." August murmured, confusion clouding his expression. "I–I don't understand. So were you..."

"Filthy creatures," she continued. He watched in fascination, as the skin on the back of her hands, then her arms, began to smoke. "I told you before," she said slowly, her lips curling in derision, "*he* is coming for you. He will bathe you in flames. You will burn. As I did. As all unholy things must."

August took a step back, then another, as she closed the distance between them. He watched, as her teeth, two sharp, gleaming points, descended over her bottom lip. He stood transfixed, as her eyes darkened, as the veins beneath bubbled to the surface, dark and pulsing. As the script appeared, starting with her hands, flowing up her arms. The scent of sulfur hit him first. Then burning flesh. And something darker, underneath. Rotten and long left to fester. To decay.

"He is our savior. The one true King. Repent, and he will bless you with his fire. All will be well. It is not too late, *Upir*. It is not too late, to save what's left of your soul."

The back of August's knees hit something solid, and he nearly yelped before realizing that he had backed into the foot of the bed. Maryanne seemed to grow larger now. Swirling shadows danced around her form. She leaned over him, smiling, her expression shifting, as she lifted her eyes towards the ceiling. Thunder cracked directly overhead, causing August to jump. Maryanne's face went slack for a second, her lips parting. She no longer sneered, as her eyes widened, and the corners of her lips curled. Her expression became blissful, transfixed, almost one of rapture.

Her pupils, which had at first appeared to August from a distance to be pitch black, were clouded, swirling with an inner mist. No. He realized. *No*. Her hands reached forward, landing on his chest. And he leaned away, heart pounding in his throat, unable to peel his eyes from hers.

It was not mist that swirled within. He peered closer, unable to resist, as thunder broke overhead once more. A deep rumbling, that seemed as though it would never end. August stared into Maryanne's eyes, into a roiling mass of flanges. Tentacle-like appendages that twisted and squirmed over each other like worms. Snakes. Foul and writhing and wriggling. She grasped his shirt, her claws digging into flesh. *"He is here,"* she hissed. But August couldn't look. He couldn't drag his eyes skyward, to where she stared. For on each coiled, slithering tentacle that writhed in her pupil, where the suckers should be, were unblinking, blood-red eyes.

August tried to wait until daylight to leave. But the storm would not let up, and each pounding crack of thunder reverberating in his chest drove him further over the edge.

He dressed hastily, pacing back and forth, peering out the window periodically. The clouds above remained devoid of anything unnatural, yet still, he could not shake the deep-seated feeling of unease that overwhelmed him. After several minutes of this, he shoved his hat on his head, grabbed an umbrella, and stormed out of the apartment.

August stalked through the streets as fast as he was able, the wind and rain lashing at the umbrella, practically ripping it out of his hands on more than one occasion. His trench coat was soaked by the time he made it to Miss Gray's house.

He stood there, outside the iron gate, staring at the foreboding, stately home, as the rain poured down, and the tree limbs overhead were tossed to and fro in the wind. He gazed up at the small window on the upper level, in the little turret, recalling the figure that had watched them on their first visit. No one stood thus now. At least as far as he could tell. He waited for the next flash of lightning, to be sure. There. A blank wall across from the window, revealed by the brief illumination.

August felt more than a little foolish, now that he was actually here. But he forced his dwindling momentum to carry him forward, until he stood before the front door, and had pounded his fist three times, hoping to be heard above the storm. He did not hope long.

He expected the door to be opened by Lottie, perhaps in a nightgown and robe, blinking in confusion, having been startled from sleep. But Miss Gray herself stood there before him, fully dressed. Immaculate. She stared at him, eyes wide. He found it oddly satisfying, to see that he had managed to startle her for once.

"Miss Gray," he said, sweeping his sodden hat off his head, in a theatrical flourish Jack would have been proud of. "My apologies, for calling so late. Or rather, so early." He glanced at the sky behind him. "I suppose you'll think me a fool. But I had the most unpleasant dream. And I could not wait until morning, to be sure you were unharmed."

The hint of a smile curled Miss Gray's lips, and she inclined her head. "I appreciate your concern. As you can see, I am quite unharmed." She stepped back, pulling the door open wider for him. "Although I must say, if you're going to be in the habit of showing up unannounced at 4 AM, you may as well get used to calling me Vivienne."

August sat comfortably ensconced before the fire in the library once more. Miss Gray had insisted on draping a blanket over his lap, after taking his soaking trench coat and hat to hang up to dry.

She had made them tea as well. August murmured his thanks as she pressed a delicate teacup and saucer into his hands and joined him.

"Now," she said, blowing on the surface of her tea, "tell me about this dream. What was so horrifying that it drove you here, on a night like this?"

August had begun mentally preparing himself for just such a question as he sat there. He had been in such a rush to arrive, that he had hardly planned for what he would say when he did.

He cleared his throat, lifted the teacup to his lips, and then placed it gingerly on the saucer once more, holding it awkwardly aloft. He couldn't help but think it looked like a doll's cup in his broad hands.

"Well, I..." he started, then trailed off. "It was a series of dreams, really. Upon each new iteration, I could hardly be certain whether I was truly awakened or still dreaming."

"I see," Miss Gray said thoughtfully. "And *I* was the subject of these dreams?"

Was that a hint of amusement August detected in her tone? His cheeks colored faintly, and he cleared his throat once more. "In part." He sighed, setting the saucer down unsteadily on the small table beside him. "I dreamt of a figure, ghostly in appearance, crouched in the center of the room. A woman. A girl. Mumbling, or chanting something. But at the same time, I saw you, lying back in an armchair, as though... as though possessed, once more. As you were on the night Jack and I first visited. You were saying something... crying out. You seemed distraught. Perhaps, in pain. I... I wasn't sure how much of what I saw was real." He paused. "Maryanne appeared to me next, and the experience was rather... unsettling."

"Maryanne?" Miss Gray raised an eyebrow at him. "Maryanne Cole? How?"

August shrugged. "Just like last time." He indicated the golden rope that hung beside the fireplace. "A bell pull. This time, hanging in the middle of my bedroom, just where the... apparition had appeared."

"What did she say?" Miss Gray asked, expression rapt.

August opened his mouth to speak, then paused, thinking. "Her manner was very... odd. Her affect... it was as though she had no interest in what had happened to her. I told her I was trying to find the murderers, and she seemed to feel no desire to help me." He frowned for a moment. "Do you think she has changed, somehow, in death?" He scoffed slightly, then shook his head. "I cannot believe I'm saying such things. This was more than likely a continuation of the dream. An apparition. A phantom of my imagination. Nothing more. How can it be otherwise?" It was easier to tell himself that, warm and comfortable by the fire, now that he saw Miss Gray was safe.

"I know you still struggle to believe, even when you have seen it for yourself, with your own eyes." Miss Gray settled back against the chair, her eyes glazing slightly. "As far as Maryanne's temperament... her father described her as an innocent, sweet young thing. Although, I got the impression that she was a fairly serious, perhaps even rigid, child. She spent most of her time either at the shop, at home, or at church."

"Yes." August nodded. "I have the impression she was very religious."

"Devoutly so, I think." Miss Gray tilted her head. "Which is somewhat unusual, for a vampire."

August shifted uneasily in his chair. "Yes, well. Most who find themselves in my position find their faith... altered, by the experience. I can speak to that."

Miss Gray nodded thoughtfully. "You say she seemed to have no interest in helping you. Do you have the impression she felt she deserved what happened to her? Her father said he was not ashamed of what she was... but yet, he kept it a secret. I have to wonder what that does to a young woman's psyche."

August paused, looked away. He bit his lower lip, as he stared into the fire. He turned back to Miss Gray. "Let me ask you, Miss Gray, what do you know of The Many-Legged King?"

Miss Gray's expression flickered briefly, then she lowered her teacup to her lap. "Please, August, call me Vivienne. I really must insist." He watched her, unmoving. She sighed. "The Many-Legged King..." she repeated, then stared into the fire herself. "A myth, I suppose. A fairytale. A legend. One repeated around many a fire, such as this, but not a name I have heard uttered, in a long, long time. How do you know it?" She raised her gaze to meet his.

"I heard it first from your own lips," August retorted sharply.

"That isn't possible," Miss Gray said.

"I assure you; it is." August leaned forward intently. "When you were first in a trance, down in your dining room. I caught you, as you fell out of your seat. You looked right at me and uttered that name. In a warning. Who is he, Miss Gray?"

"Vivienne," she murmured, her expression clouding. "I have no memory of this."

"Still, it happened," August insisted. "I saw the name, later, written on a wall downtown, mixed in with anti-vampire graffiti. Epitaphs of hate. There was a quote. Something about blood, and a cleansing fire. And just now, tonight, Maryanne mentioned something similar. She looked up at the sky, at the storm, overhead, and said *he* was here. She said he would cleanse me, with his fire. She called me a filthy creature. An *Upir*." His tone faltered, thick with emotion. "As though it were a curse-word. All along, since that night downstairs, when you claimed you, *channeled* her, quoting scripture... I thought she was referring to God. Christ. But now... I'm not so sure." August leaned forward further still, his eyes boring into Miss Gray's. "I saw what you summoned in the clouds, that first night at the graveyard," he whispered, "tell me what you know."

Miss Gray straightened, as though she had been slapped. "I see," she said. "Was it my welfare, that concerned you tonight, or your suspicions?"

"Answer the question, Miss Gray," August said calmly, although his heart was pounding once more beneath his ribs. He saw a clear flash of himself, as he had appeared in the mirror. His beating heart, exposed. His expression, half-drunk on pleasure. Debauchery. Sin. Miss Gray stood stiffly, and moved past him, walking to the far side of the library. He caught her familiar sent, that spoke to him of magnolias and peaches, jasmine, and midnights, and madness. August closed his eyes. The scent made his head spin.

"As I said," she continued, her voice cool and formal. "It is an old story. Nothing more." August swiveled to watch her, as she searched the shelves. She elevated herself, rising on the tips of her tentacles, to grasp a tome from the top shelf. She made her way back to him, and August felt an involuntary shudder shoot down his spine as he stared at those writhing appendages that conveyed her forward with an almost grotesque elegance.

She seemed to catch his glance, her lips pressing in a thin line. She held the ancient-looking book out to him, and he took it, with an expression of faint embarrassment.

"Here; a fine re-telling of the story of The Many-Legged King," she said softly. "He reigned eons ago, in a world far older than this one. A kingdom of darkness, malice, and madness. He was said to be an eternal being. Practically a god. He sat on a golden throne. They said he was a monster. They said he could not be killed."

She stood over him, as he skimmed through the pages. He turned to the next and found a story-plate. A dais; a raised, golden throne. A man sat there, in the regal garb of a king, a crown of thorns on his head. His tentacle-like limbs draped and curled over the throne beneath him. He stared straight ahead, as though he were staring back at August. The red eyes on his many limbs, stared back as well.

August felt suddenly weak, his stomach twisting. Miss Gray slid a hand under his chin, lifting it gently until he met her eyes. "I told you, didn't I? Once you lift the veil, it is not so easily replaced. Not again, as it once was. Those things you see, on the other side are half-truths. Portents of what has been, what may be." She studied him closely, her eyes flickering back and forth over his. "Whatever you see there, you may always share with me. For I have seen a great many things, August. I am not easily disturbed. And nothing I see, when I look at you, makes me want to turn away." August didn't dare so much as breathe, as she held his gaze. "Just remember that, when the time comes."

"When the time comes for what?" August managed to choke out the words.

Miss Gray only smiled a wistful sort of smile. "When the time comes, you'll know. This isn't over yet, August. Far from it." She looked away from him, staring vacantly into the distance, as thunder rolled nearby. "I see a figure... cloaked in shadows. His face is always hidden from me, just out of view. I see an open sky, stretching to the horizon. The clouds and stars above. The sound of something... a tent? Flapping, in the breeze. Flashing lights. Music. A feeling of hopelessness. Despair." Miss Gray shuddered. "Something dark is at work here. An evil, that grows stronger by the day. I fear it will take all of us, to stand a chance of weathering the storm." Thunder rolled again, as if right on cue, and August felt a shiver down his spine.

Miss Gray's hand fell away, and she looked down at him with consternation. "You look run ragged, August. Drink up! Your tea's getting cold."

She returned to her seat by the fire, lifting her cup and saucer in one smooth motion.

August let out the rush of air and obediently picked up his saucer and cup once more. The cup rattled as he attempted to steady it without crushing it in his grip.

Miss Gray smiled at him as he lifted the cup gingerly to his lips. "How is it?"

"Delightful, Miss Gray," he managed to murmur.

"Poppycock," she said, with a knowing smile. "And I told you, for the last time, call me Vivienne."

20

THE BULLET CATCH. THE POLITICIANS.

Jack drove them to the carnival on the outskirts of town. There was something about the countryside lately, August admitted, that he found abhorrent. He was inclined to attribute it to Dixie. It was difficult not to think of her, as he stared out over the fields. It was something about the places in between. The wild, overgrown hedges and thickets, the borders, between carefully cultivated farmland. Those narrow places that had gone back to nature.

They'd found her body, in just such a place. Spread out like an invitation. Almost like she'd been placed there, just for him. As they flew past a tall sea of cornstalks, August studied the shadows beneath the nearby pines, oaks, and dogwoods with a growing sense of unease.

The sound of cicadas, humming away their mad, droning tune, drifted through the open window. Jack blew a column of smoke into the air that was quickly snatched away.

"Remember, we'll only get into questioning him if we can get him on his own. We can't have an audience. Waverly will flay us alive." Jack took another pull from his cigarette at August's expression. "Poor choice of words," he said. "If we can't isolate him, we'll tell him we need to speak with him. Invite him to the station tomorrow." August remained silent. "That may make him more likely to want to speak with us tonight," Jack mused. "I can't imagine he'd appreciate the press getting wind of him paying us a visit."

Jack seemed to become conscious of August's lack of response. "You alright Sully?"

August shook his head and returned to staring out his window. "It's the goddamn country air. Makes me sick."

"I agree; it's quite nauseating," Jack said flippantly. "You're sure that's it? You seem to be brooding again. I wouldn't have expected it from you, so soon."

August stared with unfocused eyes, in the direction of the bleak horizon. "It's just something Miss Gray said. She might have seen something happening, at the carnival."

Jack stiffened, glancing in August's direction. "Tonight? What'd she say exactly?"

August shook his head. "I dunno, it was too vague to retain, much less repeat. But it's stuck, in my mind. That's all."

Jack frowned. "Wait, when did you see Miss Gray?"

August just shrugged, a slightly bemused expression on his face.

"You sly dog..." Jack trailed off.

The V8 slowed, gravel now crunching beneath its tires. Jack eased the car to the right, pulling off the road and onto an open swath of dirt mixed with gravel. A low cloud of dust hung over the parking lot. The heat somehow seemed to be intensified here.

August rolled up his window, and Jack soon followed suit, tossing his cigarette butt out the window before it closed.

"You ever been to a carnival before?" Jack asked.

"Can't stand them," August said.

Jack grinned. "Of course you can't. Come on, it'll be interesting, at least."

They drifted into the crowd bleeding onto the fairgrounds. August kept his hat pulled low, attempting to shield himself from the intensity of the late afternoon sun, as well as the stares from passersby. His senses were overwhelmed by the babble, the excited chatter of the swarming crowd, the crunching of feet on gravel below, the heat, and the dust. The swirling scents of humanity, mixing with fair-ground fare; popcorn and fried dough, beer and lemonade. Music tinkled and lights flashed. A Ferris wheel rotated slowly in the distance.

As they strode down the main thoroughfare, a trio passed by, riding on unicycles, their enormous wheels appeared impossibly tall. A woman bent down as she rode, handing children balloons with practiced balance. August watched their faces; the little cheeks bunched by wide smiles, their bright eyes. A young girl pulled on her mother's dress and pointed at the balloons. August felt his throat tighten oddly, watching them. He tore his focus away and scanned the sea of tents. "Where do we think Boone Radcliff will be speaking from?" he asked tersely.

"I hear he has a stage set up. Keep an eye out," Jack responded nonchalantly. "Why, are you already in a rush to leave?"

August narrowed his eyes, scanning the crowd. "No reason to linger, is there? Let's talk to him and get out."

"I dunno." Jack shrugged. "If Miss Gray had a... premonition about the carnival, perhaps we should stay. Keep an eye out."

August sighed deeply. "I'm already regretting having said anything."

Jack grinned. "What else is new? You're chock-full of regrets old boy."

August turned to him with a sharp retort on his tongue, but it left his mind as he eyed a crowd gathered off to the right. A large sign read, *'Bullet Catch'* in fancy scroll. A man stood beside the sign, just off the main drag, waving and calling out, "Step right up! Step right up, folks! You've never seen anything like it!"

The crowd ambling past parted and thinned, as people dropped off to stop and watch. Jack caught August's focus, and his grin widened. "Come on," he said, changing directions. August sighed deeply and followed him.

Thankfully, they were both tall. They managed to weave between the onlookers until they had a clear view. A young man sat on a black horse. Its flank brushed and shining, its hair braided with ribbons. The horse snorted and stomped and bucked its head. The man who sat astride the horse urged it forward. August watched as he nudged it with his feet, and the horse bucked, clearly on command, causing the crowd to gasp, while the young man grinned broadly.

He was striking. Practically beautiful. Twin dimples framed full lips and straight white teeth. His dark eyes sparkled beneath a strong brow. He wore his black hair slightly longer and swept back from his forehead. He was dressed in a sparkling blue jacket with gold stripes across his chest, and golden tassels on his shoulders. His chest appeared bare, underneath, a glimpse of tanned skin and rippling muscles visible. The horse bucked once more, rising on its hind legs and walking forward several steps, its front legs curled, kicking slightly for balance. The crowd exclaimed. The horse fell back down on all fours to the sound of applause, while the young man bowed at the waist and took a turn around the circle.

"That's it folks, step right up! Welcome, welcome!" The man who had been flagging people down pushed his way through the crowd to the center of the circle. He was dressed in a similar gaudy fashion. He held up a hand and pulled a revolver from a pocket. The crowd fell into a hushed quiet, with pockets of murmurs here and there. "Folks, this is a real, loaded revolver. It is loaded with a .38 special cartridge." He paused for dramatic effect. "You, good sir, can you confirm that the gun is properly loaded?" The man walked over to a large burly man he had pointed to in the crowd. With his back to August and Jack, he leaned over and presumably popped open the chamber and displayed the loaded cartridge.

The showman stepped back and strode in a circle, holding the revolver aloft once more. "Is it in fact loaded?"

"Yes Sir," the man said.

"Louder please!" the showman called out.

"Yes, Sir!" the man raised his voice, "gun's loaded alright."

"Good, thank you!" The showman continued his pacing, holding the gun aloft for all to see. "I would be remiss, if I did not remind all of you, that we are professionals, and what you are about to see is *not* to be attempted by you fine folk."

The showman turned and gestured to the young man on the horse, who directed the horse to turn and canter off to the far end of the circle, away from the showman.

The crowd behind the young man and his horse parted like the red sea, as the showman lined up and leveled the gun in his direction. "Ah ha!" The showman turned, waving his other arm. "I see, I see how it is. Ya'll don't trust my aim!" This elicited a scattered, nervous sort of laughter from the gathered crowd. The young man on the horse laughed as well. "Thankfully, my partner here does." The showman turned his focus once more on the young man, who had moved to a crouch on the saddle, and then stood to his full height. He shrugged his flashy blue jacket off his shoulders and tossed it to the ground a few feet away. Then he raised both arms out to the side, and puffed out his bare chest, offering himself as a target.

The commotion in the crowd changed, the excited chatter hushing, to a low susurrus. Those gathered stilled, all eyes on the pair in the center.

The first shot was jarringly loud, causing half of those gathered to startle and jump. Several people cried out. August's gaze remained fixed on the young man. He had jerked slightly to the right, as the gun went off. His right hand was now a fist. August watched, as he opened his palm, and resumed his previous pose, a dark hole now visible in his palm, blood dripping freely to the ground below. The crowd gasped, ooh'd and ahh'd. The young man appeared unaffected, a grim smile on his face.

A smattering of tentative applause began, until it was cut off abruptly, by the showman opposite, who held up his free hand once more to call for silence.

This time, the crowd seemed slightly more prepared for the shot. But still, there was a brief, nervous commotion afterwards. This time, the young man's left hand jerked back, and he performed the same trick, revealing a small gaping hole in his left palm.

The showman paced back and forth, allowing the commotion to continue slightly longer this time. Eventually he called for silence once more, and one could have heard a pin drop within that circle, as he took aim once more.

This time the young man's upper body jerked back, and he wobbled slightly, recovering his balance as the crowd began to exclaim. A small dark hole was visible in his chest, off to the left side. August watched as a geyser of blood flowed down his bare skin. He appeared, still, practically unaffected, although August noted a sheen of sweat now visible on his forehead. The muscles in his abs and arms appeared strained, and he seemed to tremble slightly, before recovering his composure.

"Holy shit," Jack murmured in August's ear.

"He's a vampire," August murmured back. "Has to be."

"A vampire with no fear, apparently. He seems practically unaffected. No veins... He's quite handsome, too." Jack trailed off.

August shot him a sideways glance. "Falling in love, are you?"

Jack pursed his lips and shrugged. "Perhaps. But I have exacting standards... I'm afraid no one has managed to measure up. Yet," he added, grinning slightly.

August gestured towards the young man, still standing on horseback. "But what's next, hmm? How do you top being shot in the chest, standing on a horse, while barely flinching?"

"I have no idea, but I can't wait to find out," Jack said.

A boy was now making the rounds with his cap turned upside down, as the crowd tossed spare change in, the showman attempted to elicit further donations on the young man's behalf. "The amount of training this requires, is intense, ladies and gentlemen. My partner, Holden Swift, has disciplined his body to endure a massive amount of pain, all while keeping his balance, while keeping both himself and his trusty steed, Lightening, calm. This takes an enormous amount of discipline folks. To demonstrate further..."

The showman once more held up a hand for quiet, and positioned himself facing Holden, as he stood stoically balanced on his horse. August, despite himself, was transfixed, and watched in fascination as Holden appeared to steel himself once more. This time a volley of shots rang out, unexpectedly.

The crowd stared at Holden as he swayed, tilting backwards, his arms cartwheeling. Lightening shifted slightly beneath him. There was a gasp, as he nearly fell, but managed to recover and remain standing. He let out a sharp exhalation, and swallowed, his jaw clenching tight. Sweat dripped down his brow, as three dark holes appeared across his gut. Holden tilted forward slightly, and August was sure he was going to collapse. He swept an arm before him and lowered his upper body, with control, into a deep bow.

The crowd went wild, clapping and pointing. Coins and bills were tossed into the hat, faster than the assistant could keep up with. Jack stood transfixed, then caught August watching him, and shook his head. "Not so much as a whimper. Can you imagine?"

August shook his head, expression grim. "No. I can't. The level of self-control is unfathomable. I've been shot before. Trust me, it hurts us just as much as it hurts you. The only difference is, we can recover from it more easily." Jack shook his head, still staring in Holden Swift's direction in admiration. "Come on." August patted him on the shoulder, as he turned back towards the main drag. "We have a politician to question."

Just the sight of Boone Radcliff made August's stomach churn. His speech was well underway by the time they managed to locate the rally stage. It had been built out of raw-cut lumber, unfinished, but sturdy enough to suit the purpose. Red, white and blue banners hung from the front of the make-shift stage. Boone stood behind a podium, with a megaphone held to his lips.

Boone had a clean-cut appearance. He wore his thick brown hair cut short, and while his blue eyes were bright and engaging, his words undercut any warmth that might have been interpreted by his gaze. There was something shifty in his features that made him appear untrustworthy, at least in August's opinion. The crowd gathered certainly seemed to feel otherwise.

They clapped at all the right times. They cheered and stomped their feet. They booed and hissed on command. August wasn't sure what sickened him more, Boone's speech itself, or the crowd's reactions.

Jack glanced surreptitiously at August, more than once, as though gauging whether his partner was preparing to launch himself at the stage. August, for his own benefit, chose to tune out as much as he was able.

He attempted to distract himself by watching the crowd, at first, but that only made him more irate. He watched a young woman, blonde ponytail gleaming and bouncing whenever she rose up on the balls of her feet. She glanced excitedly at the young man beside her, clasping her hands together.

Boone's voice droned on. "They preach acceptance, as though we should all just lie down, and give up. Let the monsters in. Let them take over. Let's invite them to our tables. Let's offer them sustenance. Let's break bread with them, as our neighbors." Boone paused, licking his lips, surveying the crowd.

"But who will protect us, when that neighbor, returns, in the night? Who will protect us, when that neighbor, unsatisfied with his meal, returns to take from us, what we refuse to give freely?

Will Mayor Dorsey protect you? Will Chief Waverly protect you?" A chorus of angry voices shouted, *"No!"* August clenched his jaw harder.

"No! That's right. No, they won't protect you. They can't. They can't be everywhere, at once. And the monsters, folks, the monsters, are already inside. They're already here. They're in your grocery stores, they're in your library, they're living on your street... hell, they're patrolling your street, some of them!" Boos and hisses from the crowd. August practically bit through his tongue.

He thought of Holden Swift, balanced on his horse, and willed himself to display an ounce of his fortitude. The sweat rose on his brow, and he felt a flood of anger and grief wash over him. But he willed his veins to stay hidden, and his willed his eyes to remain blue.

"They're out there, trying to catch a murderer," Boone continued, his voice heavy with sarcasm. "Who's been murdered? You ask?" Boone chuckled. "We've got a string of... of *vampires,* murdered... bodies drained of blood, that's the latest, in the papers. So, they've been killed, by a *vampire,* murderer, and we've got a– a *vampire* detective, chasing after them."

Boone shrugged, his gaze sweeping over the crowd, as scattered laughter rose. He chuckled along with them. "I swear, you can't make this stuff up." He flashed his million-dollar smile. "You know what I say, to that? I say, good. A pack of varmints, chasing after each other, killing each other..." he shrugged. "I say, let them. Let them chase each other's tales then. If it keeps the filthy mongrels occupied."

Jack glanced at August once more. "Steady on, old boy," he murmured.

August looked away, fixating on the horizon. He watched the Ferris wheel, as it rotated lazily in the sun. A bird, flying overhead. Anything, other than the man standing on stage in front of him. "We shouldn't have come here," he managed to murmur. He felt nauseated, suddenly. Weak.

"Why don't you go," Jack said, "I'll hang back here, try to pull him aside afterwards."

August shook his head. "No. I want that bastard to know I was here. To know I heard him."

Jack only nodded and sighed resignedly. August attempted to dissociate, for the remainder of the speech.

When it finally ended, Boone retreated from the stage to a chorus of applause. Jack grabbed August's arm, as he attempted to move forward. "Wait. Wait until the crowd dies down."

"Fuck that," August snapped back. "Let's confront him, now. In front of everyone."

"No, August." Jack's grip tightened on his arm. "We can't do that. Remember what the Chief said."

"I don't give a shit what he said. He can suspend me, for all I care," August replied.

"Yeah? You cause a scene right now, it's going to fall back on *me*. There's no way Waverly will buy that it was *you*, causing a raucous, and explicitly disobeying orders. So why don't you cool it for a minute. Okay? Besides, neither of us can afford to be benched right now."

August stayed where he was. Jack moved in front of him, attempting to place himself between him and Boone.

Ten minutes went by, perhaps more. August's patience was wearing thinner by the minute. Boone was making his way through the crowd, shaking hands and kissing babies, while August fantasized about ripping his throat out.

As he moved closer, Jack turned to him once more and fixed him with an intense stare. "Let me take the lead on this one, okay?"

August looked away, fixating back on Boone. Jack moved back into his line of sight, forcing him to make eye contact. "I said I'm lead, you understand?" August's jaw tightened, his eyes turning black. "No," Jack said to him. "Not here, not now. You hang back, let me do the talking. I'll owe you one, okay? If this sonofabitch is involved, he's going down. Hard. But first, we need to get him where we want him. Got it?" August forced himself to nod.

Boone's smile was so bright it could have powered a small city, but it faltered, when Jack Quinn stepped into his path. "Detective Quinn," he recovered, holding out his hand and greeting Jack with a flash of his teeth. "I didn't realize you were a fan."

Jack took Boone's hand and pumped his arm up and down. From the expression on Boone's face, and the way he held his arm, August had a feeling Jack was practically crushing the politician's hand. He felt a brief surge of appreciation for his partner break through the haze of red pulled over his eyes.

"That's a good one, Radcliff. Seems like you're full of one-liners today. But that's not why I'm here," Jack responded blithely. The gathered crowd seemed to be all ears, hanging on every word exchanged between the two of them.

Boone surveyed his supporters nearby, and his expression shifted slightly. "Oh? Well, I hope you enjoy the carnival. I hear they're putting on quite a show. Not just the main attraction, either. Did you hear about the young man catching bullets? How fascinating." The surrounding crowd murmured at this.

Boone's eyes shifted to August briefly as he continued. "Although, I've heard they don't feel pain, as we humans do. So, when you factor that in, it does become somewhat less impressive, doesn't it?"

"Speaking of impressive," Jack said, finally releasing Boone's hand, which he cradled against his side for a moment, before sliding it into his pocket. "I heard the cuisine at The Black Sheep is just–" he made a chef's kiss motion in the air with one hand. "What did you order, when you were there, the other night? I hear the foie gras is to die for." Jack's grin turned wicked, the corners of his mouth stretching just a tad too far.

Boone's facade truly faltered for a moment, but he recovered his composure quickly. "Is it? I'm afraid I haven't dined there."

"You mean, recently?" Jack frowned. "See, that's why I'm here. I need to speak with you. Let's say it's about your... dinner plans."

"As riveting as that conversation sounds, I'm afraid I'm busy. I have an agenda to adhere to, after all. The campaign does not pause for any man. Not even me, detective." Boone flashed his smarmy grin.

"That's a shame." Jack moved closer to Boone, and August watched with grim satisfaction as he visibly fought the urge to recoil. "See, we were hoping to speak with you informally, off the record, as it were. If you can't find the time in your schedule for us... well, we'll just have to have you come down to the station. Make it official."

Boone's eyes flashed and he turned to the campaign aide that hovered over his shoulder. "I'll need a few moments," he muttered, then turned back and gestured magnanimously forward. "After you, Jack. Let's take a little walk. See some of the sights."

August fell in behind Jack and Boone. The campaign staff looked flustered but attempted to hold back the crowd of onlookers from following. The men chatted for a moment or two about the carnival, while August focused on breathing evenly.

When they'd left the stage behind, Jack paused, then turned, and waved Boone to follow him. He headed towards a large oak tree, on the outskirts of the fairgrounds. "Perfect." He smiled, as he stepped into the shade beneath the branches. "A little spot of shade. And a modicum of privacy. Now." He turned to smile at Boone. "I would like to know why you, of all people, chose to frequent Madam Beaufrey's fine establishment, to engage the services of none other than the infamous Dixie LaRue."

Boone's face turned a shade that matched his white shirt. "I don't know what you're talking about. Dixie— Dixie LaRue? But, but that's... she... that's the first victim. What are you implying, son?" He scoffed, then laughed, gaining steam. "You think I had something to do with this?" He shook his head, his white teeth flashing once more. "Oh God." He slid a hand down his face, and turned, looking out over the barren field behind them. "Who put you up to this? Huh? Was it Dorsey? That sonofabitch..." Boone shook his head once more, both hands on his hips. "I have to say, I'm oddly impressed. I didn't think he was capable of fighting dirty."

"Nice try, Radcliff," Jack crooned, he lifted both hands and clapped slowly, "that was quite a performance. But I'm afraid I'm not buying it. See, we have evidence that puts you on site, on multiple occasions. What I'm not sure of, are all the details on the night of the murder itself. What did you order that night at The Black Sheep? Was I right? Was it the foie gras?"

Boone's visage was turning red now, as he struggled to look calm. "I don't know what you're talking about, Quinn. I wasn't at The Black Sheep that night. Whatever evidence you think you found, it's a lie."

"Oh really? Wouldn't that be convenient for you."

"Think about it for two seconds. Do you really think I'd be seen in public, with a whore?" He moved closer to Jack, his voice dropping low. "And not just any whore, but a– a vampiress?" he sneered. "Are you mad? That would be a career-killing move. I'd never do something so recklessly stupid, not in a million years."

"So, you claim that you weren't at the restaurant, that night." Jack held his hands up, "Fine. Are you trying to deny that you were a client of Dixie's? Because we have proof that you were. Lie to your constituents all you want; the evidence doesn't lie," Jack snapped, taking a step forward himself. "I have dates, locations, all the details–"

"*Fuck,*" Boone cursed, turning away and taking a few steps out into the field. He set both hands on his hips, his chest rising and falling rapidly, head hanging towards the ground, then he turned back to face them. "Yes. I was a... a client. Okay? Of Dixie's. But I didn't kill her, if that's what you're–"

"You son of a bitch," August growled, taking a step forward. "You liked it, didn't you? You paid her to feed from you, and you *liked* it." Jack grabbed him by the shoulders, stopping his forward progress.

"Fuck you," Boone spat at him.

"No, *fuck you*, you lying, hypocritical sack of shit." August pointed at him. "I'm free tonight, you pathetic asshole." His eyes turned black, and the veins beneath his eyes rose in seconds. He snarled, his tone guttural. "Give me five minutes, I'll tear your throat out, while you get off. For *free.*"

Boone recoiled from the fury written across August's features, his visage twisting in hatred.

Jack held him back. "That's enough," Jack said in his ear. "You need to get yourself under control. Now. Don't ruin this."

August drew in a deep, steadying breath, through his nostrils, and willed himself to stand down. He could smell the scents of aftershave, mingled with sweat, and something off, like fear, beneath the politician's skin. His heart was pounding wildly in his chest, beating rapidly in time with the pulse in his neck. And August took grim satisfaction, that he'd managed to rattle him.

"Call me a hypocrite... call me whatever names you want." Boone raised his chin defiantly. "Either way, I'm not a murderer."

"You preach hate, from your pulpit of lies," August sneered back. "Whether you killed these girls or not, their blood is on your hands."

Boone had the decency to flush slightly.

"Where were you that night?" Jack asked, voice even, as he turned back to Boone.

Boone paused, seemed to think. "I was working late." He wiped a hand over his forehead, his brow clearing. "That's right, I was working late, with my campaign staff. My campaign coordinator was there– they can all vouch for me."

"Until past 4:00 AM?" August snapped.

Boone's expression faltered. "Well, no, I–I was home by then, my driver dropped me off, sometime after midnight." He looked at the ground for a moment. "My wife though, she woke up when I went to bed. Around one."

"You have a wife. Of course you do," August said.

Boone shot him a look. "She can vouch for me. I was there all night, woke up next to her around six the next morning. I swear it." He shook his head, looked Jack in the eye. "I swear to God, I didn't hurt Dixie. I wouldn't have... I wouldn't have been able to do that. What happened to her... I– I've read the papers, heard things. I'm not a monster."

"You sure talk like one," August said, his tone clipped.

"Does the name Earnest Bunbury, mean anything to you?" Jack asked.

"Bunbury?" Boone frowned, looked down at the ground, his brows creased. "Earnest Bunbury? I don't think I know anyone by that name... never heard of him before." Jack glanced pointedly at August.

"Really?" August asked, eyebrows raised. "*The Importance of Being Earnest*? Oscar Wilde?" He held his hands out.

Boone shook his head. "Never heard of him either."

"For fuck's sake," August said.

Boone seemed to be recovering his composure, as he pulled a handkerchief out of his pocket and ran it over his forehead, then pressed it against the back of his neck.

"Look," he said evenly, "this can't come out, boys. I'm at your mercy here, and I realize it, but this can't come out. If the truth about this were to be leaked to the press, my career in this town would be over." He swallowed thickly. "Who else knows about this?"

Jack's eyes narrowed, and he glanced at August, expression grim. "The two of us. Chief Waverly. Obviously, the people who provided the evidence," Jack said tersely. "Why, you planning to bump us all off?"

Boone scoffed. "I told you; I'm not a murderer."

"No. But maybe your friends are," Jack said.

Boone licked his lips, glancing away towards the fairgrounds. "I want to speak with Chief Waverly. I'll come down to the station tomorrow, or ask him to meet me at City Hall..." he trailed off, looking into the distance. "I'll cooperate with the investigation. I have nothing else to hide," he said, lifting his chin defiantly. "I don't want to stand in the way of justice." August didn't bother trying to stifle his laughter. Boone shot him a look, cheeks reddening, as he continued. "But this– the part about Dixie and me, this can't come out."

August's stomach roiled. The nerve of this asshole. He should leak the information to the press himself. Tonight.

Jack glanced at August, as though reading his thoughts, then stepped forward. He tapped one finger lightly against Boone's chest, for emphasis. "I want you at the station. Tomorrow. We're going to bring you in, officially, for questioning. I'll make sure Chief Waverly is present, and aware of the... delicacy, of the situation. But make no mistake, Radcliff. If you so much as harmed a hair on either of those girl's heads, you won't have to worry about your career being over." Jack leaned forward, his mouth curling in a too-wide smile, full of sharp teeth. "You won't even have to worry about going to trial. They'll never find you." His voice dropped dangerously low. "Do you understand me?"

Sweat beaded down Boone's forehead once more, and he nodded swiftly. "Yes," he murmured. He took a step back, eyeing them both nervously. "Just make sure Waverly's there, tomorrow."

He turned and began to stride away, walking backward, as though afraid to turn his back on Jack. "One o'clock," Jack called after him, a faint smile on his lips.

August was filled with rage. His brain simply couldn't seem to fathom the level of hypocrisy involved. Jack, seeming to sense his mood, remained silent at his side as August stalked through the fairgrounds.

When August caught sight of Boone once more in the crowd, followed by his entourage and approached by smiling face after smiling face, he fell naturally into step behind them. He stayed a distance away, but when Boone looked over and they made eye contact over a sea of heads, August felt a jolt of grim satisfaction at the expression of ill-concealed fear.

"So," Jack said glibly sometime later, "are we going to follow him around for the rest of the evening? Because if so, I'm going to need some provisions." August glared sideways at Jack, as he eyed a nearby refreshment stand. "I'll be right back."

Jack dined on the finest cuisine the carnival had to offer, munching on an elephant ear, and sipping lemonade, making conversation with any random passerby that happened to recognize the pair. August stalked.

"He knows we're here, old boy," Jack said sometime later, clapping a hand on August's shoulder. "He knows he's our number one suspect, and he knows we're watching him. I'm not sure I see the point of this venture."

August grit his teeth, watching the crowd. The sun was sinking low now. In the dim light of dusk, in the elongated shadows of the tents, the faces of the men and women who passed in pairs and groups appeared distorted to August. Their smiles no longer full of excitement and thrill, but malice and hatred. Their laughter echoed in his ears, and he watched them in disgust. How many? How many of them were full of hate? How many of them were like Boone? Which of them had stood there, cheering and whistling and clapping, while he yelled from his pulpit, spittle flying. A false preacher, spewing hatred. It sickened him.

When Mayor Dorsey swam into view, August had to blink several times, before his mind cleared, and he was able to recognize the man.

"Detective Sullivan," Mayor Dorsey said, perhaps even, repeated, August wasn't sure, as he shook the extended hand numbly. "Jack." He turned and nodded to Jack, as he leaned over and shook his hand as well. "Listen, I just wanted to thank you both for your service. The people of Atlanta are able to sleep more soundly, knowing the two of you are on the case."

August breathed deeply, a slow controlled inhale, letting his shoulders drop, as Jack responded for both of them.

"Just doing our duty, Mayor, nothing more."

Mayor Dorsey glanced away, over towards the setting sun, now just a sliver on the horizon. "That's just it, boys. That's all that stands between us, and anarchy, just a few good men, doing their duty." He turned back to them, his gaze flickering back and forth over their features. In the awkward pause, August could think of nothing clever to say. Mayor Dorsey nodded, seeming satisfied with the brief exchange. He shook their hands vigorously once more and disappeared into the crowd.

August felt oddly calmer, after that, although he continued to trail behind Boone and his entourage, he did so with less malice.

As the shadows lengthened and spread, he could sense Jack growing restless. "What's our plan here, Sully? Do we follow him home? Ask to sleep on his couch? Or are we going to sit in the car all night? Sleep in shifts in the street?"

"I don't know, Jack. I don't have a plan."

"So what is this, then? Because I have to say, I doubt he'll attempt to commit another murder. Not tonight. If he even had anything to do with the others."

August turned to glance at Jack. "You don't think he's involved?"

Jack watched Boone schmooze for a moment. "Honestly, right now, my gut says no."

"So, it's a coincidence he was one of Dixie's clients then?" August meant his tone to carry more derision, but he was tired.

Jack shrugged. "Coincidence, or something else…" he trailed off. "But my gut says he's not a murderer. Just a coward, in an expensive suit." He studied August for a moment. "What about you? It's rare, old boy, but I suppose I've been wrong before."

August thought about it. He tried to isolate his hatred of the man from the facts of the case. From his mannerisms, his body language, during their conversation beneath the tree. August swallowed and surveyed the crowd around them. Thinner now. He watched an open tent, as it flapped in the breeze, lifted by a gust of wind that seemed to rise as a portent, bringing with it the scent of earth and rain, of cooler nights, and darker mysteries. August turned finally to Jack. "My gut... my gut tells me that something is coming. Something bad. Here. Tonight."

21

THE HUNT. THE FERRIS WHEEL.

"You're just as melodramatic as Miss Gray, you know," Jack said, his eyes fixed straight ahead, as he stared through the windshield into the night. "I don't ever want to hear you naysaying her predictions again–"

"It's hardly the same thing, Jack," August shot back. "Besides, she's partially, if not entirely, to blame. She's the one who planted the idea in my head, quite frankly."

"Well, I'll be sure to thank her, when I see her next. Sitting in a car, in a deserted field all night will surely solve the case. Can't believe I didn't think of it sooner."

"You're only giving me shit because it wasn't your idea this time."

Jack chuckled.

August sighed deeply. "I say we wait another twenty minutes or so, and head back on foot."

"You mean creep back on foot."

The pair had waited until Boone Radcliff left, with his pack of enablers in tow. They'd followed him to the parking lot, watching as he and his team departed in a cloud of dust. August enjoyed the difficulty Boone was having concealing his feelings, as the two of them stared stoney eyed, after him. He had shot them a parting glance before climbing into his car that had challenged August's ability to keep his poker face intact, the corners of his mouth twitching. As soon as Boone's car disappeared in the distance, he and Jack turned to each other and had a good laugh. Then they climbed into their own waiting V8, and took off.

Jack had driven maybe a mile or so before going off-road. He parked the car behind a copse of trees, pointing it in the direction of the fairgrounds. And there they had sat ever since. He'd hardly stopped complaining for more than a few seconds at a go, but August knew it for what it really was. Jack had nothing better to do, and got half of his enjoyment out of life by taking the piss out of August.

"The fairgrounds closed at nine," August said a few minutes later. "We wait another twenty minutes or so, and any stragglers should be long gone."

"And then what? We wander through the abandoned carnival for the next eight hours, and hope we stumble across the murderers?"

August thought for a moment, then shrugged. "Something like that."

Jack let out a long-suffering sigh. "I bet you wish you'd eaten a corn dog earlier when I offered you one."

"This is so stupid," Jack muttered into the grass.

They lay on their stomachs, beside a little clump of trees, watching the fairgrounds for any sign of activity.

"There've been no cars heading back this way, old boy. I think you need to give it up. Your gut is wrong. I can't say I'm shocked."

"Maybe there have been cars. Maybe they turned their headlights off. Or, maybe they were already here, and they never left." August glanced over at what appeared to be an empty stretch where the make-shift parking lot had been.

"I just want it to go on record, that when *I* planned a stakeout, it included tea, and provisions. And we didn't have to slither on our stomachs through the grass like snakes."

"You know I despise tea. Besides, it wasn't as though you brought it, was it?"

The pair went on like this for some time, until Jack suddenly gripped August's arm, and went still. "There," he whispered, pointing with his free hand towards the fairgrounds. "Did you see that?"

"See what?" August attempted to press himself lower to the ground, as though that were possible, as he stared in the direction Jack had pointed.

"I saw a light, moving. Just there."

"You're sure? I can't see anything now."

"I'm sure," Jack said, his voice pitched low. "There's someone there, moving about."

"Should we go check it out?"

Jack turned to him, the whites of his eyes stood out starkly in the darkness. The hum of cicadas whirred away, and the breeze lifted August's hair. "No, I'm rather cozy just here."

"Fuck off," August said. "Come on then, let's see what's going on."

They rose to their feet, stiff and groaning. August limped for a moment as his legs recalled how to move.

"I bet it's just carnival folks. They must stay on the grounds, overnight. In tents or trailers, or what have you." Jack waved an arm. "This has all been a complete waste of time."

"Oh come off it, what else were you going to do tonight?"

"Sleep, you daft idiot. We need to be sharp for Boone's interrogation tomorrow. At least, one of us does. I don't know that I can risk you being in the same room with him, behind closed doors."

"Hush," August murmured, and they quieted as they approached the fairgrounds.

August had to admit, it was more than a little unnerving, being here at night. The abandoned fairgrounds had taken on an eerie, surreal quality. The wind, which had continued to blow with gusto, filled August somehow with dread, as though it carried with it the promise of foul, twisted things. It was partially the scent, he admitted. That smell in the air, just before it rained. And sure enough, dark storm clouds gathered in the horizon, and August prayed the rain would hold off for another few hours. Otherwise, he would never hear the end of it.

As the wind picked up, a tent flap lifted and fell, lifted and fell. August watched it with a growing sense of malaise. He lifted his gaze briefly to the sky overhead, and spied a single star, at first. Then another. The distant lights seemed to wink and sputter, as traces of clouds spun overhead. August thought of faraway worlds. Dying stars, and ancient, mad kings.

Jack grabbed his arm once more, practically causing him to jump. And just then a sound broke through his consciousness. The steady background drone of the cicadas was broken by a faint noise. A voice. Laughter.

Jack looked back at him and pointed, then fell into a crouch. August fell into step behind him, head swiveling and eyes wide.

He needn't have been so alert. Their quarry made no attempt to remain hidden.

There, as they rounded a large tent, a group of figures, roving in the dark, came into view. Jack glanced back at August once more and pointed to a concession stand that stood several feet away. August nodded, and one at a time, they ran across the few open feet of ground to crouch behind the stand.

A group of men. Perhaps seven or eight of them. At least some of them appeared to be drunk, or well on their way. Several were armed. Long guns, perhaps shotguns, worn over their shoulders. One man stood leaning on his gun, the muzzle pressed into the ground. They spoke in hushed tones, but otherwise did little to conceal their presence. Their voices rose and fell on the wind. A chorus of muffled laughter was released once more. August peered around the corner of the stand, and Jack moved to hover over him. August watched, as a flashlight beam was fixed on the side of the tent the men were gathered around.

A man stood there, a paint brush in one hand, a bucket in the other. Sure, confident strokes, as he added to the tableau of hatred already well underway. As the flashlight shifted and moved, several of the men laughing, August read the words scrawled at the bottom of the tent; *'Bow to The Many-Legged King.'*

"For Christ's sake, hold the flashlight steady," the man painting called out. "Idiots." He turned back to the tent, and as the flashlight beam centered on his back, August stared. There, on the man's neck, was a mass of scar tissue; raised, curved lines, radiating out from a center.

Jack whispered over his head. "Hank." Before August could respond, or formulate a plan, Jack was past him, leaving a rush of air behind.

"Evening boys," Jack said amicably, strolling towards the group, both hands in his pockets. The flashlight spun and was fixed on Jack. He squinted and attempted to shield his eyes. "Hank, isn't it?" Jack addressed the man holding the paint brush aloft. He dropped it on the ground.

"What do you want?" Hank hissed.

The barrels of several shotguns were pointing at Jack.

August tensed, balanced on his feet in a crouch, as he slowly removed his revolver from its holster. They didn't seem to realize he was there.

"Just wanna to talk to you, Hank. Maybe, about this fine art-work of yours." Jack gestured towards the tent, and the text and symbols scrawled there. "And about that mark, on your neck."

Hank smiled, a merciless, cruel sort of smile. "Though I am weak, so shall he strengthen me. Though I wrong, so shall he right me."

"Come again?" Jack leaned forward, tilting an ear towards the young man.

His skin was shiny, forehead and cheeks slick with sweat, as his chest rose and fell. He raised his voice louder. "Though I sin, so shall he cleanse me. Though I am afraid, so shall he steel me."

"Yes, that's all very wonderful for you, I'm sure." Jack waved a hand dismissively. "But what do you know about Dixie LaRue? Hmm? Were you with her that night, Hank? Did you arrange a meeting, at The Black Sheep? Perhaps with this Many-Legged King?"

"I shall not fear, for he is my shield, my sword," Hank's voice rose louder, he was practically shouting now. The men gathered moved restlessly around Jack.

"Did you lure her to her death, Hank?" Jack sneered, leaning forward. "Did you get your girl killed, Hank?"

Hank paused, sneering back. "She wasn't my girl." He spit onto the ground. "She got what she deserved. Better, than she deserved. She was cleansed. Filthy whore."

There was a click of a hammer being pulled back. August swiveled to a man standing towards Jack's rear. He stood with an arm outstretched, a handgun pointed at the back of his head. Time seemed to slow. Then chaos reigned.

Jack tore through the group with a deep growl that August felt in his chest. The flashlight swung wildly. Paint went flying. Hank was down on his back. Jack jumped away, as the blast of a shotgun and a handgun echoed, followed by a second shotgun blast, then a third.

August gripped his revolver, his heart in his throat. He watched as one of the men lunged at Jack from behind, arm raised high. "Jack!" he cried out, his voice lost in the cacophony. But Jack spun at the last second, and a scream rent the night. Something wet sounding and solid was thrown against the side of the tent.

Another shotgun blast, and August watched, hardly breathing, revolver aimed at one dark figure after another, as Jack's movements became a blur. He seemed to anticipate their next moves, dodging and leaping. Now he was diving towards another man's feet. He took him out, and a shotgun went flying a moment later.

"Fuck," August muttered, as he trained his revolver on another dark figure. The roving flashlight beam briefly illuminated a man standing directly across from him, shotgun leveled at Jack's chest.

August hesitated for a split second. Was he really going to shoot this man? They needed to bring Hank in for questioning, but they couldn't leave a pile of bodies in their wake.

August pulled the trigger, and watched as the man cried out, grabbing his knee and falling to the ground. When the next shot rang out, it hit August in the gut. He pitched forward, with a moaning, keening sound as the pain hit him and drove through him like a lance made of fire. *"Fuck,"* he gasped. He attempted to raise his revolver, but was shot once more. This time, the round buried itself in his upper thigh.

Jack was by his side, dragging him backward to the stand. August felt suddenly weak. Inexplicably so. And the fire was spreading. Seeping through his veins, into his bloodstream, like poison. He writhed on the ground, as Jack leaned over him. "Jesus Christ August, where are you hit?"

A volley of shots rang out, smacking into the stand over their heads. August managed a gasping intake of air. The veins in his chest, under his eyes, swelled and pulsed, itching and hot, lit from within with that same, unnatural burning flame. "Silver," he managed to gasp. "Silver bullets."

"Fuck!" Jack patted him down, his hands on his chest. "What do I do?" He shook him slightly by the shoulders. "August, what do I do?"

August shook his head, clenching his teeth. "Nothing. I'll be alright. Didn't hit anything major... I don't think. I'm just... weak."

Jack pulled in a rush of air, steadied his breathing. He glanced back towards the men, as another errant shot went wide overhead. "You're sure?"

"I'm sure." August nodded. He managed to focus, blinking, on Jack's face. "Where are they?"

Jack straightened slightly and turned. "Looks like they're on the run," he said gruffly.

The clouds rushed overhead, the wind lifting the hair on August's forehead, now slick with sweat, as he writhed within his own skin. "Go," he said, taking in Jack's pitch-black eyes, and too-wide mouth, full of elongated teeth. Jack looked back down at August, eyes fixing on his partner as he stilled. "Go get him."

He remained overhead for only a second, and then he was gone. August heard a swish, the vacuum of air and the movement of grass, and then, from somewhere off to his left, a howl.

It rent the night, and even the cicadas momentarily ceased their endless drone. A cold sluice of primal terror went down August's back, at the bone-chilling, unnatural cry, and for a few seconds, the night was still. Then the sound of answering screams floated to him, carried on the foul wind.

August drifted, in and out of consciousness, and in and out of time. He couldn't look away. Couldn't close his eyes, as their faces swam before him. Maryanne. Dixie. Their eyes, cold and lifeless. Dead and staring. He saw flames. An unnatural fire. Burning flesh and dripping fat. He twisted to his side, heaving, and retching, at one point. Adelaide's face. She spun towards the door, in her bedroom upstairs, her features lit from below by the fire in the grate. Her eyes went wide in terror. "You!" She gasped and was lost to the darkness.

Miss Gray, seated at her table. A crowd of dark figures, heads turned in her direction. August lay on the table. He ached. He writhed and moaned. The scent of sulfur filled his nostrils. His flesh burned. A line of fire ran up his gut, his innards torn by something sharp and jagged. Tears streamed down his cheeks. The figures around the table did not so much as glance his way.

Miss Gray was chanting, now. Her lips moving fast and sure, her voice rising and falling in a rhythm. She raised both palms, towards the ceiling, and her eyes opened, filled with white, as her head tipped back. Flames blossomed from her open palms, from the top of her head. She smiled, an awful smile. *"He is here,"* she uttered, and her face was bathed in a flickering, sickly green light. Her smile broadened in rapture. *"He is here!"* Her eyes fluttered closed then opened once more. Her head snapped down and she stared at August, pupils swirling. *"Wake up!"*

August woke. He stared up at the swirling sky. Clouds rushed overhead, blotting out the stars. August pictured himself, some-where out there. On a distant cold rock, that circled a dying sun.

He lay there, alone, in the dust. On a rock that hurtled through empty space. The thought comforted him, oddly.

But then he recalled where he was. Here. On Earth. With humanity. A humanity he was part of. Whether they wanted him or not. And he sat up.

August took his time, getting to his feet. He held one hand, clamped over his gut, in the spot where his shirt remained sticky and damp. He walked. Bent forward, practically doubled over. It was agony to move. But he found that he could. He could feel the poison, still leaching from his system, as his unnatural body worked overtime to heal itself.

His first cohesive thought was of Jack. How many rounds had been loosed, before he'd taken off after them, into the night? Were they out of bullets? Had Jack been shot? Was he lying in a field somewhere, bleeding out into the dirt?

August walked. Where he was headed, he didn't have the slightest clue. He paused, thought for a moment. Forced his sluggish mind to catch up to his current predicament. The car. He needed to make it back to the car. He could call for back-up. Get help. The Chief had fought to have the two-way radios installed just last year. He could use the radio, call the station. Perhaps Jack was still out there. Perhaps it wasn't too late.

August stumbled forward, unsure for a moment, whether he was heading in the right direction. He surveyed the fairgrounds, eyed the Ferris wheel, and reoriented himself, turning back towards the direction they'd approached from. As he did so, he paused. Froze. Then turned back slowly. The Ferris wheel was moving.

August stood beneath the Ferris wheel, as he shivered in a cold sweat. Music played, and lights flashed, the cheerful melody so at odds with the scenery, it made the hair on August's neck stand on end. Goosebumps rose on his arms.

A figure turned, rotating endlessly, nearly reaching the apex now. The man hung upside down. August's head moved in unison with the great wheel.

When the splayed figure was on its downward arc, he broke out of his stasis and rushed to the controls. He admitted swiftly to himself that he had no clue what he was doing, but the big red button seemed to beg to be pressed. So, he pressed it. The wheel ground to a halt with a screeching sound that was hardly comforting.

August approached the figure, affixed to the wheel. Ropes, tied to wicked black hooks, pulled his skin taut, affixed to the metal spokes of the wheel on either side. The chest cavity yawned like the mouth of a cave that led down to hell.

As August moved closer, forcing himself to take each step, despite the way he trembled, he gasped. A quick intake of air, as he studied the man's features in the moonlight.

He struggled for a moment to recall the young man's name. Holden. Holden– *something*. The bullet catch.

His dark hair was damp, falling in waves over his forehead. His head hung limply. The veins beneath his eyes, and over his chest, which he had so carefully controlled, kept in check, during his act, were webs of darkness. His eyes were closed.

August felt his chest filling with a hollow sort of grief. Cold and numb. Senseless. Utterly senseless. He thought of the young man's figure, as he balanced on the horse. The picture of youth and health. The peak of life. Destroyed. Violently. Ended too soon, in pain and suffering. He only hoped the young man's pain tolerance had served him well, in the end.

August blinked rapidly, clearing his eyes, clenching his fists, and as his gaze traveled down the body's length, he stiffened, staring at his exposed ribcage.

His heart. His heart was still in his chest. Still beating. Barely. Weakly. Sporadic and stuttering.

August shot forward, held a hand beneath the man's nose. Was there a faint puff of air against his hand? He lifted one slack eyelid, then the other. The pupils were dilated, dull, without consciousness. But did he live still?

August raised his bloody palm and slapped him across the face. Nothing. He stared at his palm, painted red from his own wound, in the moonlight, and pressed it to the man's lips. Pressed it under his nose. He slapped him on the other side of his face, as he did so. A small intake of air, the man's exposed lungs expanded slightly. His eyelids fluttered. August let out a rush of air, stared at his own wrist, and steeled himself. His eyes darkened, and his canines grew. He bit into the flesh beneath his palm, attempting to ignore the revulsion that flooded him. His stomach lurched, and he swayed on still-weak legs. He pressed his wrist, blood flowing freely now, between the man's lips, and willed him to drink.

22

THE INTERROGATION. VISIONS.

August sat at his desk. Jack paced. The windowpanes ran, streaked with rain. The storm raged, and the day dragged on.

"You should go home," Jack repeated, his words clipped.

August shook his head stubbornly. "I'm fine."

"You aren't fine." Jack removed a cigarette from the inner pocket of his coat. He rested it between his lips. He caught August's expression and held up his lighter. "If I smoke, will you go home?"

August frowned at him. "I told you, I'm fine. You saved my life, from what I hear. Quit worrying. I think you've done enough."

Jack snorted and resumed his pacing. "Yes, well. I would have rather saved what's his name– Mr. Swift's life, if I'm being honest." He sighed. "He would have owed me his gratitude, and all. But no, you had to swoop in under me, didn't you? You had to be the hero. Foolish. You practically let him drain you dry. And that, after being shot."

"Twice," August said. His head was pounding. His pulse was weak. He felt strangely hungover. Jack had managed to hunt down Hank, the night before, chasing him through the fields and woods. He had carried him, alive, but unconscious, back to the fairgrounds, to find August, lying on the ground at the foot of the Ferris wheel, nearly drained of blood.

Holden Swift had made it. Barely. He was lying under guard in the hospital up the street.

Jack was anxious, waiting for Boone Radcliff to arrive. He was also furious at August, who had reported for work that morning as usual. On time.

"How much did you get out of him, last night?" August asked. He sipped gingerly at the terrible burnt coffee from the break room.

"Holden?" Jack sighed, running his hands through his hair. "Not much. He was able to mumble something about hoods, and tentacles. He kept losing consciousness. I'll visit him again, later today. But I'm not hopeful, Sully. I don't think he saw their faces. I'm not sure he'll be able to give us much to go off."

"I'll come with you," August said. The mention of tentacles made his blood cool.

"No, you won't. You look like shit. You shouldn't be here."

"What about Hank?" August changed the subject. "Did you get anything more out of him?"

"Hank…" Jack chuckled, trailing off. "Oh, I got a lot out of him. He wouldn't shut up, in fact. But it's all rubbish. A lot of religious mania and crazed ranting. Mostly about this '*Many-Legged King*'." Jack sighed and jerked his head. "He's cooling his heels back in a holding cell. Thinks he's some sort of Renfield-type character. Keeps going on about how his *master* is coming for us all. Says he's going to come claim him. Cleanse him with fire."

August forced himself to swallow the sip of coffee in his mouth. He felt sick to his stomach.

"So, that's what we're dealing with, it seems. Some sort of cult situation. This self-styled 'Many-Legged King' must be the ringleader." Jack sighed again, folding his arms, and staring at the rain-streaked window. "How unoriginal."

August couldn't help but release a snort of laughter. "You think that's all this is? A cult?"

"Our friend Hank in there, sure sounds like a religious twat who's half off his rocker." Jack turned to August, studying him for a moment. "When you're feeling better, maybe you should talk to him. You might have more luck with him than me."

August raised an eyebrow. "Why? Because I was a preacher? You think I'm delusional enough to get through to him?"

Jack grinned, cigarette still hanging from his lips. "You believed in an almighty power once. Perhaps the two of you have more in common than you think."

August looked away, choosing to de-escalate, for once, rather than escalate. He picked up the sheaf of papers on his desk and set his coffee down. "I've been going over the list, from Madam Beaufrey," he said. "Looking for any other names, any patterns." August shrugged. "I copied out all the entries for Boone."

"And?" Jack moved over to August's desk.

"Looks pretty random, in terms of any sort of pattern. But I'd say on average, Boone visited Dixie once or twice a month. No more frequently than that. Dates and days of the week are random, from what I can tell. Again, I find it odd he didn't use a fake name.

The other thing that stood out to me, is that our Earnest Bunbury, whoever he is, appears only once. On the night Dixie died. That name was never used previously."

"So, either he never visited her before, or he simply never used that name during previous visits."

"Right. And we know it was the first time Dixie ever met a client at The Black Sheep. So there's no pattern there we can search for." August shrugged. "I mean, I did try looking, but the restaurant is never mentioned. Dixie met clients several other places. Mostly hotels."

"How long had Boone been going to see her? Did he ever have her come to him?" Jack frowned down at the list.

"Going back about a year and a half, it looks like. The records themselves only go back two years though. I don't know how long she'd been working there. This may not be a full history."

Jack nodded, his eyes glazed. "I can't remember for sure, when I first started hearing about her." He shook his head, glancing at the doorway, as though he expected to see Boone walking through it at any moment. It was only 11 AM.

"Dixie did meet up with him, outside the cathouse. Not often. Just twice. Both times, at a hotel here in town. At the Biltmore, nonetheless."

Jack's eyebrows rose. "No expense spared by Mr. Radcliff."

"Apparently not when it came to Dixie," August said, setting down the list. "I still don't get it. How could he have done this? Assuming he is involved. He was hooking up with Dixie for what, a year and a half, and then he just decides to off her? As part of some... ceremony?" August massaged his temples, both elbows propped on his desk. "He doesn't strike me as the cult type."

"No, I'd have to agree with you there." Jack sighed deeply, and plopped into his chair, lifting both feet onto his desk. "So. Where does that leave us?" He met August's gaze, both eyebrows raised. "We still have two dead bodies; a call girl, and a future spinster. A half-mad graffiti artist, who won't stop spouting off about kings, and the end of the world. A lying politician. A half-dead carnie, who witnessed his own murder, and still can't identify the killers..." Jack trailed off. "Fuck me," he said. "It's enough to make even me feel slightly discouraged."

August remained silent for a long pause. "Don't forget, we have an autopsy report that may have been tampered with," he added.

"True," Jack stated, nodding. "But it feels like we've hit a dead end there. Could have been anyone. Anyone could have snagged that report off Marcy's desk. They had at least a half an hour, likely more; that's just all she would admit to. Anyone with access to a typewriter, and there are many in that building, could have quickly copied the report. Where do we go from here? Where does that leave us?"

August only shook his head. He didn't have an answer to that.

"Up shit's creek, that's where," Jack mused. "I almost forgot; we also have a medium, and her admirer. Both of whom claim to see visions of the dead."

August's eyes narrowed, as he fixed on Jack's expression of faint amusement. He stared at the cigarette that clung for dear life to his lip.

"And here we sit," Jack said, cigarette bobbing, as the rain pattered on the roof. "No closer to solving this thing, practically two weeks, and two and a half murders later."

August paused, frozen, with a thought half-formed in his mind. "We need to go back to the drawing board," he said. "What do the first two murders have in common? What's different about the third victim?"

Jack stared over at August, his expression rapt. "The first two were female," he began slowly.

"Yes, yes, not that." August waved a hand, feeling a surge of energy, despite his bone-deep exhaustion. "How were the victims chosen?" Jack stared blankly back at him. "Presumably, the first two victims were selected carefully. Or at least, not at random. The killers knew who they were. Knew enough about them, to know that they were vampires. To know where they lived, or at least worked, and how to gain access to them."

Jack sat up straighter. "Everyone knew Dixie was a vampire."

"Yes." August nodded in agreement. "The same can't be said for Maryanne. At least, not according to her father."

"Whoever chose Maryanne, had inside knowledge. They knew she worked at the shop. They must have known that sometimes she stayed late, after closing. She let the killers into the shop, most likely, of her own free will." Jack stared thoughtfully at the grimy windowpanes.

"Yes. And when did the carnival arrive in town? The day before it opened? Two days before?" August continued. "How did the killers go about selecting their third victim? They can't have had intimate knowledge of the victim. Not this time. Not in advance of the carnival coming to town."

"The third murder was a crime of opportunity," Jack said, his eyes widening. "It was planned at the last minute. Perhaps even spur of the moment. Perhaps that day, as the victim was seen performing for the crowd."

August nodded. "Yes. Exactly."

Jack seemed to deflate, sighing, and slumping in his chair. "It's a good catch, Sully. It's a break in the pattern for sure. But where does that get us? From what I can tell, it brings us no closer to uncovering the killers. If anything, it still points to Boone."

"He was there." August nodded in agreement. "And he specifically mentioned Holden Swift to us, remember?"

Jack locked eyes with August, his expression turning grim. "Two hours, until he gets here. He won't leave this station until he confesses what he knows."

Boone arrived promptly at one. He was accompanied by an entourage once more. This time, consisting of several lawyers, in dark suits. Chief Waverly had arrived in advance. He shot Jack a warning look, before they marched down to the conference room.

August felt a little dismay at not being included. Jack was right. He should go home. As the minutes and hours ticked on, he found himself growing weaker. More faint. His stomach swam and his pulse alternately raced and seemed to trip over itself and pause. He saw pinpricks of rainbow; dots of bright colors, when he moved his head too fast. It felt like one of the worst hangovers he'd experienced in his life. There was a reason he didn't drink. And he knew that it could mean only one thing. He had lost far too much blood, the night before. And he would continue to suffer, to grow weaker, until he fed again.

He thought about leaving. But where would he go? Home would do him no good. He pictured himself arriving on Miss Gray's doorstep, and his cheeks flushed hot. He could think of only one alternative.

But he delayed. Waiting, at his desk, nursing a second cup of now lukewarm, burnt coffee. Voices rose and fell, in the conference room down the hall. August's eyes swam as he stared down at the list. He leafed through the crime scene photos, while he waited. He read the inscriptions, burned into the victim's flesh. Mumbling the words in Latin to himself under his breath. He recalled the scent of sulfur, and melted flesh, from the night before. Would Holden's skin bear the blemish of his torture? Or would it heal fully, miraculously? Time, and some internal, ungodly magic, wiping him clean?

August stared down at Maryanne's death mask. The inscriptions carved into her arms. The mark, on her forehead. That swirl, so reminiscent of eight, curved limbs, filled him with a deep sense of malaise. He thought of Miss Gray, once more. Of the image in the tome she had handed him. The mad, many-legged king, on his golden dais. Ruling over a dying world.

It continued to rain, the sky drowning the city below, and the voices, angry now, rose and fell in the background, growing fainter and fainter.

When August looked up from his desk, the golden rope hung before him. Was it larger, this time? Thicker? It looked as though its girth had grown since the last time he saw it. He swallowed, in a throat suddenly parched, and dry.

No. He was too tired. Too weak. To see such things again. Not right now. But he stood, on trembling legs, and moved cautiously over to the rope that waited for him.

Who would be summoned, this time? The third victim had been snatched from the jaws of death. By luck, more than anything August himself had done.

When he pulled on the rope, he listened to the bell that rung, far in the distance, oddly cold, and hollow sounding somehow. It was louder than it had been, previously. Not a faint tinkling of bells. Not a chime. A loud, deep reverberation. One that echoed and caused his heart to flutter in his chest. He had the sudden image of the Many-Legged King himself, descending from his throne to meet him. Demanding to know why he had been summoned, and who dared to do so.

But the door to the station swung open. The little bell chimed. And there she was.

Maryanne appeared no more eager to see him than she had the first time around. "Not you again," she said evenly.

"Me," August said wearily, lifting his chin. "I want to know who did this. Who is *doing* this. Who is The Many-Legged King?" August felt a sudden surge of anger, as his mouth opened, and the words tumbled out.

Maryanne watched him with a bemused expression. "You will know him soon enough."

"Tell me," August demanded. He moved a step closer to her, than another. His eyes began to change, and his veins, drained as they were, pushed to the surface. He ran his tongue over his slick, sharp teeth, as he stepped face to face with the dead girl. "No more games. Tell me what you know."

"What I know?" Maryanne hissed, her eyes darkening in turn. "What I know?" Her voice rose, incredulous and trembling, stumbling on the words. Her hand shot out, and she gripped him by the throat. "This, is what I know."

August was drowning. Unable to draw a breath. His vision faded to black, and he was filled with an unfathomable horror. All he heard, before he lost consciousness, was a roaring filling his ears, and his soul, with terror; the sound of water, being sucked down a drain.

When he opened his eyes, he was sitting in front of a mirror. His hair was long, golden. He brushed it with a comb. His black eyes stared back at him. He lifted one hand, gingerly, touching the veins beneath his eyes. He let out a sob. The girl in the mirror, her name was lost to him, began to cry, her bottom lip trembling. The door behind her swung open, and there was the tailor, standing there, a look of horror on his face, as he turned to face him.

"Oh, God..." he murmured, dropping to his knees on the hard floor beneath. "Oh God, no. What have you done? What have you done?" The image faltered, beneath a swell of tears, and faded away.

He was at school. The other children sniggered. Laughed, and grinned secretively to each other. He could feel it. Feel his veins, pulsing beneath the surface. Did they know? Had he slipped? An errant thought, a flood of emotion... all they'd have to do was look at her, and they would know. His stomach roiled, and he knew, suddenly, that he was going to be sick. He bolted from his chair, made it nearly to the door, before he spewed a spout of vile, burning liquid all over the floor. His classmates screamed and shouted behind him. His teacher watched in horror, as he turned back to face her. "Go," she said, one shaking hand pointing to the hallway.

Now he was in church. He sat there, back erect, against the hard wooden pew. He clutched the bible he held in both hands, digging a corner beneath his thumbnail. The pain focused him. Sharpened his intent. He stared, enraptured, at the man who preached from the pulpit. His face was young. His eyes were kind. The man's gaze swept over his congregation and landed on him. When their eyes met, he felt it. A blossoming of warmth. Of peace, deep in his chest. He relaxed slightly, his pulse slowing. The panic that was his constant companion, seemed to ease. The blue-eyed preacher did not look away. He seemed to speak only to him. *"For all are welcome, in the Kingdom of heaven."*

August sat in front of the mirror once more. He stared at his reflection, willing his veins to contract. They obeyed. Slowly. A bible was spread out before him, on the small white vanity. He stared down at the pages below. His lips moved, uttering prayer after prayer. A drop of water fell on the page. Blurring the text beneath. Then another. Tears slid down his cheeks. August strained. He clawed. He pulled away. Away from the *other*. He lifted his gaze and saw a face that wasn't his. Maryanne. Maryanne was her name. And she was dead. She had been killed, in a horrible way. She had been tortured. And he knew. He knew in the pit of his soul, that she had given herself up. Willingly. Her faith had been twisted, and she had come to believe herself to be the monster, in her own story.

"No." August spoke, but it was Maryanne's mouth that moved. Her lips that uttered the words to her own reflection. *"No. You aren't a monster. They used you. They twisted you. With falsehoods.*

Lies. You never needed to be cleansed. You never needed to be found. You were never lost, in the first place. You were never broken."

August swayed on his feet and felt a great rush of air sucked into his chest. He was drowning. Drowning. He clutched at his throat, and the roaring in his ears... the roaring of rushing water seemed to fade and subside. He opened his eyes and scanned his surroundings. The station. He was back in the station. There was his desk.

He turned back to face the street. The bell pull was gone. He was alone.

August had just managed to return to his desk, knees wobbling, when a door down the hallway burst open, slamming against the wall. He watched, as a group of men filed out of the hallway, and into the office, weaving between desks as they went. He felt weak. Disoriented. He recognized one of the men as Boone Radcliff. Boone shot August a triumphant sort of withering stare, before he exited the station through the door held open before him.

August turned to see Jack and Chief Waverly standing side by side, both with their arms crossed over their chests.

"That was bullshit." Jack turned to Waverly with an explosion of emotion. "We're going to let him just walk right out of here?"

"Let it go, Jack. His lawyers are right. We have nothing on him." The Chief raised a hand and pointed at Jack. "I warned you to be careful, to move with caution. This man is powerful. He has friends, in high places. And a team of lawyers. What do we have? A list? A handwritten list, proving he liked prostitutes? So what? It doesn't put him at the crime scene, and it doesn't implicate him in the murder."

"Like hell it doesn't," Jack muttered.

"It doesn't, Jack. It's not enough. Not on its own. You get something real, something irrefutable. Otherwise, it's our word against his, and he claims he has alibies."

"They don't span the entire–"

"Do they need to? His driver vouches for him until up to 12:30 AM. His wife vouches for him coming upstairs to bed sometime after 1:00. The murder took place, per our own coroner's report, sometime between 12:00 and 4:00 AM, all the way on the other side of town, in the middle of nowhere, in a farmer's field."

"He might have had enough time," Jack started.

"How'd he get there, Jack? Did he fly?"

"I don't know," Jack said.

"No, you don't know. His driver didn't take him. Did he hail a taxi, at two in the morning?"

"Possibly," Jack muttered, staring at the floor.

"Then get out there and find out, yeah?" Chief Waverly flung his arm out, his face turning red. "Get out there, and start canvassing taxi drivers. See if anyone happened to pick up the infamous Boone Radcliff, and drive him out of town, to the scene of a murder. Maybe they forgot to come forward."

"Fine," Jack snapped. "We don't have enough on him."

"No, you don't," Chief Waverly agreed, his anger seeming to fade as quickly as it had come. "I like him for it, Jack. I really do. But I don't think he's our man."

Jack hung his head, nodded. "We'll go back to the drawing board. Go over everything again. I'm going back to speak with the third victim, Holden. I'll try again with Hank. He must know who did this." Jack's expression turned slightly murderous.

"You do that," the Chief said, studying him. "Carefully, this time. I can't afford to have any more collateral damage. Not right now." Chief Waverly turned to look at August, who watched with wide eyes, his hands wrapped around his hollow, aching gut. "And you, get out of here. Go home. Go…" his voice trailed off, "go, take care of yourself. Do whatever you need to do, and get your ass back in here when you don't look like you're on the verge of death."

August ended up at the only place he had left to go. When Madam Beaufrey opened the door, he expected her to laugh in his face, or turn him away. It was a new door. Or at least, perhaps, a patched door, with a fresh coat of paint.

But she only eyed him warily and stepped aside. He followed her up the stairs to Adelaide's room.

August managed to make it to her bed, before he collapsed. His vision swam, as he stared up at the canopy. The gauzy curtains were pulled by an unseen hand, falling around him. Like a shroud.

"Take care of him, dear. Keep him here for the night." Madam Beaufrey's voice echoed in his ears, as he lost himself to darkness once more.

23
A REVELATION.

It was dark when August woke. He had drifted in and out of consciousness for what felt like several hours. He knew only that Adelaide was close by. He breathed in her scent. She cradled him to her, when he stirred. He fed. Life and strength flowed through his veins once more.

He glanced over at Adelaide now. Her form draped with only a silk sheet. Her skin gleamed, pale in the moonlight. He stared for several seconds, marking the rise and fall of her chest and let out a sigh of relief.

He tried not to wake her. But he stirred, unable to get comfortable. Admitting finally that sleep would not find him, he rose and sat on the edge of the bed. He felt a hand slide down his upper back.

"You're awake," she said, still blinking sleep from her eyes. "Do you feel better?"

August smiled down at her. "I do. Thank you, Adelaide."

"You don't have to thank me." She grinned, as she ran her nails down his back once more. "I told you before, I like it."

August's smile faded. "It's dangerous, you know. What happened tonight. I could have drained you... I wasn't... fully aware. Wasn't in control."

Adelaide sighed, propping herself up on one elbow. The sheet slid to reveal her bare chest. August tried not to stare.

"I trust you, August. I don't believe you're capable of something like that."

"Even when I'm not conscious?" He frowned down at her.

"Even then," she said, a knowing curve to her lips. Her smile faltered slightly, as she studied him. "You were mumbling, you know. Saying things, in your sleep. It was almost like you were feverish. You were pouring with sweat, shaking. I couldn't get you to wake up enough to feed, at first."

"I'm sorry you had to deal with me like that," August said, his cheeks burning hot. "What sorts of things was I saying?"

Adelaide thought for a moment. "Something about a king, and a throne. Dying stars and planets. It was hard to make any sense of it. But you spoke of other things, too. You talked about people. Maryanne. I heard Dixie's name. And Jack's." She cocked her head to the side, studying him. "You said the name Hank, several times. Hank... with an 'H'... was that the name of Dixie's beau?"

August looked away for a moment, recalling the haze he had been in. He could only partially remember it. A night full of pain and agony. It was probably for the best if he forgot. He nodded, after a moment. There was no harm in telling her. "Yes, Hank, was his name. *Is* his name. We have him down at the station."

"He's the one who did this to her?" Adelaide sat up, pulling the sheet and blankets around her as though she were suddenly chilled.

August shook his head. "No. I don't know. I'm not sure he was directly involved. But I think he knows the people who were." August sighed. "He's spouted nothing but gibberish so far. He appears to be in a religious sort of mania. He keeps going on about saving our souls, cleansing them with fire…"

Adelaide frowned, as she stared over at the window, and the stretched rectangle of moonlight that shone onto the floor below. "How strange."

"Yes, his behavior has been bizarre, to say the least."

"I wonder what happened to him," Adelaide mused. "He never used to act like that around here. But then, I suppose he was always religious, wasn't he?"

"Was he?" August asked, his gaze straying from the moonlight to Adelaide's innocent brown eyes.

"Well yes, that's where Dixie met him, after all. At church."

August felt himself still. Even his heart seemed to pause for a beat. He recalled the hard wooden pew, against his shoulder blades. The bible clutched in both hands, the corner, stabbing beneath his nail.

"Which church, Adelaide?"

24

THE REVEREND BLACKSTONE. A STORM GATHERS.

It seemed oddly appropriate, he supposed, as he clung to the back of the passenger seat with one hand, and the door handle with the other.

Miss Gray took the turns as though they were a challenge. She refused to give an inch, never slowing, and rather seeming to speed up, as she rounded each bend.

August had arrived back at the station on foot, in the middle of the night, to find Jack asleep at his desk.

Jack had listened to what he had to say, then he sent August home to sleep, promising to pick him up first thing in the morning.

But it had been Miss Gray's long Cadillac that had come to a stop in the street below his apartment. August found himself hoping, once more, to make it as far as the churchyard, at least, in one piece.

"He never saw their faces," Jack mused bitterly. "They kept them hidden. They wore long, dark red robes. Pointed hoods, dark holes for eyes."

"They're more crimson, than they are red," Miss Gray said, turning to glance over her shoulder at August. "Do you believe yet, August? Didn't I describe them exactly as such?"

"Watch the road, for Christ's sake!" August cried out, pointing as a car turned out into traffic in front of them.

Miss Gray somehow managed to avoid it. She laughed, her voice low and husky. "Someone is on edge, this morning,"

"I would be more concerned if he wasn't," Jack mumbled back.

"I heard that," August sighed, his heart rate returning to normal, as he leaned back against the seat and tried to relax. "What about their voices? Anything they said, that might be helpful? Did they use any names? Would he recognize their voices again?"

Jack shrugged. "Perhaps. The main one, the leader; he spoke quite a bit. A lot of chanting and carrying on, of course." Jack waved a hand, glancing back at August. "He was able to repeat some of it. It was about as helpful as the jargon Hank has been spewing non-stop since I tackled him in that field."

"Did you enjoy that?" August asked, one eyebrow raised. "It's rare now a days that you get to give chase like that."

Jack laughed ruefully. "It was fun while it lasted. He made it too easy."

"Have you really learned nothing else?" Miss Gray asked incredulously. "One attempted murder victim, and one suspect. One who saw the killers, and one who must know them, and no new leads?"

"Other than the church," August added morosely.

"Yes, other than the church," Miss Gray conceded.

"We know the ringleader has tentacles," Jack said, "that's not nothing." He glanced sideways at Miss Gray.

"I don't know him, if that's what you're getting at," she replied stiffly. "We don't all know each other, you know." August was grateful he wasn't on the receiving end of that glare.

"Right," Jack said, with a huff of air. He pulled a cigarette out of his pocket, lighting it, along with a second, for Miss Gray.

"Is that really new information?" August asked. "He's referred to as 'The Many-Legged King'..."

Jack glared in his direction now. "We have the church. We aren't dead in the water. Not by a long shot."

August heaved a sigh of relief, and gave himself a minute to compose himself, before exiting the car. An odd sense of Deja vu swept over him, as he stood in front of the humble church, in the empty field. The headstones, just where they had last seen them, stretched towards the treeline.

Miss Gray and Jack headed for the stairs that led to the front entrance. August eyed the wooden doors and their black handles with resignation. "You aren't coming in, are you?" Jack asked, one eyebrow raised.

"What, shall I wait outside?" August spread his arms wide. "What was the point of enduring the car ride then?"

Miss Gray stared coldly at August, although he thought perhaps she was trying not to smile.

Jack shook his head. "Why don't the two of you wait here. I'll see if the good Reverend would be willing to take a turn with us outdoors."

The good Reverend was not willing to take a turn with them outdoors. He was in the middle of crafting his next sermon and had in fact attempted to avoid speaking with them at all, Jack informed them, somewhat breathlessly. He had been able to convince him to speak with them for a few minutes inside.

There was nothing for it. August steeled himself and trudged up the stairs behind Miss Gray. He knew exactly what would happen to him in the church, although he liked to think he'd gotten past all that, part of him knew, deep down, that it wasn't so.

August's heart rate climbed as he passed beneath the eaves into the yawning front entrance. It appeared much larger inside, than it did without.

It was all too familiar. All too achingly familiar. The rows of pews and the cross that hung at the far end of the sanctuary, framed by stained glass windows. The silence. The way the smallest sound echoed and traveled within. The way the light itself fell. It all combined to infect August with a sweeping sense of claustrophobia.

It had happened every time he'd attempted to enter a house of God. No matter the denomination. He had quit because of it. Most assumed, it had been because he was a vampire, naturally. But no. It was the panic that swelled in his chest. Thick, choking, blind panic. You couldn't reason with panic, August had come to learn. You couldn't talk your way out of it. You couldn't modify it. Change it. There was nothing to be done but to endure it. And he could not.

He felt himself beginning to shake. To tremble. And he fought to keep himself under control. He wouldn't break down. Not now. Not in front of Miss Gray. Jack. He would suffer in silence. He must. He stared at the hard wooden pews as he walked past, in a haze. Maryanne had come here. Every Sunday. She had endured the awful guilt. The shame. She had endured it all, for her faith, and for this man, who sat before him now.

The Reverend Blackstone rose to his feet, and pressed his hands together, nodding at each of them in turn. "Please, come in. Have a seat, be welcome." He held his hand out, indicating the chairs that faced his large desk. "I apologize, for my reluctance to take a break. I fear that my concentration is such that once broken, it can be nearly impossible to recover. But alas, I understand the importance of this visit." His expression grew grave. "Poor little Maryanne. May her soul rest in peace. She was one of God's true children. Called home to him too soon, as is so often, sadly, the case."

The Reverend appeared stricken, his features faltering with what looked like true grief. August was struck again by his apparent youth. He had a strong jawline, long blonde hair that fell in waves past his ears. He was dressed in simple black robes. The office itself was equally plain and humble. It likely spoke to the strength of his character, August mused. He recalled the feeling of comfort, of warmth, in his chest, as he sat in that pew, as Maryanne. And looking at the Revered, he felt some of that warmth now, breaking through the blind panic that threatened to consume him.

"Did you know Maryanne well?" Jack asked smoothly.

"Ah, yes. I did. I did. She was devoted; Maryanne was. She was always willing to help. Take on extra duties. We feed the needy. We have several charitable enterprises. Most of our events take place downtown, you understand. We cannot expect those who need our help to make their way out here. I could always count on Maryanne to pitch in. Her sense of service was very strong."

"And what of Miss LaRue?" Jack asked, leaning forward. "Did you recognize her, amongst your flock?"

"Miss LaRue," the Reverend repeated, seeming to think for a moment. "Yes, Miss LaRue. I do remember her. I had forgotten for a moment. Of course. She was one of the victims as well." He sighed deeply. "I hadn't seen Miss LaRue here for quite some time. But that's common, you see, for many who attend. They come infrequently. Not like Maryanne. She was one of our regulars. Miss LaRue did attend several times, though, this past year. She was more likely to attend around the holidays." The Reverend shrugged.

"Did you ever see her with her boyfriend, Hank?" Jack asked, eyes narrowing as the Reverend glanced away briefly.

"Hank... why yes, I recall Hank spending time with her. They sat next to each other... that may have been the last service I saw Miss LaRue attend, now that I think about it. Hank's one of those who's hit or miss as well, when it comes to attendance. Sometimes he comes with a few of his friends." The Reverend frowned. "A bit of a rough-looking crowd, if you catch my meaning." He held up his hands in a gesture of supplication. "Not that I judge, but I suspect he hangs around with Red's gang." The Reverend shook his head. "Nothing good comes of violence. And young men like Hank, unfortunately, seem to be particularly drawn to it."

"And you were... aware, of Dixie LaRue's status? In the community?" Miss Gray asked, one eyebrow raised.

"I was," the Reverend Blackstone said slowly. "All of God's children are welcome within these walls." His gaze shifted to August as he uttered those last words, in a way that felt deliberate.

August swallowed thickly. He ignored the sweat beading on his brow and hoped the Reverend wouldn't notice it either.

"How inclusive of you," Miss Gray said. "And Maryanne, were you previously aware of her... condition?"

The Reverend Blackstone turned to look at Miss Gray, as though he were really seeing her for the first time. He cleared his throat. "Her condition?" He said slowly.

"She was an upir," Miss Gray said, "a vampire. Did she not confide in you?"

The Reverend frowned, lines appearing between his brows. He stared down at his desk, his eyes moving rapidly back and forth. "As I said, all are welcome here." He inclined his head. "The poor child was clearly struggling. But no, Maryanne did not share her... troubles, with me, although I knew something was bothering her. Naturally, I did my best to alleviate her feelings of woe. She seemed to be harboring some deep-seated guilt. Perhaps that was it. Perhaps she was holding herself accountable for her condition." His gaze had landed on August as he spoke. "But if so, it was not her burden to carry." August stared into those clear blue, earnest eyes for several seconds, his stomach roiling, before looking away.

The Reverend sighed deeply, his voice sounding suddenly much older, and tired. "If only I had gotten through to her. Whatever burden she carried with her, it weighed heavy on her soul... and she would not put it down."

"Is Boone Radcliff a member of your congregation, Reverend?" Jack asked swiftly.

The Reverend bowed his head, and he lingered on his notes, scrawled in cursive on the pages before him, in a longing sort of manner. But he lifted his focus once more to Jack, and his eyes seemed almost to sparkle, with a gleam that had been absent previously.

"Boone Radcliff," Reverend Blackstone repeated thoughtfully. "Yes. It appears you already know the answer to that, Mr. Quinn. And I'll answer what I predict your next question will be, if you'll allow me."

"I will. Be my guest." Jack swept an arm out. August was close to fainting now. Or puking. One or the other. He didn't know how much longer he could take it, sitting here. But he didn't want to miss what the Reverend was about to say.

"My answer is yes, to your next question. If you're wondering whether I ever saw Boone Radcliff speaking with the victims. My answer would be yes. On both counts."

August had excused himself, then. He made it to the side of the church, before he retched his guts up at the base of the wall. He had been hoping to make it to the treeline but it was too far away, and he hadn't wanted to vomit on some poor soul's grave.

He wiped his mouth on his sleeve and walked away from the church. He felt slightly better already, having emptied his stomach and exited the church. August moved towards the treeline eyeing the grave that bore the name 'LANGSTON' that Miss Gray had brought them to that first night.

August frowned, as he moved past the familiar headstone, and surveyed the stones closer to the treeline. Why hadn't he noticed it before? Last time they had been here, admittedly, he had been somewhat distracted. But it was now very obvious that the last few rows of graves were far more fresh-looking. They were set at the very back of the churchyard, practically beneath the trees they had hidden within.

August read the names, murmuring them out loud, as he went, and scanned the dates. One of them struck him as oddly familiar, although he couldn't quite place it. All fairly recent dates, as he had suspected. Several were dated within the past six months.

The row before, was dated in the past year. And the row before that, within the past two years. It seemed like an awful lot of graves, in a short time, for one small church. How large was the Reverend's congregation, at this point? August frowned as he peered back at the church. Only so many people could fit on the pews inside.

Dark clouds seemed to gather and swirl once more, directly overhead. August recalled how Miss Gray had called them down, in her anger. The memory of the massive alien limbs that seemed to curl inside, still made his stomach twist in knots. Was she angry now? What were they learning, within those walls? Had Boone Radcliff hunted here, like a predator? A cat among mice. Taking advantage of the faithful, the downtrodden. August felt himself filling with blind, unreasonable anxiety once more. The roaring sound, like water being sucked down a drain, came to his memory unbidden. He shook slightly. The aftereffects of his panic, no doubt. And the illness that always followed.

August heaved a sigh of relief, as the figures of Miss Gray and Jack stepped out onto the worn footpath that led to the church. He eyed the fresh headstones once more and made his way back to them.

The storm was upon them by the time they made it to the station. "It has rained rather an inordinate amount recently, has it not?" Jack called out to August, as they fled from Miss Gray's car, into the harbor of the station.

They found it deserted. At least, the front office was empty. There would be at least one officer on duty, in the back, keeping an eye on their friend Hank, in his holding cell.

"I can't recall it ever storming this much in such a short span of time before." Jack continued to grumble, as he shook out his trench coat and hung it, along with his hat, up to dry on the coat rack.

August joined him. "I have a feeling I know why," he mumbled under his breath.

"What's that?" Jack asked, turning back to him as he strode to his desk.

"Nothing," August said. He sat heavily at his own desk. "What do we do now?"

"I really don't know, old boy." A cigarette had materialized and found its way into Jack's mouth. He stared glumly at the rain lashed window. "I hate to admit it, but I feel quite stuck. You heard Chief Waverly; we haven't got enough hard evidence to implicate Boone."

"But now we have a connection between Boone and both victims," August said.

"True. The Chief doesn't know that yet. The Reverend gave us enough to draw a connection between Boone and Maryanne. Says he saw them speaking on one occasion, at least." Jack sighed. "But that may not be enough. It was at one of their charity events. Here, downtown. It doesn't really prove that he *knew* Maryanne."

"No, I suppose not. Boone talks to a lot of people, doesn't he?" August mused. "What if we go back and speak with Maryanne's father? Maybe we'll uncover further evidence of some connection between Boone and Maryanne."

Jack tilted his head, pressing his lips together. "Not a bad idea. It might not even need to be a direct connection to Boone. What about to Boone and his staff? Maybe Maryanne volunteered with his campaign." Jack sat upright. "There could be some paperwork, somewhere, right? If that were the case..." he got to his feet, paced back and forth. "There has to be something, some connection we can prove. In Dixie's case, it was Hank. Boone may have interacted briefly with her as well, at the church, and obviously, we know they did much more than that. But I have a feeling it was Hank who Boone ultimately used to get Dixie where he wanted her. The same could be true for Maryanne. Boone strikes me as someone who doesn't like to do his own dirty work. Maybe he made the initial contact, or connection, but he used an intermediary from there. To distance himself, you know?"

"It has the ring of truth," August said. "But this is all just speculation."

"The Reverend seemed to think Hank worked for Red. Or rather, was associated with him, and his gang." Jack slammed his hand down on a nearby desk. "Dammit, I really thought we'd ruled that angle out. I hate to go back and stir up Red again, not unless we have to."

"I'll tell you right now, I'm not up for that tonight. I'm still recovering from the carnival," August said. He left out the part about puking his guts out at the church. The car ride back hadn't been a pleasant one, either.

"No." Jack shook his head, as he continued to pace. "No. I don't think we need to. I think he's mistaken, the Reverend. I think it's Boone we need to focus on."

"I think we should speak with Maryanne's father again, personally," August said slowly. "I can't help but think there might be more there that we're missing. He may know more than he realizes."

"Yes." Jack nodded as he spoke. "Yes, we'll do that. But first, I think I'd like to give our good friend Hank another go."

The storm seemed to have followed them back to town. Thunder boomed overhead. Flashes of lightning were clearly visible through the narrow window set high in the holding cell. Whenever the thunder rumbled, Hank smiled.

He seemed to relish the chaos that raged outside. He stopped and turned, staring out the window at the churning sky, waiting for the next stroke of lightning, and crack of thunder.

"He's completely and utterly mad," Jack murmured to August out of the corner of his mouth.

August found it difficult to disagree. Hank had no reservations about talking to them. Jack had been accurate in his description of the man. He wouldn't shut up. He babbled on and on about the fires of hell, and the cleansing flames. About how they needed to repent. About how their souls could still be saved.

Jack turned eventually to August. "You must feel right at home, old boy. Imagine if you'd had Hank around, during your preaching days. He'd write all your sermons for you."

"I was never one for fire and brimstone myself," August said, with a long-suffering sigh. "Did you ask the Reverend Blackstone about this?" He turned away from Hank and dropped his voice lower. "About his... religious mania, I mean? Has he always been like this?"

"Oddly, no," Jack said, keeping his voice low in a similar fashion. "I did ask him, and he said he had the impression that Hank was never particularly devout. I think you heard him saying how he only would show up here and there, at church. The Reverend didn't seem to know what I was talking about. I got the distinct impression that this is a whole new Hank we're seeing now."

"Did you injure his head when you tackled him?" August asked lightly.

Jack grinned. "I swear, he was like this before I got to him." He shook his head, folding his arms over his chest. "No, I can't account for it. It must be whatever he got into, with this 'Many-Legged King'... some sort of cult-induced fanaticism, or whatever you want to call it. Clearly, it's addled his brains."

Hank continued to babble as he paced his cell. "*He* is coming. The time is almost here. *He* is coming. He cannot be stopped. He will not wait. His time is near. He is coming. He will cleanse me. He will cleanse me. His fire will cleanse me." He repeated himself more than once, as he stared up at the little window, rocking his body back and forth.

Jack slammed against the bars of the cell suddenly. "Listen," he growled, letting his eyes turn black and his mouth grow wide. "We need to ask you a few questions, Hank. Can you focus, for once? Can you do that for us?"

"*He* is coming," Hank whispered, as he cowered against the wall.

"It's not worth it, Jack. Look at him," August said.

"Can you do it for *him*?" Jack crooned, still focused on Hank. "For *him*. See, we want to help him, when he arrives. Tell us who he is. Tell us who you work for, Hank."

The men waited, as Hank, for once, fell silent. Jack might be on to something, August realized. Although he cringed slightly, as he took in the wide-eyed look on Hank's face. He seemed to earnestly be considering Jack's request. It felt like lying to a child.

Then Hank's expression shifted, his lips parting in a sneer. "*He* is coming. *Him*. He who will carve out your heart. He who will blacken your flesh and cleanse your soul. He is coming, with his fire." Hank stood, straightened. He appeared to be fixed on August, ignoring Jack completely. His chest expanded, with a great intake of air, and then he was yelling, his lips stretched taught, his white teeth gnashing. *"He will break you! He will remake you! He will cleanse you in the pit! In the fire that never ends! He. Sees. You!"* Hank lunged forward, slamming into the bars, spittle flying in August's face.

At that moment, thunder, loud and low, radiated from over their heads, and August could have sworn the very walls of the station shook. The lights went out, and they were plunged into darkness.

25

A HAND IN THE DARK. A PROMISE. THE KEY.

Jack called out to the officer on watch. His name was Smith. There was no response. They waited, hoping Officer Smith would appear in a moment or two, perhaps with a flashlight in hand. But they had no such luck.

"Jesus Christ," Jack said. "Do we always have to do everything around here?"

They made their way slowly in the dark, down the narrow corridor towards the front office.

August nearly tripped over Officer Smith's body. "What the fuck?" He hissed, crouching down, patting the mound of soft flesh that lay before him. Lightning flashed, and just enough light made it back into the opening of the corridor, to reveal the officer lying face down on the floor.

August felt for a pulse, while Jack swore, removing his revolver from its holster. "For fuck's sake," he said, "keep your eyes peeled, Sully. Is he dead?"

"Not yet," August whispered. "He appears to have been knocked out."

"Now what?" Jack whispered back. "It's practically pitch black in here, but I don't see anyone. I can smell them though. There was definitely someone else here."

"I hope so. Unless Officer Smith managed to knock himself unconscious."

"You're so witty, Sully. Really. Why do you always pick the middle of a crisis to start trying to be funny? You have a very odd sense of comedic timing, you know that?"

"Oh, you're one to talk," August hissed at him. "And what crisis, exactly? The power's gone out, during a thunderstorm. I don't know what, or should I say *who*, you're smelling, but I'm not picking up anyone else's scent." August bent in a crouch as he removed his revolver from its holster as well. "We must have flipped a breaker, that's all. Should be simple enough to fix."

"Then why are you getting your gun out?" Jack asked haughtily.

A hand wrapped around August's mouth from behind. At the same time he began to struggle, Jack let out a muffled cry beside him. August willed himself to let loose. He didn't have to try very hard.

His teeth were suddenly too large for his mouth, pressing against his lips, and the hand that held a damp rag tightly over his mouth and nose. He caught the scent of something acrid and chemical on the rag, and bucked his head harder, catching himself from instinctively drawing in another breath. He grabbed the man behind him with his free arm, and using all his strength, he leaned forward and flipped his assailant over his head. The man landed with a muted cry on top of the body of Officer Smith.

Jack's strategy had been somewhat different. He had elected to let his mouth widen beneath the hand that pressed a rag over his face, and then he bit it off.

Jack spit the hand out onto the floor of the corridor, and turned to August, blood flowing down his chin, with an expression of pure disgust. He spat at the ground, spraying blood. "God awful," he said, "what sort of lotion do you use?" He turned to the man who was screaming bloody murder behind him and punched him square in the face. His head bounced off the floor of the corridor below, and he stopped moving.

"Well then." Jack shrugged and turned towards August's assailant. "Let's see what our new friend can tell us."

The second assailant was scrambling away from them, shuffling backward, and bumping into desks. He held a hand out in front of him in supplication. Then he glanced down at the severed hand he held in his own with look of pure horror and dropped it hastily. He wore a back cap, pulled down low over his forehead, and what looked like a dark woolen scarf, wrapped around the bottom half of his face. He was dressed in a tight black, short sleeved shirt. The dim moonlight revealed tattoos covering both of his muscular arms. "No," he said, "please, no. I'll go. I won't cause you any more trouble."

Jack pounced. Leaping forward, over the desk the man had managed to put between them, landing with his feet on either side of the man's chest. The man in black let out a blood-curdling wail and attempted to shrink into the floor.

Jack lifted him with one hand, and held him there, suspended in air, as he turned back to locate August. "Let's see if this one can give us something we can use."

"Who do you work for?" August asked, moving closer. "Who sent you?"

"I–I c–can't... please, I can't tell you..."

Jack's fist buried itself in the man's gut. "We're going to find out anyway, might as well save yourself some pain."

"Who do you work for?" August repeated, his voice strained. "Why are you here?"

"We're here for him! Hank! In the cell!" the man moaned, as Jack pulled him closer, his teeth gleamed in the faint light from the streetlamps shining through the windows. The scent of urine filled the air.

"Not again," Jack said. "I need to find a balance between threatening them and making them piss themselves."

"You aren't there yet," August said matter of factly.

"Clearly," Jack said. "We're going to ask you one more time. Who sent you here tonight?"

"*He* did," the main stammered. "*The Many-Legged King.*" The words came out as a whisper.

"And who is he?" Jack growled, breathing in the man's face once more. "You know, when he's not going by his... official moniker... what's his real name?"

The man shook his head, eyes going wide. "I– I don't know!"

"You don't know, or you won't tell us? There's a massive difference, my boy."

"I don't know! Truly! That's all they ever call him! I've only seen him once, and not his face!" The man held his hands up. "Please, I swear."

"Where did you see him?" August asked urgently.

A clatter and a rusty squeak emanated from the dark corridor behind them. "God damn it," Jack said. "How many of you are there?"

"Here?" The man stammered. "Just four. Me and him." He pointed to the one-handed man lying unconscious on the floor. "And two in the back, taking care of Hank."

August and Jack turned to look at each other. "Taking care of…" Jack repeated.

A shot rang out from the corridor behind them. Then a second.

"Fuck." Jack stared down the corridor for a moment, then turned back to the man suspended in the air before him.

"Wait," August said slowly. "You said there were four of you, *here*. Are there more of you, somewhere else?"

The man's wide eyes swiveled to August in the dark. "Please, I'm injured. I thinking I'm bleeding internally."

Jack shook him like a rag doll. "Did they send more of you somewhere else?"

"The woman," the man gasped, "the witch. They sent the rest to take care of the witch."

August took a car this time. He drove like Miss Gray herself, not daring to slow down, even on the turns. The Ford V8 screeched to a halt in front of her gate, wheels spinning and sliding on the wet pavement.

He raised a fist to pound on the door, but realized in the flash of the storm overhead, that the door was already open a crack.

August pushed his way inside, heart hammering in his throat, breathing rapidly. He tore from one room to the next. He held his revolver aloft, aiming at chest height as he entered each room. He cleared the lower level with an increasing panic building in his chest.

He breathed in deeply, as he ducked into the dining room. Miss Gray's place at the head of the table was empty, as were all the other seats. He entered the kitchen next, and caught a faint scent. It was subtle, but there. Blood.

He found a trail of it, in the next corridor. The power seemed to have been cut here, too. And he moved as fast as he dared through dark halls, being sure to remain silent, balanced on the balls of his feet. The blood trail ended at a dark figure slumped against a wall. A man dressed all in black. August heaved a sigh of relief and continued forward. He found another man, dead, his eyes bulging, in some sort of parlor room, with what looked like thick ligature marks around his neck. He found a third man in similar conditions on the stairs.

The first level cleared, he mounted the stairs quickly, hope beginning to bloom in his chest.

He found her in the library. She sat perched on a chair by the fire. Miss Gray smiled, as he entered the room, as though she had been expecting him.

"Miss Gray," he exhaled, his chest still rising and falling rapidly. The veins beneath his eyes ached and strained, while those on his chest itched. He took in Miss Gray's cool collectedness with coal-black eyes. "I see you had visitors tonight. So did we, at the station."

"Did you?" Miss Gray raised an eyebrow. "And I see you appear unharmed, although, quite disheveled, I must say. And Jack?"

"He's alright." August forced himself to breathe more evenly, his cheeks flushing slightly. "Unharmed, as well. I left him waiting for back up. I'm sure they've arrived by now. I can't say the same for Hank, unfortunately."

Miss Gray frowned. "Hank was killed in the fallout?"

August shook his head. "Looks like they were there specifically to make sure he didn't talk," August said darkly. "We found him doused in gasoline. He'd been lit on fire, from what we could tell, then shot, twice, for good measure."

"Heavens," Miss Gray murmured. "Well." She stood and gestured across the room at the fire. "Have a seat. It looks like you'll be joining me once more, for a late-night cup of tea."

"I must say, I'm rather impressed, Miss Gray, I counted at least four assailants downstairs. Equal in number to those they sent to the station. They must have deemed you a formidable target."

"Indeed, August," Miss Gray said primly. "And they weren't wrong."

August set his full teacup down on the table beside his chair. "Did you get any information out of any of them, beforehand?"

Miss Gray shook her head swiftly. "I'm afraid we didn't speak." She shrugged. "Well, not meaningfully, at least."

"That's too bad. I must admit, I'm more than slightly ashamed of our lack of leads. Once more, we've had a brush with the enemy, and I can't help but feel we've come away even more empty handed then we were before."

"But still alive," Miss Gray said, and sipped her tea.

"Yes," August conceded, "there is that."

"You're down a witness now, though, unfortunately. Possibly a valuable witness, seeing as they risked more of themselves to make sure he didn't talk."

August sighed deeply, shaking his head. He stared down at the floor. "Our quarry seems to be always one step ahead of us. It's getting to the point of utter ridiculousness."

Miss Gray set her cup and saucer down on the coffee table by the sofa and got to her feet. She walked over towards August, coming to a stop in front of him. She reached down and tucked her hand under his chin. "Chin up, darling. At least the night wasn't a total loss. I got to see you arrive with your teeth bared, ready to rescue me." A smile curled the corners of her lips, as she spoke. She stared down at him, as he attempted to control the erratic pounding of his heart.

Miss Gray's thumb slid up, to caress his cheek, and he cursed himself as his veins swelled and darkened beneath her touch. She didn't look away. She only smiled once more.

"You shouldn't do that," August murmured.

"Or what?" Miss Gray asked. "You once dared me to show you my worst. Shall I dare you the same?"

August swallowed thickly, willing himself not to move. But she reached up, and with the very tips of two delicate tentacles, she began to unbutton his shirt. He pulled her into his lap then, as he pressed his lips to hers, kissing her deeply, before he could stop himself.

As he released her lips, and migrated to her throat, breathing in the intoxicating scent of her, she laughed. That low, slightly husky laugh, that drove him half-mad. "I swear, if you still call me Miss Gray after this, I shall never offer you tea again."

He grinned against the hollow of her neck. "Is that a promise?"

Miss Gray's low laughter filled his senses, just as her scent surrounded him. "Yes." She turned his face to hers, laughing down at him. "That's a promise."

He silenced her laughter with his lips.

August was walking the streets of Atlanta once more. He'd elected to go by himself, to speak with Maryanne's father. After spending the night with Miss Gray, the pleasantness of the memory, still lingering in his mind, he had first returned early the next morning, almost reluctantly, to the station.

The station had been turned into a command center, during the night. Cops were on patrol at all hours, assigned in shifts. Both August's assailant, and the man who'd lost his hand, were still alive. The one-handed man was now being kept under close guard in the holding cell with his partner in crime, having been seen by a physician at the hospital. Both swore they had never seen the Many-Legged King's face. Furthermore, they insisted they didn't work directly for the Many-Legged King and knew nothing about a cult. The pair took their orders from someone else entirely.

"Someone they refuse to name," Jack had said darkly, giving August a knowing glance. "I know of only one person who commands this kind of muscle."

"Red," they had said at the same time.

So, Jack was on his way to pay Red a little visit. He insisted he was capable of doing so solo, but August wasn't buying it. He had threatened to go to Chief Waverly, who had spent the morning glaring over in their direction often enough, that August knew without asking they were both on his shit list.

"Fine," Jack had snapped. "I'll request a few officers to accompany me. But I'm telling you, the odds of me getting through to Red with company, are slim to none."

"I'm not beating up a bunch of his goons again, Jack. Do you want to hear my suggestion? Ask to speak to Rose this time, instead. I suspect she's the one who's really in charge anyway." Jack had frowned, but then thought for a moment, and nodded his agreement.

Now, August walked through sodden, rain lashed streets, in the direction of the tailor's shop, over on Edgewood Avenue.

When he arrived, Mr. Cole appeared startled, or at least surprised, to see him, August realized this with a faint pang of guilt. They'd been spread too thin. Hadn't taken the time to return and speak with the man properly, as they should have.

August enquired politely after his health and asked how the arrangements for Maryanne had come along. Mr. Cole gave a description of the wake, which had been closed casket, of course, as well as the funeral service that followed.

He heaved a deep sigh, as he stared off into the distance. "And the Reverend Blackstone, he did a wonderful job, delivering her eulogy. He wrote it special, just for her. Didn't use his typical material, his usual quotes." Mr. Cole waved his hand. "I've been to enough funerals in my time. I know all the typical material. This was different. He..." the man trailed off, struggling to speak. "It got to me, though, that speech." He reached up and brushed the tears out of his eyes.

"I'm so sorry, Mr. Cole," August said. "I'm glad he was able to bring you some comfort, with his words. I met him, you know, just the other day. He struck me as a kind-hearted man."

"Oh, that he is," Mr. Cole said. He removed a white handkerchief from his pocket and blew his nose noisily.

"Listen, did Maryanne..." he paused, unsure how to word what he wanted to ask. "Did Maryanne, have anyone she was close with? Anyone at all, that she might have confided in? I know you mentioned that the family kept it a secret, that only immediate family knew about her condition. But, if I could get a— a full list of names. Anyone you know of, that knew, even if you trust them. That would be just, so helpful."

August felt his chest deflate slightly, at Mr. Cole's expression. "A list? Names? You mean family?" he asked, one eyebrow raised, his voice gruff.

"I do, Sir. Family. Anyone at all. Anyone Maryanne might have met, either at the shop, or through school, or even through church. Anyone she spent time with, that she might have confided in."

"I told you before," Mr. Cole said, shaking his head. "It was only family that knew. I can't think of anyone else she would'a told." August sighed. "Well, besides the Reverend Blackstone, a'course. He knew about Maryanne. He's the only one she told, besides family. But, well," Mr. Cole scoffed, "there's just no way he's the murderer."

26

THE REVEAL.

August burst through the door to the small office at the back of the sandwich shop just as Jack was rising to his feet. Rose shot him a curious look, her lips curving, as she took in his dark eyes and pulsing veins.

"Damn it Jack, we're idiots."

Rose raised an eyebrow. "I won't argue with that. Your partner here, just had the audacity to accuse me of consorting with this *'Many-Legged King'* I've been hearing so much about. I told him to fuck off. If I find out who that bastard is, I'll stitch his many legs into a skirt that I can wear on Sundays. He's caused us nothing but trouble." Rose sighed. "Turns out, my father is also an idiot. I can't believe it... Jack says he's been loaning out some of his crew to the rotten King's cause. I oughta make a skirt out of him, too, come to think of it."

Jack held his hands out to the side. "There you have it, old boy. She claims neither she nor Red know the identity of the murderers. Yet, it certainly seems as though Red may have loaned some of his goons to the cause. I find it all to be a little too much to swallow."

"That means a lot, coming from you." Rose gave him a sideways grin. She turned and began to stack folders on the desk.

"None of that matters now," August said, "I know who he is."

"You do?" Jack stared at August, both eyebrows raised.

"I do," August repeated swiftly.

Rose paused in her stacking, leaning forward. "Who?"

August glanced at her, then decided he was past caring. "The Reverend Blackstone."

"The Reverend Blackstone?" They both repeated.

"Not possible," Jack said, shaking his head. "How? What evidence do you have?"

August paused, then swore. "Fuck. Zero evidence, now that you mention it. But I know it's him."

"How do you know?" Jack crossed his arms over his chest.

"I believe you," Rose said, almost reverently. "That man's a snake if I ever saw one."

"See!" August pointed at Rose.

"Out with it already," Jack groaned.

"I just finished speaking with Maryanne's father, Mr. Cole. He insists, swears, that the only person, aside from immediate family, who knew Maryanne was a vampire, was the Reverend Blackstone." August glanced behind him, at the empty shop, and closed the office door. "He lied to us!" he exclaimed, turning back to them. Jack shook his head slowly, but his eyes widened. "We're bloody idiots, Jack."

"But is that enough?" Jack frowned. "So, he's the only one Maryanne confided in? At least, according to her father..."

"Fathers don't know as much as they think they do," Rose murmured, shaking her head.

"No, don't you switch sides." August pointed at Rose. "He fits perfectly, Jack. Think about it. He knew both victims; both were members of his congregation. And he knew Hank."

"But how does Boone fit into all this then?" Jack said slowly. "Did he go through Boone, so he could book Dixie for the night? Lure her outside?" Jack frowned, "But why? He was their Reverend, after all. They trusted him. Couldn't he have gotten both victims to meet him somewhere all on his own?"

August sighed. He had a point. "We don't know that Boone was even involved for sure, remember? The man who met Dixie at The Black Sheep that night could have been anyone."

"Antoine described him as tall, with brown hair, and blue eyes..." Jack said slowly. "It couldn't have been Hank. I still suspect it was Boone. Antoine may have been trying to protect him. He certainly seemed like he was protecting someone. And whoever it is, they must be powerful, that man has no spine." Jack frowned. "And even *I* couldn't get him to crack. Boone makes sense."

"Yes, but Boone had a point," August reminded him. "Would he really allow himself to be seen, in public, dining at The Black Sheep, no less, with his call girl vampire girlfriend?"

"No!" Rose gasped. "I knew it! I cannot stand that man. Oh, poor Emily. His wife will be devastated. What a hypocritical–"

"We don't know that it was him," August said to Jack, then aside, to Rose; "He is a hypocritical bastard. He was definitely a client of Dixie's. But we still don't know the identity of her client that evening. Whoever booked her to meet him at The Black Sheep, used a fake name; Earnest Bunbury."

"Earnest Bunbury?" Rose frowned. "As in Oscar Wilde?"

August gaped open-mouthed at Rose. He held out both hands. "Yes! Thank you!"

"Yes, yes, you can quote pretentious literature to each other later." Jack glanced between the two of them. "Nude, for all I care. But getting back to the case–"

"Right." August snapped his mouth closed. "The case. My point is," he moved his hands up and down for emphasis as he spoke, "The Reverend Blackstone, or at least the church itself, seems to be at the center of all of this. We were halfway there. We knew the church was the meeting place. We knew it was the common thread that tied the victims together. But until that moment, sitting there across from Mr. Cole... until he said only the Reverend knew about Maryanne... it just didn't occur to me. He said, 'but of course, *he* couldn't be the murderer'... and it all clicked."

August turned to Jack, his expression earnest, pleading. "Jack, I'm telling you. You always accuse me of being too cautious, of refusing to follow my gut. I'm following my gut now. It's him. The Reverend Blackstone, is the Many-Legged King."

"Okay," Jack said. "So, what do we do about it?"

"We confront him. We go to the church; tell him we know what he's done."

"With what army?" Jack asked, spreading his arms out. "I don't know about you, but if Blackstone really is the Many-Legged King, I'm guessing it's going to take a hell of a lot more to pull a confession out of him than just, you know, telling him we know."

"We'll bring back up," August replied rapidly. "We'll go to the Chief–"

"Who will say that we have zero evidence. We can't arrest a man, any man, but especially someone of the Reverend's standing in the community, without a shred of evidence."

"Who said anything about arresting him?" August leaned forward. "I just want to accuse him, Jack, and I want to see his face when I do it."

"You're sure, aren't you?"

"Yes. I'm sure. Think about Hank; the fire and brimstone he was spouting; he didn't make that up himself. He was quoting someone else." August paused, "The graffiti I've been seeing, around town... I saw some the other night; it had an actual quote, chapter at least, maybe verse, if I'm remembering correctly. And it was quoting the Many-Legged King. As though there's some... some religious text, he's written. Who does all of this sound like? A preacher, Jack. A preacher. I'm telling you; Blackstone is our man."

"Okay." Jack nodded. "Then we confront him. You and me. We break him. Get inside his head. Force him to talk."

August let out a rush of air. "Okay. Me and you. We can do this."

"No," Rose said, shaking her head. August had forgotten for a moment that she was still there. "No, you can't. This sounds stupid. You're going to walk into... what? The lair, of this evil, twisted king, and call him out? Just the two of you?" She stood abruptly, glancing between them. "No. My men will go with you.

I've had enough of this bastard, stringing up women. Not in my town."

For the first time since August had burst through the door, he smiled.

"Did we really need to bring Miss Gray along?" August asked, swallowing thickly.

"I told you, you ungrateful barbarian, it's Vivienne," Miss Gray said.

"If you're right, August, I think we can use all the help we can get," Jack called back to him.

"But did you have to let her drive?" August said faintly.

The car lurched around a curve, taking it much too fast. August groaned in the backseat.

Jack twisted his upper body, peering out the rear window, angling to see past August.

"I'm fine, thanks for asking," August muttered.

"Just checking on our entourage," Jack said, shooting August a wink, as he monitored the line of black cars trailing behind the Cadillac.

In addition to feeling more than a little nauseous, and anxious, August felt himself succumbing once more to the weight of melancholy as he stared out the window at the desolate land-scape. Grey clouds hung low, stretched to the horizon, but a nexus seemed to have formed in the sky directly above the plain church. August noticed immediately that the doors were flung wide open.

As the Cadillac turned down the worn tire path that led to the humble church, August hoped it would be the last time he would make this trip out. If he never saw a dirt road again, it would be too soon.

The trio climbed out of the car and stood, staring up at the church. "This is it," Jack said, "right back where we started."

"See?" Miss Gray turned to them with a feline smile. "I was right all along."

In the end, Jack elected to have Rose's gang wait for them out-side. Two men were to take point; directed to wait just outside the doors, in the shadows under the eaves. They were told to rally the others at any sign of danger.

As they stood at the foot of the steps, Jack turned to August. "You don't have to come in, you know. I'll have Miss Gray for back-up. You could wait by the door." Jack glanced at the burly men who had already taken their positions. "I'm not sure how many brain cells this pair has between the two of them."

"I'll be alright, Jack." August heaved in a deep breath, then exhaled. "I can do this," he said flatly.

"You don't have to, though, old boy."

"Yes," August replied firmly, staring up at the steeple, against the backdrop of swirling clouds. "I do."

Jack studied him for a moment, then grinned. "If I end up having to carry you out of there puking your guts up, just try not to vomit on my trench coat."

August narrowed his eyes, first at Jack and then at the yawning doorway that loomed above them. He glanced over at Miss Gray, and she nodded back, giving him a small smile.

"Let's get going. Before I lose my nerve."

August had expected to find the nave empty, as it had been during their last visit. As his eyes adjusted to the darkness that filled the foyer, he took in flickering candlelight in the sanctuary. Large free-standing candelabras stood to either side of the pulpit. More candles lined the far sides of the pews, and a large, circular, lit candelabra hung from the ceiling.

A lone figure stood high in the sanctuary, behind the pulpit. Billowing black robes fell to the floor.

August froze, as his brain seemed to do a double take. In the flickering candlelight, he had briefly interpreted the dark shapes filling the pews as shadows. He blinked rapidly, and stared, open-mouthed, as it dawned on him. The rows of hard wooden pews were full of people. They sat silently, unmoving. An entire, frozen congregation, dressed head to toe in hooded pitch-black robes.

"Ah, the good Reverend Thaddeus Blackstone," Jack called out as he sauntered down the aisle. "Do you mind if I call you Thad?"

"Detective Quinn," Reverend Blackstone called back to him from his place behind the pulpit. "I would say I'm surprised to see you back so soon, but obviously," he swept his arms with a smile, "I've been expecting you."

"I can see that," Jack said calmly. "And you invited all of your friends."

"Yes. We are many, detective. My flock has been part of this all along. They deserve to be here, to witness my ascendency."

August trailed behind Jack, making a point of putting himself between the Reverend and Miss Gray. He stared at the backs of the silent hooded figures in the pews. Still, not one of them moved.

"Your ascendency, huh?" Jack mulled over the word, as he planted his feet in the middle of the nave, and crossed his arms over his chest. "That's a funny term for surrender." He turned to August. "Have you heard that one before, Sully?" August shook his head, but his eyes never left the Reverend.

The Reverend Blackstone smiled, a patronizing, patient sort of smile. His blonde hair fell in perfect shiny waves. His blue eyes, which August had seen before as full of warmth, held the glint of something else. Some inner fire, that smoldered and bided its time, below the surface.

"What has been foretold, must come to pass." He raised his arms to the side, palms towards the heavens. "There are those among you, who seek the truth. The truth that calls to them. Whispers to them, in the dark. That little voice, deep in your mind, that knows all, that sees all. It does not lie, that little voice. That voice you hear, I speak with now. For I am truth, made plain. I am wrath, made whole. Fire, made pure. I am that voice, that you have long denied, which tells you, when you stand on the edge of the cliff, to throw yourself onto the rocks below. For it is only in death, that you shall be made whole, once more. It is only in your suffering, that you shall be redeemed." The Reverend paused, his gaze fixed on August, who at that moment, could not have looked away if he'd tried. "I am the fire, that calls to you, in the night. Cast yourself on me. And I shall set you free."

August's heart was pounding, trapped in his throat. His eyes burned, and he realized he had not blinked. Not once, since the Reverend had started talking. It was as though he cast a spell, with his words. Woven with his inner thoughts, that had remained hidden in shadows, their forms only vaguely hinted at, even to him, until now.

A sudden noise made August jump, and he swiveled to see Jack had both hands raised. He was slow clapping.

"Fascinating stuff, old boy, although, to be honest, you lost me at the cliff part. I've never been one to feel tempted by *l'appel du vide*... But I can see it, though. I can see why these sheep have gathered here to lap up your words, not recognizing it for the poison that it is." Jack smiled. "But enough of all that. You know why we're here." He spread his arms. "You're wanted for the torture and murder of two young women. Dixie LaRue, and Maryanne Cole. Your third victim, was snatched from the jaws of death by our intrepid detective work." Jack turned and winked at August before turning back to face the Reverend. "So, we can skip," he gestured around vaguely, "whatever *this* is." His voice dropped into a lower, more serious register. "Because you're going to have to come with us."

The Reverend smiled his patronizing smile once more. "I won't be going anywhere, detective. For these charges you would lay at my doorstep, I am afraid, you have no proof."

"I'd argue this little... gathering, is proof enough. But, let's do a quick recap. *You* are clearly at the center of all of this. The victims were members of your congregation." Jack paced back and forth in the aisle as he spoke. "You had ties to both victims; you knew Maryanne Cole very well. In fact, you were the only person who was aware of her status as a vampire. We have that on good authority. But when it came to Dixie LaRue, you needed an intermediary. Someone who she would come to trust, so you could lure her where you wanted her, when the time was right. You wouldn't risk your own reputation, getting close to her. That wasn't an option, like it was with Maryanne. I suspect you attempted to use Boone Radcliff, at first." Jack came to a stop, his eyes darting to the Reverend.

Reverend Blackstone remind stoic. He stood with both hands pressed flat on the pulpit. August's stomach twisted and turned. He wiped the sweat from his brow. He swallowed down his gorge, as it threatened to rise. He tried to ignore the rising panic that fought to take over his nervous system and focus on Jack's words.

"You must have known, somehow, that he was... involved with Dixie. You intended to get to her through him. Perhaps you even blackmailed him. Threatened to reveal his secret." Jack's eyebrows rose, as he studied the Reverend's reaction. "But something must have gone wrong. Perhaps you found Boone too difficult to control. So, you turned to Hank."

"The boyfriend," Miss Gray murmured.

"Yes." Jack turned to her. "But he was never really her boyfriend. He was courting Dixie with only one goal in mind: to lure her out on the night of her murder. But Hank's mind was soft. Much softer than Boone's. And I'm afraid it turned rather into mush, as you bent him to your will, filling his brain with more of that, drivel, you were muttering earlier..." Jack trailed off. "Yet again, your plan must have failed. Hank wasn't able to deliver the goods. And you could only access Dixie here, at church, on Sundays. You couldn't very well snatch her in broad daylight, and dragging her from the cathouse was out of the question."

Miss Gray frowned. "Was it, though? It seems like that would have been the path of least resistance."

"I can assure you," Jack said briskly, "Madam Beaufrey is much more formidable than she seems. Besides, the alarm would have been raised. The law would have been called in. The one thing you needed, was time. Time with the victim, with none the wiser, and no one interfering, while you completed your macabre little tableau."

The Reverend Blackstone droned, in a bored sort of voice. "I suppose you will, eventually, get to the point, in this recitation?"

Jack held up a finger. "Patience, is a virtue, dear Thad. Now, where was I? Oh yes... I thought at first that it was Boone Radcliff, who had booked Miss LaRue for the meal at The Black Sheep. You see, we knew that Antoine was protecting someone. When we asked for a description of her mystery date, he described the man as being tall, with brown hair and blue eyes." Jack shook his finger. "Here's where I slipped up. You see, something was nagging at me, although I couldn't quite figure out what. If it had been Boone with Dixie that night, and Antoine was protecting his identity, he would have made an effort to describe a man who looked nothing like Boone." August frowned at Jack's words.

"But, he described a man who was actually similar in appearance to Boone, with brown hair, and blue eyes." Jack shook his head. "I should have caught that little detail, at the time. I would have expected a man in Antoine's position, to describe someone who was the *opposite* in appearance of the person he was trying to protect. We wasted too much time focusing on Boone." Jack sighed. "Antoine was clearly afraid. Afraid of someone with influence, in a position of power. But Boone, while influential, has limited power, at least for now."

"This is all circumstantial," the Reverend said thickly. "Conjecture. You have nothing on me." He made a *tsk-tsk* sound, and there was something in the rattle of his vocal cords that struck August as slightly off. Inhuman. A shiver ran down his spine. "What would Chief Waverly say?"

Jack surveyed the first few rows of pews, shaking his head. "Oh for fuck's sake... don't tell me he's here?"

The Reverend paused in his evil musing and frowned for a moment. "No. But that would have been perfect, wouldn't it?"

"No, he isn't," a voice called out, and a hooded figure rose from the first pew, turning to face them. "But I am." The man raised his hands to his hood and struggled for a second to remove it.

He was clear-eyed, but his brown eyes were cold and full of malice. He appeared slightly disheveled, his salt and pepper hair mussed, he ran a hand through his hair and it fell perfectly back into place. Then he glanced down at the severed hand, gripped inexplicably in his own, and dropped it with a horrified gasp.

"*Why* does that keep happening?" Jack asked.

"Mayor Dorsey?" August gasped, his jaw dropping open in disbelief.

"The one and only," Jack said grimly. "With his salt and pepper hair and brown eyes... nothing like the brown-haired, blue-eyed man Antoine described."

"*You're* Bunbury?" August asked incredulously.

Jack shook his head. "It took me far too long to see it. You were the perfect accomplice. You booked Dixie LaRue for that night. She was likely more than a little surprised when she saw you sitting there at The Black Sheep, waiting for her. As far as I know, you'd never spoken to her before that evening. But that wasn't important. The important thing, was that she trusted you."

"Of course she did," August said thickly.

"With your campaign in full swing, running on peace and acceptance, your entire platform hinged on embracing the vampire community. If there was one person, who could have led Dixie, like a little lamb to the slaughter, into a field in the middle of nowhere, in the dead of night, it was you."

"But why?" August sputtered. His building nausea and panic were momentarily forgotten in his shock and outrage. "Why would you do something like that? Why on earth would you help... *him*?" He glared up at the Reverend and felt himself suddenly on the edge. His nerves and panic fading into something far more primal.

Mayor Dorsey raised his chin, eyes cold as steel. "I don't expect you to understand, son. But I did it for the good of the city. For the good of its' people."

"Bullshit," Jack spat, "you did it to secure the election."

"What?" August frowned. "How do the deaths of two innocent women help win an election?"

Jack laughed. "Fear. He thought if he could stoke fear of violence against vampires, he would have a chance of beating Boone. The only thing greater than hatred, is fear."

Mayor Dorsey sighed. "He would have won. Boone. He was going to win. I could feel it. Do you understand what would happen to this city, if Boone were to take over?" Mayor Dorsey stared intensely at August. "Far more innocent people would have died, would have suffered, if I hadn't done what needed to be done."

"Oh fuck off!" August's pulse pounded in his temples. He felt a headache building; a vise-like grip, like a band, tightening around his forehead. The veins beneath his eyes rose to the surface, black morphing to purple. His fists clenched at his sides. "All that bullshit about a few good men, doing their duty... you're fucking psychotic." August felt a hand on his arm and turned to find Miss Gray standing calmly beside him.

"He's wrong," she whispered. "It's hope. The only thing stronger than hatred, stronger even than fear, is hope."

August felt as though a cold bucket of water had been tossed over his head. He felt a swelling behind his eyes, and for a brief second, had the absurd feeling that he might cry.

Miss Gray continued to hold his gaze as Mayor Dorsey continued. "It would have been anarchy. An unfathomable anarchy. I did what needed to be done. I don't expect your thanks for it."

"The only thing I'm not sure of, is who did the draining." Jack glanced from the Reverend Blackstone, who stood like a stone behind his pulpit, to Mayor Dorsey, then back again. "We know a vampire was involved. Or rather, we assume. Both victims, as well as the near-miss third victim, were drained of blood, yet someone altered the first autopsy report to hide that fact. What I can't figure out, is why exactly."

"To hide the motive for the crime," August said thickly, turning to Mayor Dorsey. "You wanted to stoke fears of upirist violence, not promote hatred of vampires. It was you. You didn't just lure

Dixie. You drained the victims. You're a closeted vampire." Mayor Dorsey glared back at him with steely eyes. "You doctored the first autopsy report to hide the fact that a vampire was involved."

"How'd you alter the report? We suspected a new copy was made. How did you do it?" Jack asked curiously.

"Gladys," Mayor Dorsey replied gruffly.

"*Fucking Gladys...*" Jack moaned, slapping a hand over his forehead. "We never talked to her.

"But, it was her birthday," August frowned. "They were all singing to her... how'd she manage to get away?"

Dorsey shrugged. "She pretended someone knocked cake onto her. Had to leave to go get it cleaned up."

"Damn it..." August murmured.

"But why drain the victims in the first place?" Jack asked. "It seems an unnecessary addition, quite frankly." Mayor Dorsey stared stoically at Jack.

August spoke up. "You fed on them so they would be too weak to fight back, didn't you? And you wanted them to be too weak to recover from their wounds, in case you were interrupted, mid-ceremony."

Jack's eyes lit up. "Ah... and that's exactly what happened with the third victim. When the gunshots started going off, you fled the scene, before you had a chance to remove Holden's heart."

"Yes." August nodded. "Leaving him technically still alive. There are only so many ways to kill an upir, as we know. Removing the heart was the final, necessary act, made much easier by first draining the victim to a point they can't recover from."

"And he wouldn't have recovered, if you hadn't happened to come along right when you did." Mayor Dorsey shook his head. "That young man would have been perfect. A beautiful, tragic symbol, in death. The town would have been outraged."

"You're a monster," Miss Gray said flatly.

"Well, now that we're at the name-calling phase, I think we've dallied quite long enough, don't you?" The Reverend Blackstone intoned from behind his pulpit. He flashed two rows of white teeth. "Shall we... wrap this up? I grow weary of the self-righteousness."

"Talk about self-righteousness," August fumed. "You have called yourself a *King*, fashioned after *The Many-Legged King*... revered as a *God*." August paused, took a shuddering breath. "*'Thou shall not worship false idols'.*" He glared up at the robed figure, his chest heaving. "*You* are the false idol you worship." He turned to Mayor Dorsey. "And *you* are the worst sort of hypocrite. Even worse than Boone. At least he knows he's a fraud. You still haven't figured it out."

"As I've said, when the children have resorted to name calling, it's time to conclude." The Reverend swept out from behind the pulpit and glided forward with a low slithering sound. From beneath his black robes, many limbs unfurled, curling and smoking. Tendrils rose into the air, as August stared in dread at the sinuous tentacles, with their many roving red eyes. "You see," the Revered smiled down at August, his lips curling smugly, "I haven't fashioned myself after The Many-Legged King... I am *he*. And I've come home. At last."

The ends of his tentacles glowed red-hot, and August watched in disbelief as flames rose on the tips. The scent of sulfur filled August's nose. *No.* It couldn't be. It wasn't possible. He was gripped with an overwhelming sense of desperate panic, in that moment.

August recalled the writhing tentacles, swirling in Maryanne's pupils. The feeling of drowning, as she sucked him under, into a world of madness, darkness, and obscurity. The sound of water, being sucked down a drain, as though his soul was being flushed into oblivion, filled his ears. Was that it? Was that what happened, in death? Was that all that awaited them? Madness and chaos? A black tunnel into the void?

August's gorge rose, and he struggled to breathe. He watched, as though from far away, with an odd sense of surrealism, as Jack reached into the front pocket of his trench coat. He pulled out a cigarette and placed it between his lips.

Jack glanced up at The Many-Legged King. "Do ya have a light, Thad?"

27

BAPTISM BY FIRE.

Thaddeus Blackstone smiled down at them, palms pressed together, as though in prayer, as he lifted two curving appendages. The flames flickering there seemed to pulse and expand. He flicked the ends of his tentacles in a motion similar to the snapping of fingers, and two glowing balls of flame shot upward. He bounced them on the ends of his undulating appendages, keeping them balanced and suspended as they grew.

"It would be my pleasure, detective."

August dove to the floor, just as a ball of flame launched in his direction. It passed where his head had been a split second before.

He rolled on his back, scanning for Jack. But he was nowhere in sight. Miss Gray stood farther down the aisle, her head tilted to the rafters.

August followed her gaze upwards and couldn't suppress a small grin. Jack hung there, upside-down, like a spider, from the swaying circular candelabra. The candles sputtered and flickered around him. He pulled the cigarette from his lips with one hand and lit it on the nearest candle. "Never mind. Once again, looks like I'll have to do everything myself." He took a long puff, then launched himself.

The spell that held the ominous, black-robed congregation in stasis seemed to have broken. The first rows of cloaked and hooded cult members stood and surged forward.

"August!" Miss Gray cried out, pointing behind him. August took in her wide eyes and rolled to the other side of the aisle. Flames crashed in his wake. He watched in horror as the floor where he had lain smoked, then bubbled. With a hissing sound, sickly green fumes rose into the air. August was momentarily overcome by the sulfurous miasma. He coughed and sputtered, attempting to hold his breath, he slid forward on his stomach, grabbing onto the pews with clawed hands as he pulled himself away from the unearthly green flames that had begun to lick the side of the nearest pew.

August rose to his feet, as balls of flame flew past him. He waved an arm to clear the smoke in the air and watched with a faint surge of relief as Rose's men streamed into the nave, guns raised.

Bullets flew and the fire spread. August watched Miss Gray for a brief second. She stood in the center of the aisle, perfectly still. He moved a step closer, as though to lunge at her, to pull her out of the line of fire to safety. But her lips were moving rapidly. Her head tilted back, and her expression became rapt. August's brow creased in confusion, as a pale mist seemed to gather around her. As the cloud spun faster, he began to make out swirling figures in the mist. They twisted and rotated, forming a shield around Miss Gray. August's jaw dropped open, as he caught a glimpse of pale limbs and mournful eyes. Open mouths, as though the phantoms were mid-wail.

Jack's laughter rang out from somewhere behind him, and August turned, ducking, as another, particularly large ball of fire flew over his head to crash into a phalanx of black-robed minions, sending them sprawling

Jack landed next to August, balanced on a pew. "You alright old boy?" Jack called out to him. "You haven't puked yet!"

"What's with the black robes?" He called back to Jack. "I thought they were supposed to be crimson?"

"We have more than one set of robes." Mayor Dorsey had materialized in the aisle before August. He shrugged. "We figured black would be more dramatic, for the final scene." Dorsey's sharp canines gleamed in the firelight. Black veins covered his cheeks and his chest above his collar. "It's a shame, we couldn't see eye to eye, you and I." He smiled apologetically at August. "We would have made a good team." He leveled a gun at August's forehead.

"I already have a partner," August growled. His fangs lengthened, and he tensed to pounce.

Jack barreled into Mayor Dorsey, just as the gun went off, knocking his arm aside. They landed in a crash onto the pews. Black robed figures scattered, some of them shrieking.

The round pierced August in the gut. He gasped slightly, lifting his palms to the red stain that was already spreading rapidly through his white shirt. He felt a now familiar burning spreading through his veins. *"Oh for fuck's sake..."* he murmured.

Jack was on his feet. Mayor Dorsey's gun had been flung several feet away in the scuffle. August watched as Jack lifted Dorsey and tossed him across the nave. He hit a pillar on the far side of the pews, back first, and slid to the floor in a heap, where he lay, unmoving.

Jack turned to August. "I hate politicians."

August's hand fell away from his gut, covered in blood, and Jack's coal-black eyes seemed to darken. The Reverend Blackstone's voice, which had been a low susurrous in the noisy chaos of the church, was rising, growing ever louder, breaking in a crescendo.

He was airborne, now. Floating high above his pulpit. Only the whites of his eyes were showing, as six of his extra appendages flicked and flamed, generating and bouncing balls of fire that rained down on the pews below, leaving puddles of poisonous-looking green goo in their wake.

Whatever alien tongue he spoke in, it was certainly unknown to August, and he was left with the distinct impression that it was not of this world.

Thunder cracked overhead, rumbling and breaking amidst the gunfire and cries of pain. The whole church shook. Windows shattered. Candles fluttered out in the ill wind that bellowed through the shards of stained glass. The only light now came from the balls of flame that rotated on curving tentacles, illuminating the unblinking red eyes below in a hellish glow.

The Reverend Thaddeus Blackstone, The Many-Legged King, laughed then; a deep, throaty laughter, that grew and swelled. That rattled and reverberated deep in August's chest. He could feel it; the silver, as good as poison in his veins, as it continued to spread, worming and twisting, its tearing black fingers of fire burning through his core.

August turned to Jack, his vision starting to swim. "Jack..." he said. "I never told you–"

"Save it, old boy. It's not over yet." Jack gave him a mournful grin, the lines between his brows creased. "You're not going down that easily."

August surveyed the destruction wrought in the church around them. The black robed figures swarmed and fought. Some of Rose's men were wide-eyed with fear, but they continued to fight. They weren't about to lie down and die. Still, they seemed to be scattered thinly throughout the nave, now fewer and far between.

The wind howled through the broken windows, and August watched in fascination as an impossibly large, black shadow, that seemed to hang, suspended from the very clouds above, curled and writhed in the chaos of the storm outside.

"It looks quite hopeless, at the moment, Jack," August called out, turning to find his partner. His vision lagged to catch up, bright dots of rainbow light sparkled in his periphery.

"It's never too late to hope, old boy," Jack said, with a wry grin. "What am I always telling you?"

A crack sounded behind August. Close. Too close. And he jerked, as a round entered his back. Then a second. Then a third. He swiveled to Jack, and he watched in horror as a dark hole appeared in Jack's chest. Then another, in his stomach. *Jack!* He cried out, one arm stretched towards his partner.

Jack glanced down at his chest, then up at Mayor Dorsey, who still held the smoking gun pointed in his direction. The click of an empty chamber sounded. Jack laughed, his mouth splitting to his ears, his teeth gleaming in the twisted firelight. He dropped into a crouch, then pounced.

Jack became a blur of motion, of limbs and snarling teeth. Dorsey's eyes went wide, his mouth forming a perfect 'o' in surprise. An odd wet thunk reverberated, followed by tearing and cracking.

Dorsey swayed on his feet, his chest a hollow bloody cavern, as Jack held something deep red, thick and globulus, aloft in one hand.

Jack was painted in a steaming spray of blood as veins and arteries emptied like firehoses. Dorsey managed to lift an arm in August's direction, his coal-black eyes seeming to lock onto him, just as the light within them faded. August couldn't help but stare into the open cavity that yawned in his chest. The jagged ends of cracked ribs, and the sight of the still deflating, papery lungs, brought his stomach roiling up his throat.

August fell to his knees in the aisle, gagging, as Jack's laughter echoed in his ears. He coughed and retched, gasping for breath. He glanced up to see Jack launch Dorsey's heart at the Reverend Blackstone. It hit him in the face with a sickening squelch.

Blackstone let out an inhuman shriek of rage. Blood-curdling, and bone-chilling. August watched, his jaw dropping open, as the man's face seemed to split, rending itself in two, a thick line of red running through his chiseled cheekbones, just above his lips.

The Many-Legged King's face cratered in on itself, then yawned wide, revealing row after circular row of teeth. A mass of flanges burst out from the dark void in the center, blood red eyes whirling, searching for them down below. He released the rotating balls of flame he had been coaxing in one massive blast. August pressed himself against the floor as a wall of heat moved over him in a wave that pulsed outward through the nave.

He turned and twisted, searching for Jack, and found him once more hanging upside down from the chandelier high above, his mouth open wide, tongue hanging out. Jack panted heavily, then shook himself, as he let out an answering chilling howl.

August managed to turn on weak, shaking limbs, and raised his gaze towards the ceiling to look for Miss Gray. She floated there, hanging in midair, directly across from The Many-Legged King. The figures made of fog swirled and twisted, nearly obscuring her from his view. August watched as an errant ball of flame hit the swirling cloud and bounced away uselessly.

They would make it. They would win. Somehow, they would win. He just wouldn't be there to see it.

His vision shuddered and seemed to narrow, as though he were looking down a dark tunnel. A tunnel of black. A tunnel of darkness. A tunnel that led to nothing. He would be sucked down that awful drain once more. Into the void. Only this time, he wouldn't be waking up.

When August glanced towards the open doors of the church, he was hoping for one last look. One last glimpse of the sky outside.

But his gaze fell on something that obscured his view, and he felt a brief flutter in his chest. In his gut. A brief flutter of hope.

August fell onto his hands and knees, and then onto his chest. He pulled himself along, with a soft squelching sound, leaving a trail of blood in his wake.

His vision continued to narrow, as the silver bullets did their work, but he kept his eyes fixed straight ahead.

When he reached the golden rope, the bell pull, that hung in the middle of the foyer, he was overcome in a moment of doubt by the sheer size of it. It was massive. He knew if he were to rise on his feet, and wrap his arms around it, his hands might not touch on the other side. And that was exactly what he would have to do.

August used the last of his strength to slide himself forward, until he lay just beneath the bell pull. He gripped the tassel that hung, suspended overhead, with both fists, and pulled himself upwards, one agonizing inch at a time.

Then he used his claws, dug them into the side of the massive rope, and clung there, breathing heavily. His vision was narrowed to practically a pinhole. But he wrapped his arms as far as they would go, around the massive rope, as he managed to slide his feet, blindly, beneath him. He summoned every ounce of his willpower, and took a deep breath of the malodourous, sulfurous air. Then he used all of his body weight, and the last of his remaining strength, to pull.

August was floating now, too. Watching, from somewhere high above, held down by only the roof of the nave. He was pinned there, against the rafters, when the first of them entered through the front door of the church.

Dixie LaRue strolled in. No, strutted, in. As though she was on a catwalk. She raised her gaze to the ceiling, gracing August with a brief, satisfied smile, in thanks. Her eyes were pitch black, and her veins were beginning to spread.

She was followed by two more women. August could see their fangs and darkened veins from his perch on the ceiling. He didn't recognize them, but he had a feeling their graves lay just a few yards away, out by the treeline, on the edge of the woods.

Soon there was a crowd. They surged through the doors. They filled the nave. At first, no one but him seemed to notice them. They rolled over the black cloaked figures. August watched as they were torn to shreds. Lines of red appearing in their chests. Their hoods were sliced open. Their mouths gaped in horror. They swatted at unseen assailants, eyes wide in terror. They died with a scream on their lips.

Maryanne entered the church last. She surveyed the chaos, and then turned to find August, up at the ceiling. August expected her eyes to be hard, like shards of flint on his. But they were soft. Wet with tears. She almost smiled, the corners of her mouth twitching. But then, she was never one for smiles. She nodded solemnly, once, to August. He nodded back, blinking his own tears away.

August watched as her eyes turned black. As the veins seemed to run down her cheeks, spreading to her chest. Her hands clenched into fists, and she turned and locked onto the eldritch form that floated high above the pulpit.

August heard it starting, then. And he felt a pang of dread, as the roaring of rushing water filled his ears. As he prepared to drown. But he saw Dixie LaRue, with Maryanne not far behind her, stalking through the nave, bent on their revenge. He saw Jack, standing beneath the Revered Blackstone, lowered into a crouch, readying to pounce. He saw Miss Gray— Vivienne, arms spread wide, head thrown back, eyes closed, a secretive smile on her lips. Just like a Cheshire cat, full of mystery, and power. August was smiling too, when he was finally pulled under.

28

ANOTHER DAY.

Jack Quinn sat with his feet propped up on his desk. An unlit cigarette hung from his lips. It was affixed there, on his bottom lip, hanging by its own paper skin. It would rip off when he removed it, leaving a bit of itself behind.

"It's been a whole week," Jack said, his eyes glazed over. He roused himself and stared down at the folder that lay open in his lap. "A whole week. And not a single interesting case has fallen into our laps."

August Sullivan chuckled, watching his partner as he turned another page in the file. "And that's a bad thing?" He asked, unable to hide his amusement.

Jack shrugged. "Well, it's boring, isn't it? I mean, we defeated an unknowable, ancient evil." He sighed. "What do we do next?"

August just shook his head. "You really are insufferable, you know that?"

Jack shot him a look. He reached into his pocket and removed a golden lighter.

August glared at him. "I swear, Jack, if you light that thing, so help me God..."

Jack's eyes remained on August's, as he flicked the lighter open with a flourish, and held it beneath the tip of his cigarette. Just as he pressed his thumb down, the bell above the door clattered.

THE END

ALSO BY

Dread House, 2024
Possession, 2024
Mount Snow, 2025
Carl: An Easter Horror Thriller Novella, 2025
Jumpers, 2025
MANIMAL, 2025

ABOUT THE AUTHOR

A.C. Hessenauer describes herself as an author of horror thrillers with gothic romance vibes. A.C. is an active member of the Horror Writers Association. When she's not participating in macabre ceremonies dedicated to the eldritch horrors out in the woods, A.C. enjoys spending time with her family; her husband, two sons, and border collie named Maximus. She loves a good horror movie, and of course, getting swallowed whole by a good book.

DREAD HOUSE PUBLISHING

Check out our website; Dread House Publishing, for news on upcoming releases, and to sign up for a monthly newsletter with ARC opportunities at www.dreadhousepublishing.com or scan the QR code below.